GARY WINCHESTER

First Encounter

A City of Silence Saga

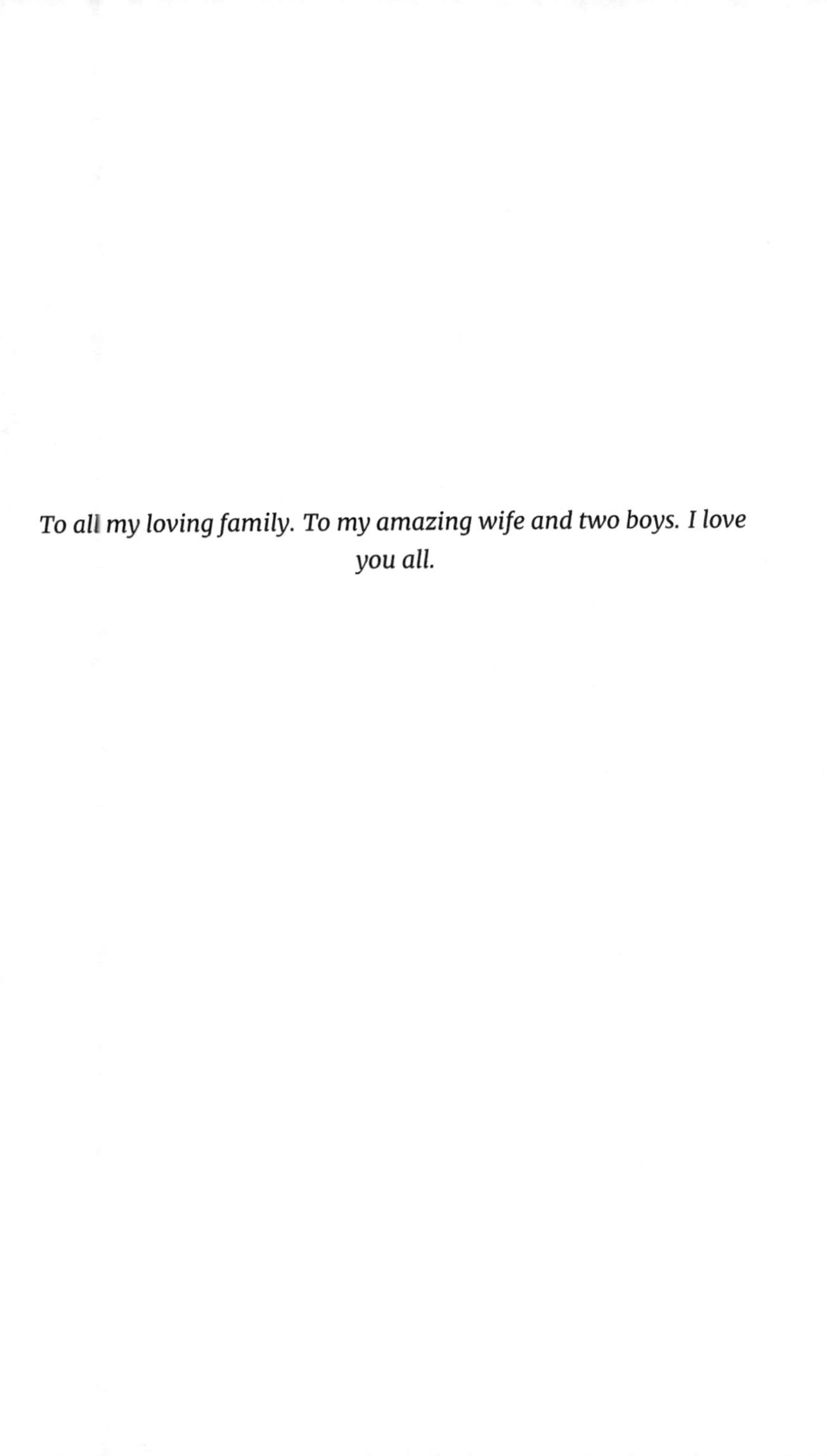

To all my loving family. To my amazing wife and two boys. I love you all.

Silence is the most powerful scream...

-Anonymous-

Contents

Acknowledgments

I would like to thank all my beta-readers; without you, I do not think this book would have turned out to be amazing. Special thanks to TM, I could not have done this without you. I cannot forget my other partner in crime; you know who you are. Thanks for your help and advice.

Prologue

Post Impact: 10 years
   December 22, 2063
   Dear Felicia,

As you may already know, between 2035 and 2058 A.D., man-made and natural species were both disastrously brought to their knees. The pestilence, famine, and plagues that followed added to the ever-present tension of war. It did not take much for the delicate balance to tip in favor of violence. Countries would fight allies for food, and the smaller developing nations were often torn apart by civil war. These times, aptly named the Dark Era, were worse than anyone could imagine. I am glad you were not there to see humanity's fall.

As many of the world's governments collapsed under political stress, the remaining world's leaders came together and formed the NWF. It was not until the New World Federation was established that humanity was brought out of total anarchy. It was believed that without a world centralized government, our species would continue to plunge further into chaos. With their remaining resources, the NWF focused on restoring continent after continent, bringing the world back to order, starting with England. With great leaps in military technology and bioengineering, England had been deemed the central hub for the NWF. Its robust infrastructure and willingness to adopt NWF ideals helped usher in a smooth transition of power.

From the hub, the NWF military invaded, and, with superior weaponry, they drove out any local militias or mob bosses that held a tight grip on the regions, ending their illegal reign. With crime declining, the NWF set up a web of military installations within the remaining iconic landmarks and had them all linked to headquarters. With each location established, the purpose of revitalizing each region had begun, starting with infrastructure and then agriculture to feed its people.

Now, in the year 2073, civilization has reached what many of us thought to be the apex of human evolution. The NWF has made unbelievable advancements in the world. It was so popular that even regions with a history of destabilization, such as parts of Africa and South America, fell beneath its ever-stretching umbrella. Within twenty-five years, the entire world followed, and there has been what has come to be called the Pax Orbis, World Peace.

But the Pax Orbis was short-lived. In the winter of 2073, many people of the world, including myself at age twenty-one, helplessly watched as an asteroid storm bombarded all parts of the globe for days. Asteroids and meteors hit with unfathomable force, causing occurrences such as earthquakes, tsunamis, and volcanoes to erupt.

In an instant, billions of my species had ended. It was indeed an extinction-level event. The power and destructive force behind these natural disasters was so catastrophic, hundreds of miles were vaporized, killing the inhabitants before they had a chance to realize what was happening to them, let alone what was happening around the world.

The asteroids opened craters miles wide, spewing up a ton of ash and debris into the sky. With each column of smoke reaching the heavens, the Sun's rays began to dissipate as the Earth was slowly engulfed by a cloak of smoke and flames. In the days that *followed, our planet burned. Eventually, the fires died, and the Earth continued to cool as sunlight failed to penetrate the thick clouds.*

It was only fifty years from today that the New World Federation had started to stabilize the crisis that had befallen our once unique world. What we once called the Blue Planet is nothing more than another lifeless heap orbiting the Sun.

I bet you, the NWF did not count on this happening! Humanity was brought to its knees once more, not by war, but from the reaches of outer space. It's now impossible to keep count of the millions of people who perished from starvation and cold.

Oh, how I yearn for Pax Orbis again. Even with the NWF's preparation for natural disasters, this was simply beyond their capabilities. Our hope now lies in EVE.

Yours Truly,
  Orion

P.S.

Buirke brought in a group of bandits today as a pack of Stalkers was attacking them. Mitch had them taken to the medical bay to be treated. And of course, we have them sedated for safety measures because we never know what outsiders are capable of. I'm not sure what Mitch plans to do with them. I suggest we put them back outside the wall and let nature do with them as it pleases. Honestly, we have no space for their kind here.

Chapter 1

The sky over Old London remained the gloomy gray atmosphere it had been for the past decade. Snow, which had fallen for countless days, had recently ceased. Even with the calming storm, strong winds often followed, picking up the fresh accumulation and creating whiteout conditions. The former bustling capital city was now a ghost town. The only remnants of its glory days were the dilapidated skyscrapers and broken face of Big Ben, which managed to stand through all the seismic activity following the asteroid showers. Ice and snow formed over the rubble of collapsed buildings, forming artificial mountains.

With the absence of the typical pedestrian noise of a bustling city, the sounds of ten bulky speeders roared across the abandoned land. With pale hands painted on their sides, the speeders were no ordinary vehicles. Each vehicle was re-engineered to traverse the desolate grounds of Europe. Crafted from an assortment of scavenged materials, they varied in size and appearance, from the compact size of a sedan to the hefty girth of a school bus.

Shock and terror had become an effective tactic against potential enemies. Razor wire, large, spiked plows, and iron sheeting for windows not only weighed down the vehicles but added to their hideous appeal.

Those who survived the impact and the aftermath were faced with two choices: either join the multitude of isolated communities that had sprung up around the Earth, or join bandit gangs roaming the planet desperately scavenging for resources. The chances of surviving alone were slim and most often meant certain death.

In the distance, the windowless towers of Old London loomed through a flurry of snow. One of the vehicles slowed down while the others continued to speed by. The black body was labeled with the word Scorpion in white paint; it had been transformed from an APC (Armored Personnel Carrier) into something resembling a miniature tank. It was the perfect vehicle for navigating through the snowy terrain. With its powerful four-hundred-horsepower engine, even large drifts were no match. The six wheels were equipped with sharpened blades, ready to slice through anything foolish enough to come close while in motion.

Moments after coming to a halt, the driver's door opened as the driver leaned out. The bandit peered into the distance, their head and eyes covered by a fur hood and snow goggles. They stood there examining the once glorious city as the wind whistled snow around them, calm breaths of steam evaporated from the purple scarf covering the figure's mouth.

"Come on, Rowan. Shit, you're acting like it's summer," a female voice shouted from inside the APC.

Rowan took a moment to scratch beneath the metal band around his neck, a constant reminder of the world he lived in. Satisfied with the reminiscent skyline, he sat back in the driver's seat and closed the door. Shifting into drive, the heavy vehicle's wheels rolled forward, spewing up a frosty white mist, giving chase to their fellow speeders.

Entering the city limits, the caravan found the roads littered with abandoned vehicles, which were ideal for parts. The *Mammoth*, the largest of the bandits' vehicles, carried a large V-plow attached to its front to push whatever it could not navigate around. Constructed from a semi-truck tractor and the rear section of a school bus, and having its tires replaced with caterpillar tracks. Painted white as camouflage, the *Mammoth* acted as the mobile center for the bandit's leader. Iron shutters were installed to cover its large windows in a combat situation, while two large steel drums fastened atop carried additional fuel for the caravan.

A few miles into the ghostly city, the *Mammoth* came to a clunking halt in front of a building in Old London's town center. Shutting off the engine, the other six speeders fell in behind their mothership, shutting off all engines. A large steel door in Mammoth's center dropped like a drawbridge, slamming into the ground with a thud, which echoed into the distance.

The door swung open, revealing a broad and muscular figure standing at six feet tall. They wore a rugged red and white flannel lumber coat, heavy work boots, and worn-out blue jeans. A single herringbone braid, the color of rich brunette hair, hung down the center of their back, while their left hand held a 1873 Winchester short rifle with a firm grip.

Unaffected by the needles of snow blowing against her exposed face, she remained silent, taking the time to examine the various buildings and shops that lined the town center. The only signs of any activity were the winds whistling between the buildings.

Grabbing the two-way radio at her side, "Marcus, I need you upfront."

Marcus Rowan was sitting comfortably in his vehicle, writing in a little green book, finishing up his thoughts, when the call came through.

"You and that book of yours. What do you write anyway? You some apocalypse poet?" asked a red-haired man with a broad Irish accent from the rear.

"Don't worry about it!" He insisted, storing the hard book in the pocket inside his coat.

"Sorry that I asked," he replied, feigning annoyance. "Anyway, what does she want with you?"

"Who knows, Spence. Either way, I hate her voice, and I'm looking forward to the day when I no longer hear it," he ranted with a deep sigh. "But that's a story to save for another time," Rowan continued.

"Sure, you will. But I do know one thing she wants." Rowan furrowed at the comment. "Who couldn't resist the idea of having a piece of chocolate in times like these?" Spence continued, his freckles curling into a smile.

"Shut up, fool," Rowan joked, opening the door, using the scarf to cover his mouth. "You guys wait here."

"Oh, I plan to," Spence laughed.

Rowan promptly grabbed his rifle, sitting between the front seats, and stepped out of the vehicle. The inches of packed snow crunched beneath his weight. With his scarf blowing wildly with the wind, Rowan took a few seconds to adjust his coat before making his way through the calf-deep snow towards the front of the caravan.

Even with his physical strength, Rowan always struggled to trudge through the heavy snow. He stopped at the bottom of the Mammoth's ramp and saw two figures waiting for him: Larissa, the fearless leader of the Pale Hand, being the first.

As the caravan traversed Old Europe, Rowan heard stories of Larissa's cruelty. She watched her family being murdered in Rassosh and was taken as a slave during the NWF's collapse. After being a sexual puppet to her captors, she eventually killed them all and led a group of slaves out of Rassosh. They became known as the Pale Hand, initially seeking to liberate other slaves but facing resource shortages that forced desperate measures for survival.

Bones, serving as Larissa's chief guard and secondary lookout, positioned himself midway up the ramp. Adorned in Viking-esque garb and brandishing a machete at his flank, his formidable stature underscored his role as Larissa's chosen sentinel. Towering over six feet and tipping the scales at three hundred pounds, he was an unspoken deterrent to anyone contemplating an unsanctioned approach. Even with vision in just one eye, he vigilantly monitored Rowan's ascent.

"Yeah, what is it, Larissa?" Rowan inquired, halting a few feet away from her.

"Watch your tone," Bones growled over him. "Have you forgotten your place?"

"Now, now, Bones — no need to get upset. Sometimes even the roaches need to be reminded of their place," Larissa corrected, reaching into her pocket, revealing a handheld device with a small bright red light and additional buttons. "Such an amazing tool. Glad I found it at the old prison," she said, waving the controller slowly through the air. "With a little push on this, that pretty face of yours will be no more. Now, why don't you try that again?" She extended her free hand to him.

The collar bomb, developed by the NWF for use on prisoners of war and convicts, incorporated a small explosive and a tracking device. This innovation virtually eradicated any attempts at escape. Initially, the design featured a timer that required resetting every twenty-four hours to avert detonation. However, Larissa modified it to accommodate the extended duration of Rowan's missions.

Rowan was familiar with the ritual Larissa had established for him, a ritual he had to perform each time he appeared before her. With every enactment, he sensed a fragment of his being eroding into anger. His gaze would often linger on the machete at Bones' side, aware that with a swift move, he could disarm the behemoth before his good eye even registered the action and sever his head. However, no matter his speed, he could never outpace the simple press of a button.

For now, he was compelled to comply with Larissa's demands, biding his time while devising a plan to remove the collar. He was acutely aware that the day might come when she would unhesitatingly activate the timer, potentially ending his life, and more critically, that of his team, in an instant.

Taking a deep breath, Rowan knelt before her. Gently grasping her hand, he brought it to his lips for a kiss.

"That's better, Marcus. Stand up and come inside," she said, turning to enter the Mammoth, leaving him kneeling.

"Didn't she say get moving?" Bones snapped, pushing Rowan in the back as he rose to his feet.

Budging only to move a few inches, Rowan stood his ground, without facing his attacker. "If you desire to keep the ability to wipe yourself. I advise, don't do that again."

"Or what, roach?" he taunted, stepping closer from behind until Rowan could feel the heat of the giant's breath.

"Bones, let him be; I have a task for him," Larissa commanded from within.

Following orders, Bones circled around Rowan, deliberately bumping him with his shoulder. "Roach," he muttered under his breath.

With the windows covered, the Mammoth was bathed in candlelight. Its interior echoed a collector's haven, with an array of objects showcased on the ceiling and walls. Each piece marked a destination Larissa had visited in her travels. Opposite the entrance lay the weapons cage, filled with an array of heavy machine guns, assault rifles, hand grenades, and pistols. The wall behind her seat was further embellished with items like fine linens, Russian dolls, and her prized Winchester Rifle.

Arriving at her seat, Larissa dramatically sank into what was dubbed the executive chair—a threadbare, patched-up recliner that had seen better days but still commanded the room like a monarch's throne. The members of her entourage basked in the opulence of her lavish mobile abode. Amidst a crowd of the less privileged, Rowan kept his gaze fixed on Larissa, advancing forward while ignoring the sneers and whispers emanating from her entourage.

"You move quite slowly for a soldier," she taunted, spinning the detonator through the air.

"Your display of power works on your cronies but not me," Rowan thought. "You know, I was bringing up the rear. I can't secure our flank if I'm not there," he said aloud, stopping a few feet from her.

"Don't be a smart ass with me," she snapped, raising a finger to silence Rowan before he could respond. "Take your team and scout the area for anything of value. While you're doing that, I'll relocate the rest to the shoe warehouse lobby across the street for cover. You've got seventy-two hours.

Report back once you've completed the task," she instructed, dismissing him with a swift hand gesture.

"That's it? I walked through a blizzard for this. She could've said that over the radio. But naw, she has to flaunt," Rowan thought to himself.

"Is something troubling you, Marcus? You have that pensive look," she said, locking eyes with his vacant stare.

Rowan remained silent, spun on his heels, and walked away. He understood that inquiring about her plans would be futile.

Despite her cruelty, Larissa managed to keep the group united and, more critically, alive—a key factor in their survival. However, it was Rowan and his team who mitigated the lethal consequences of her poor decisions. One such mistake was failing to secure the area adequately before conducting a reconnaissance mission. When he once challenged her, she ended the debate by brandishing the detonator. Consequently, he preferred to avoid disputes about tactical priorities, such as the importance of securing a site versus gathering resources.

"No problem. Is there anything else you need?"

"That's all for now. You may leave," Larissa concluded with another dismissive gesture.

Rowan turned to leave, but before he could take four steps toward the exit, one of Larissa's followers blocked his path.

"Yeah, crawl back to your nest, roach," the rotten-mouth man quipped.

Rowan gazed at the man who looked as if he had just emerged from under a rock. Despite the man's unpleasant breath, Rowan managed to smile.

"What are you smiling at, roa....?"

In the midst of a word, Rowan's hand shot upward, delivering an uppercut to the man's chin. Before the man could fully collapse, Rowan caught him by the coat collar. The sharp tug dislodged several of the man's decayed teeth onto the floor. Pulling the man back, Rowan then drove his elbow into the man's nasal bridge. The sound of a loud crunch filled the air as the man spun to the ground. The remaining thugs, witnessing their comrade whimpering on the floor like an injured canine, rose swiftly, reaching for their weapons, but they were stopped in their tracks by a series of methodical claps.

"One day, I might not be here to stop them," Larissa warned as a brief silence covered the room. "Now get out, before I feed you to the dogs."

Casting a final glance at Larissa, Rowan brushed past her, grunted, and made his way to the exit. "When that day arrives, their bodies will be stacked upon yours," he murmured, moving towards the door. In the Mammoth, a man's anguished cries echoed through the silence, dominating the atmosphere for a fleeting moment.

"Why do you continue to let him live?" Bones queried, his voice barely above a whisper.

Larissa's lips curved into a knowing smirk, a glimmer of understanding in her eyes. She was well aware of Rowan's restless yearning to break free from the group, hindered only by the collar clasped around his neck. Years of survival had honed her ability to decipher people's intentions, a skill that had safeguarded her through countless dangers. Rowan exuded an aura of danger, a simmering intensity that hinted at his capability to seize what he desired if provoked. Larissa harbored no illusions about his potential for recklessness. Instead, she strategically allowed him to unleash his pent-up frustrations on those foolish enough to provoke him, channeling his wrath towards others and granting him an outlet for his smoldering rage.

Being the leader of this band of ruffians, she guarded her innermost understanding with an iron will, a secret she wouldn't dare unveil, not even to Bones. Her authority hinged on the facade of ferocious maniacs she commanded. These enforcers, in their own menacing way, served as a deterrent for the level-headed individuals within her domain. It was an unspoken pact; compliance with Larissa's directives or risk facing the brutal wrath of her henchmen and the ominous specter of the collar looming over them.

"My crew and I could easily make up the manpower if Rowan and his team......somehow disappeared in the next storm," Bones suggested.

"In this day and age, everyone has a purpose," she responded, her eyes locked on the closing ramp.

"I understand. But whispers are circling the camp, you're goin' soft. Especially with the roach and his crew."

"Let Marcus be," she stated firmly, her gaze piercing Bones'. "To silence the gossipers, ensure there's an abundance of food and bottles tonight. Let them drown their troubles in drink. That should hush their murmurs."

"As you wish."

"Would one of you kindly assist in getting this unfortunate soul off my pristine floor and properly tended to?" she barked, indicating the man still whimpering in pain. "And for heaven's sake, clean up this dreadful mess!"

"And would someone, please, get this fool off my floor and bandaged up," she yelled, gesturing to the still whimpering man. "And for heaven's sake, get this damn blood up!"

Chapter 2

Making his way back to the Scorpion, Rowan leaned his assault rifle against the side of the vehicle and sat on the cold, yet comfortable snow beside the front tire. His Viper variant assault rifle was a more modern version of the tried-and-true M4 carbine. Rowan returned to the Scorpion, resting his assault rifle against the vehicle before settling on the icy ground near the front tire. The Viper variant weapon he carried was a sleek upgrade from the reliable M4 carbine, its matte black finish standing out against the snow-covered landscape. As he sat there, a gust of wind swept through, carrying with it a chill that seeped into his bones despite his weather-worn gear. The desolate expanse around him seemed to stretch endlessly, broken only by remnants of buildings buried under layers of frost and snow.

Leaning back against the cold metal of the vehicle, Rowan's gaze wandered over the horizon where shadows danced in the fading light. The silence that enveloped him was eerie, punctuated only by distant howls carried on the wind. His mind replayed Larissa's orders, her sharp voice cutting through his thoughts like a knife. Despite their clashes and her ruthless leadership, he knew she held sway over their bandit group with an iron grip.

The weight of their precarious existence settled heavily on Rowan's shoulders as he contemplated their next move in this unforgiving world. Beyond survival lay a yearning for something more—a chance at redemption amidst the ruins of civilization. With each passing moment, the line between ally and adversary blurred in this post-apocalyptic wasteland where trust was a luxury few could afford.

As darkness crept closer, Rowan's hand absentmindedly traced the scars etched into his weather-beaten hands—a testament to battles fought and losses endured. The scars told stories of resilience and defiance against insurmountable odds, marking him as both survivor and warrior in this frozen realm where every step forward was fraught with danger.

In this frozen wasteland that bore witness to humanity's downfall, for a brief moment, Rowan sat alone with his thoughts, steeling himself for the challenges that lay ahead. The soft glow of the sun through the dense clouds beckons the encroaching night. And as he braced himself for Larissa's task, Rowan's resolve remained unyielding—a beacon of hope amidst the icy desolation that gripped London in its frostbitten embrace.

The crunch of footsteps cutting through the icy silence drew his attention away from his thoughts. "Man, that was a quickie," Spence chuckled softly as he settled down next to him.

"You do know you have a problem, right?" he responded.

"That's what my mother always said. Well, I suspect that's what she would say if I knew her," he remarked, adjusting his scarf snugly under his chin.

"To be honest, if I were in her shoes, I'd have ditched your ass as well," a voice chimed in from the left.

Facing the sound, they encountered a slender, athletic woman standing at 5'8", her sharp features cutting through the icy air. The wind danced with her purple and black clan scarf as if in a silent waltz. This was Val, Rowan's trusted second-in-command. Known for her intense aura, she moved with quiet confidence amidst the frozen landscape. Despite being wrapped in winter cargo pants and a short parka puffer coat, Val exuded a striking presence that surpassed mere beauty within the remnants of their bandit clan.

Men often made crude remarks about her Asian background and shared inappropriate fantasies inspired by anime, targeting Val with their unwelcome advances. While she usually brushed off these comments, occasionally a bold individual would try to cross the line from words to actions. In those moments, they quickly discovered that Val's precision and attention to detail, honed through her expertise as a sniper, allowed her to shut down their advances decisively. To the men, it seemed like an abrupt end; to Val, it was simply a lesson in natural selection.

Without lifting his gaze to meet hers, Spence clenched his jaw briefly before responding. "Hold on a sec, lass, you don't have the privilege to speak poorly of her. That's not your place," he retorted, gesturing towards her with a firm finger. "And you're barging in on a fine manly discussion here. Why don't you step back and let the guys handle this business?"

Val shook her head in exasperation at Spence's words, striding past him until she reached Rowan. With a deliberate motion, she nudged some snow towards the Irishman's feet before coming to a halt.

"Hey there..." Spence began, shaking off the frost.

"Quit your crying. The cold will help make a man out of you

yet."

Spence flashed a grin, confidently remarking, "I'm a handful and then some," grabbing his belt buckle and extending his middle finger to point between his legs.

Val pivoted with a muted sigh, her gaze meeting Rowan's. "You needed me?"

Spence tilted his head, eyeing Rowan quizzically. "Hold on! You told her...?"

"Yes, he did, and from what I see, you invited yourself like always," she replied. "So, it looks like you are the one interrupting the 'man-moment'."

"Spence, hold that thought," Rowan commanded, halting Spence mid-sentence in his tracks.

Following the given instructions, the red-bearded man obeyed, crossing his arms and reclining. Rowan shifted his gaze towards Val, noting her initial annoyance fading away. Spence and Val existed as polar opposites within the group dynamics. Val maintained a serious demeanor while Spence leaned towards simplicity. Val actively avoided unnecessary interactions with Spence, a rare occurrence since he persistently provoked reactions. Their coexistence resembled a volatile mixture waiting to ignite; though one embodied gas and the other fire, they shared an exclusive understanding of Rowan's escape plan from Larissa. Their communication remained cryptic and concise to exclude others from unnecessary involvement.

Val meticulously strategized ahead of the group, often poring over any maps to gain an edge. In contrast, Spence excelled in social settings and gatherings but respected boundaries when advised against engaging. Despite his mischievous nature, he proved himself as a reliable comrade and adept soldier.

Rowan found himself in the unenviable position of overseeing their interactions to prevent conflicts or undesirable intimacy from brewing between them.

"We need to move out," Rowan pressed on, "Our leader wants us to scout the vicinity," he mentioned, his hand flexing involuntarily.

"Figured as much. Good thing I spent time going over maps of the area. I'll pick a route." Val replied.

"It's your specialty," Rowan confirmed.

"Anything else?"

"That would be a negative right now. Just find the best route and meet us in the back in five. We have a job to do," Rowan finished.

Val meticulously readjusted the scope on her rifle. "I'll handle it," she stated with unwavering focus. Glancing briefly at Spence, she caught him gesturing wildly, hands spread wide as he silently mouthed, "I'm a big man." With a subtle smirk, Val began striding back towards the vehicle. "You'd sooner spot a thriving palm tree in that city than convince me you're anything close to a real man!"

"But you agree I'm imposing, right?" Spence quipped as Val walked away. Disappearing behind the APC, her hand reemerged with a single finger raised. Spence looked at Rowan. "Yup, I'm winning her over."

"You need to stop playing with fire," Rowan warned as he stood up.

"Nah, man. It's all in good fun."

"The latest 'Darwin incident' said the same thing," Rowan replied, helping Spence to his feet.

"She's uptight, and a pain in the arse. She needs to learn how to relax, and I'm here to help her with that.

"Well, that stickler for rules is the very reason we stay alive during our scouting missions," Rowan remarked, attempting a comical Irish accent that fell flat.

"Whoa, whoa, she is part of the reason?" Spence questioned. Rowan raised an eyebrow, waiting for the justification. "I'm the team's four-leaf clover. It's the luck of the Irish that brings us home, my friend."

Rowan playfully thumped his comrade's shoulder. "I'm sorry. You are right. How could I have forgotten our lucky weed?" he remarked, then strolled towards the rear of the transport.

"Actually, it is an herbaceous plant. So, fuck your classification," Spence replied.

Rowan often found himself surprised by the occasional insightful remarks that escaped Spence's usually jesting facade, revealing a sharp mind beneath the humor. Spence, who humorously referred to himself as a "full-time Irish fighter/part-time whoremonger," sported fiery red hair and a braided beard cascading down his chest, embodying a fierce warrior aesthetic. In this changed world, his previous exploits as a whoremonger had given way to a more festive lifestyle. Raised in an orphanage, Spence possessed a unique outlook shaped by his upbringing.

The orphanage instilled in him a keen ability to decipher people's intentions. Trust was a rare commodity, and he held even fewer in favor. Following his military stint, which ended in discharge due to clashes arising from his sense of superiority, he crossed paths with the Triple Top Mercenary Corporation. It was during this tumultuous phase that Rowan encountered him, altering the course of both their lives. During their heyday with Triple Top, Rowan and Spence traversed the globe, stirring trouble for numerous tyrants only to return later and assist those same despots in rectifying the chaos they had sown. In those bygone eras, the mercenary trade flourished with lucrative opportunities abounding.

Another figure from their Triple Top days occupied the rear of the vehicle. Alistair, affectionately called Al by his comrades, sat there, a slender yet sinewy man with a face marked by wisdom and sorrow. His hair, a mix of salt and pepper, hinted at his experiences. While his appearance might not have stood out, his combat prowess was unmatched. Raised in the rugged streets of Brazil, he had honed skills and resilience that set him apart. Rowan witnessed this firsthand when he and Spence finished a mission and decided to unwind at a local bar. It was there that they saw Al effortlessly take down three opponents before being overwhelmed by their companions. In that moment, Rowan recognized that Al's demeanor aligned perfectly with the mercenary way of life. Following the incident, he and Spence visited Al in the hospital as part of their recruitment strategy.

It proved evident; while the corporation could teach someone to shoot, Al's innate combat prowess was inherent, a quality Rowan couldn't ignore. Discovering Al in the hospital, his visage swathed in bandages and restrained to the bed, they encountered him standing in the corridor amidst two prone figures and one fleeing. Al's bed, being lodged in the room entrance, had thwarted his pursuit. Following a brief discussion, Al accepted their proposal, particularly enticed by their commitment to covering his legal and medical expenses.

Al proved to be a valuable addition beyond just combat skills. Discovering his background as a former EMT in Brazil, Rowan swiftly appointed him as the team's medic without hesitation.

It always made a good story of how he admitted to getting his friends in the hospital to place him in the very same room as the ones he had put in the hospital. Unwilling to give up on a fight and able to heal people, turned out to be a win-win for Rowan.

After meticulously oiling his gun, Al peered out from the vehicle. "When's our departure time?"

"What gave away that idea?" Rowan questioned back with a friendly smile.

"Because we stopped," Al stated with his usual calm certainty. "And because the first thing Larissa has us do once we stop is get us to do her grocery list while she indulges herself at camp."

"Careful now," came Timothy Brook's voice from behind Al. "Larissa will be madder than a wet hen if she finds out you do not appreciate the 'help' she has given us."

The deep, resonant voice belonged to Timothy 'Rook' Brook, known simply as Rook. Hailing from the sun-baked lands of Southern Georgia, Rook's passion lay in tinkering with colossal vehicles. His journey led him through the ranks of the Army, where he rose to the esteemed position of Captain within the Armor Division. As fate would have it, when the catastrophic meteor struck, Rook found himself stationed in Germany, pursuing a degree in Engineering. In the tumultuous aftermath that followed, his mechanical expertise proved just as indispensable as any medical skill.

Amidst the chaos that engulfed the camp he was part of during Larissa's ruthless takeover, Rook's life hung by a thread until she recognized his worth, sparing him on the condition that he kept their fleet running smoothly. Standing tall at 6'3" and weighing 250 lbs.., Rook exuded a quiet strength reminiscent of a chess master contemplating their next move. Unyielding in his principles and unwavering in his beliefs, even Larissa's relentless attempts to sway him could not shake his steadfast resolve.

Despite being surrounded by individuals willing to compromise their integrity for survival, Rook remained an unwavering beacon of honor and dignity. This unyielding stance often stirred tensions within the camp until Larissa made the decision to transfer his care into Rowan's hands for the sake of maintaining peace among them all.

The dynamic within Rowan's team revolved around their indispensable skills and shared aversion towards Larissa. Their unity wasn't born out of a commitment to being the heroes but rather a pragmatic understanding of survival. With the exception of Rook, most members would hesitate little in dealing with Larissa's group decisively if necessary. While they acknowledged that violence wasn't always the solution, when it came to dealing with Larissa's followers, it often seemed like the only viable option. Upon seizing control of a camp, those left standing faced a stark choice: submit or face dire consequences. This mindset fostered a precarious environment lacking long-term stability. Larissa's dominance, enforced by sheer strength, kept them bound together, yet Rowan foresaw its inevitable expiration date. Thus, he took charge, meticulously preparing his makeshift team for the inevitable confrontation with their notorious leader.

"She is always mad, so what's new?" Al continued as Rook nodded in acknowledgment.

"What I care about is us. She is sending us on more excursions, further from camp, and the fact is, we are coming back with less. How long before she starts becoming paranoid and thinking we are keeping the finds for ourselves?" Rowan added

"She might be an outright bitch, but Larissa has not survived this long by being stupid. That's why we made the long trek to jolly old London." Spence emphasized by extending his arm towards the city.

Al's gaze fixed on the Irishman. "Are you suddenly on her side now? Did she promise you something special with Bones every time you defend her?" Spence folded his arms, a grin playing on his lips. "Watch yourself, mate. Remember our last spar? I had you on the floor in no time. I wouldn't mind giving you a refresher, especially if you insist on dragging Bones into my personal affairs."

"You keep bringing this up. You know I was drunk and had a concussion," Al protested.

"A victory is a victory, fella," Spence quipped.

"Why on earth does anyone bother with Spence's romantic escapades?" Val inquired dryly, smoothly weaving past them and giving a playful tug on Spence's beard. "Let's keep it together."

"Ow," Spence grumbled. Before he could respond, she had already initiated a conversation with Rowan.

"Here is the best path we can take into the city. The maps we have do not provide any specific locations, so we'll have to do it the old-fashioned way — going door to door."

Rowan looked over the map. She was right. In all the post-apocalyptic games he played as a kid, there was always someplace, conveniently marked on the map, which allowed you to get all the supplies you needed.

"This will be like going to the dentist. Long and painful,"

Rowan added, as Val nodded before passing the map around to others.

Al scanned over the map with Rook peaking over his shoulder. "What are the odds that half of these paths are even passable? The last city we went to, which was half the size of London, I might add, had the worst lanes."

"Crawling on barbed wire might have been a more enjoyable pastime than trudging through a frozen-over London," Rook quipped dryly.

"Well, find some way to get a connection back to a satellite, and I'll get you two softies a clear path using Google," Val replied, yanking the map from Al's hand.

"Did she suggest I lack courage?" Al inquired of Rook, who affirmed with a deliberate nod. "You do recall the incident with the collapsed structure, don't you? Leaving out the pack of wild dogs, I somehow missed the mattress and landed on and shattered a nightstand. My knee now throbs whenever the cold sets in," he grumbled, turning towards Val.

"Well, you're in luck. The weather station forecasted seventy-degree weather coming our way in the next three to four hundred years," Spence replied.

Al snapped a part of his gun in place to emphasize his point. "You know what I mean. Traversing a city like London is far more dangerous than what we encounter in the wild."

Right on time, Mia Hawthorne emerged from the Scorpion, completing the team's assembly. Despite lacking formal military training, Mia's survival skills in the wilderness with nomadic groups showcased her resourcefulness. Rowan believed that facing the dangers of the city was a lesser risk compared to crossing paths with her. At just twenty-six, Mia exuded a perpetual vigilance. Her sharp eyes meticulously swept over every detail in her vicinity, betraying a predator's calculated watchfulness rather than a prey's fearful apprehension. Observing her deliberate and assured gaze, Rowan recognized the unmistakable confidence born from being at the apex of nature's hierarchy.

With determined strides, Mia advanced towards Rook, her gaze unwaveringly fixed on him. She presented a handcrafted bow directly in front of the towering man's face. Rook shifted his eyes from the weapon to Mia, meeting her intense stare. Without breaking eye contact, Mia shook the bow in a silent demand. Relenting, Rook accepted the bow from her outstretched hand and inspected it carefully.

"I see some good welds," Rook commented before taking a closer look at the trigger mechanism.

Mia's lithe fingers danced in a flurry of controlled chaos, a silent language that spoke volumes. Rook mirrored her movements with a stoic grace, his gestures more composed. In a swift exchange, Mia's hands stilled, punctuated by decisive motions that prompted a nod from Rook. With a sigh, she reclaimed the weapon.

Mia stumbled upon the battered compound bow during a scavenging trip, deciding to repurpose it as the foundation for a new bow. Rook, with his extensive welding expertise and an innate knack for nonverbal communication, mentored her in the intricate repair and maintenance procedures.

Mia was born with a damaged larynx, rendering her unable to speak. Her father, recognizing the challenge, ensured she learned sign language. Though imperfect, it sufficed for her daily needs. In this post-apocalyptic world, Mia encountered adept hunters who introduced her to alternative modes of communication. Describing her as a proficient archer would be an understatement; Rowan witnessed her precision firsthand when she swiftly incapacitated six men before they could even discern the origin of her arrows. She unleashed a flurry of projectiles, turning her targets into human pincushions.

Initially indifferent to firearms, her curiosity piqued as she observed the seasoned soldiers expertly handling their guns. Gradually, she found herself drawn to the intricacies of gunmanship. Her journey began with mastering the art of handling a customized Glock that discharged reduced-caliber bullets, enhancing precision in each shot.

"Hold up, Mia; Rook is going to have to look at that later. We have orders to move out," Rowan called. The hunter turned around and gave him a look which suggested he was dinner for some wildcat. "You know our role within this community and where we stand in the pecking order. Larissa wants us to scout the area away from the camp to see what this old dump of a city has to offer. We can say what we want about our fearless leader..."

Mia raised her hand, forming a unique gesture with her thumb, pinky, and middle finger extended. This sign, though unconventional in sign language, was Mia's own creation to convey her disdain for Larissa. The thumb and pinky formed an "L," while the middle finger symbolized a universally recognized expression from centuries past in the old world.

Spence acknowledged the gesture with a loud, "Fuckin'-A."

"Group's supplies are low, and my guess is they're lower than Larissa is letting on." Rowan continued after his team's chuckle had died down. "And regardless of how we feel, that group needs us as much as we need them."

"We're not in good company here, Rowan," Rook commented.

"When have we not been?" Val whispered.

"I understand how you feel. But if we try anything, we die, so we must play ball for now. That metal collar around your neck is not a fashion statement. It's either the collar or we can go out on our own, where we will die from hunger within days," Rowan said, ending the debate.

Rowan viewed their inquiries not as a flaw but as a necessary release of pent-up frustrations. He recognized the importance of allowing his team this moment of vulnerability. His responsibility lay in maintaining control, a crucial task for the safety of all involved.

Rowan surveyed his team, studying each determined face, "We've been lazy enough today and wasting daylight. Time to head out and see what London has to offer. Finalize your gear, and pack enough resources for one night. We meet back in one hour."

Spence walked up to Rook, "Come on, I need you to grease my shillelagh."

"You could just ask me to check your shotgun, like everyone else," Rook sighed.

Spence's *shillelagh*, as he liked to dub it, was the *Herakles* — an automatic twin-barrelled shotgun with a capacity of up to thirty-five rounds. While he favored his AK-47 for most situations, in tight spaces, nothing rivaled the destructive power of the Herakles.

"What, and miss the look on your face every time I ask? Nah!" Spence chuckled, patting his friend on the shoulder.

In the following moments, Rowan's team maintained a hushed demeanor while readying themselves for the reconnaissance mission. When executed correctly, recon held minimal risks, with potential dangers arising mainly from encountering larger bands of marauders or, in more dire circumstances, cannibalistic groups. Yet, these concerns paled in comparison to their primary fears - falling victim to the unforgiving winter environment.

In the aftermath of the Impact's early years, the team had witnessed unfortunate souls vanishing into unseen crevices, being crushed under precarious ice masses, and most commonly, succumbing to hypothermia. The biting cold presented as formidable a challenge as any adversary they might face head-on.

The asteroid impact altered humanity's trajectory by propelling vast amounts of organic matter into the atmosphere. This fine dust clouded the stratosphere, triggering a sudden drop in Earth's temperatures akin to a miniature ice age. The unfolding events defied expectations, despite numerous forewarnings and apocalyptic predictions. It seemed almost as if the planet itself attempted to safeguard its inhabitants. Whether through a protective instinct or scientific oversight, Rowan found solace in the former, renewing his flickering faith in mankind and fueling his will to persevere.

Upon encountering Larissa, it became evident that she governed with unwavering authority and a lack of compassion. Two rigid decrees governed her followers, mandates that he frequently found himself obliged to enforce despite his personal reservations. The initial edict: any act of theft within the community was strictly forbidden. Violating this regulation resulted in swift exile from the group to face the unforgiving chill of solitary nights or a swift shot to the head.

The most stringent decree she enforced was the second rule: no infants allowed. Those who opted to start families faced a stark choice - abandon their newborns or remain with them. She allowed no room for ambiguity. Offspring equated to increased resource demands; more resources translated to heightened challenges, labor, and a scarcity of skilled individuals.

The shifting world demanded that Rowan adapt, a constant evolution he begrudgingly embraced.

Chapter 3

Part of readying their supplies, the team meticulously went through their standard procedures. They started by inspecting their clothing, sleeping gear, and provisions. Next in line were their knives, ropes, medical kits, and various survival implements. Lastly, they checked their weapons meticulously due to the unforgiving cold; each firearm underwent thorough scrutiny to guarantee its optimal operation. Understanding that a single misfire could mean survival or demise in this brutal environment.

Like a well-oiled machine, they emphasized the importance of double-checking each other's weapons. Rook checked Spence's AK-47 and Herakles shotgun. Mia checked Rook's machete, Spence fixed Al's pistol grip, and Rowan checked the slide on Val's sidearm.

Rowan observed Val's precise movements as she deftly secured her Beretta pistol in its holster and effortlessly slung her sniper rifle across her back. Each member of the team had their idiosyncrasies, superstitions, and rituals that held a sacred place in their routines. Rowan had encountered soldiers who shunned writing farewell letters before embarking on missions, believing it sealed their fate, while some would attach their blood type to their equipment despite the ominous connotations it carried.

Val, in contrast, had bestowed names upon her weapons – her pistol was Chloe, and her rifle she called Scott. Rowan understood the sentiment behind it. Any method that aided his team in navigating the harsh reality of their world, he had learned to accept.

"Val, you mind giving me a hand?" Rowan asked as he clicked his last gear in place on his ballistic vest.

When Spence exited the vehicle, while making sure he sauntered past Val, shooting her a lingering wink as their eyes met.

"Will he ever catch on?" she muttered, exhaling wearily as she set her boot down atop a crate to fasten it.

"Come on, Val. It's Spence we're talking about. Maybe one day he'll come to heed my warnings," Rowan replied.

The two exchanged a smile, which was quickly erased from Rowan's face as Val tightened the straps on his gear, causing him to grunt.

"Getting weak on me, old man?" she asked.

"Naw, I think you've just gotten meaner in your old age."

Val glanced behind her, a wry smile playing on her lips. "Keep it down. If Spence hears you, he might just beg for a little comination," she remarked dryly, dismissing the notion with a shake of her head.

"Well, just between us, his safe word is 'rainbow'," Rowan disclosed. Val simply turned and left, giving Rowan a good laugh.

As the Scorpion emptied, Rowan lingered inside for a moment. He paused, absorbing the stillness. Outside, his team's camaraderie filled the air with laughter and banter, solidifying their bond from comrades to kin. In this frozen urban expanse, they found a new sense of unity. Rowan's role as their leader solidified with each passing heartbeat. Drawing in a lungful of icy but invigorating air, he joined his team in the snow-covered cityscape. Excitement pulsed through him, etching a grin on his face.

"To London!" He addressed no one in particular.

Ω▪Ω▪Ω▪Ω

In the heart of Old London, where iconic structures like Big Ben and Buckingham Palace once stood amidst bustling crowds, a stark transformation had taken place. Rowan had never set foot in this city, but from the footage he'd glimpsed over the years, it was a vibrant metropolis teeming with vitality and hues.

Today, however, the landscape bore no resemblance to those lively images; instead, a desolate scene of monochrome shades enveloped the abandoned thoroughfares.

"The rats have better taste than to stick around here. And I'm not just saying that because of my charming Irish roots. This place gives me the creeps," Spence remarked.

Rowan found himself in agreement. After exploring numerous towns and cities, they discovered that the majority were eerily devoid of life. Through their expeditions, it became evident that humanity had split into two distinct groups. The first consisted of individuals striving to carve out a semblance of normalcy from the remnants of civilization. These resilient souls worked tirelessly to clear paths, fortify their surroundings, and adapt the terrain to their advantage. They stationed guards to protect their territories, yet Rowan remained unfazed by these efforts.

There was another category that caught Rowan's attention. These individuals were the ones who set traps and hunted unsuspecting victims from the darkness. During a reconnaissance mission in a district of Thionville, located on the Northern coast of France, his team encountered a band of cannibals who had prepared to ambush them. It was in that moment that Rowan realized how events had changed ordinary people, forcing them to adapt to their surroundings, going as far as to select tactical positions for lethal purposes.

Luckily, Rowan and his team of seasoned warriors were facing adversaries who had chosen what they believed to be the perfect ambush location. However, the attackers' negligence in concealing their trail proved to be their downfall. This oversight enabled Rowan's team to swiftly detect and eliminate the assailants. Subsequently, they located the enemy camp and successfully retrieved a substantial cache of much-needed provisions.

In this urban landscape, the contrast was stark. Certain streets lay barren, devoid of both vehicles and life, while others were blocked with debris. Initially appearing deserted, London gradually revealed its secrets as they scoured a small area for three hours. Bullet casings glinted in the snow alongside a discarded magazine, evidence of recent activity that hadn't been buried by the ongoing snowstorm.

Traces in the snow hinted at a significant object being dragged through the vicinity not long ago, resisting being concealed by the relentless snowfall. They crouched low in concealment, their eyes fixed on the road that stretched towards a strategic intersection, perfect for an ambush. Time trickled by as Rook, Al, Rowan, and Spence maintained their vigil, an hour slipping away without any hint of movement or presence beyond the quiet landscape.

Mia and Val returned from a quick recon, their expressions tired. "Rowan, we searched the area but found no signs of anything else," Val reported solemnly.

"Understood. Good job. How far are we from the camp?" Rowan asked as he continued to scan the roads with his binoculars.

"We are about a quarter mile as the crow flies, but that amounts to a few blocks in the city," Val said.

Rowan did a mental sigh. Searching for cities took time. Even though many of the buildings in London were in better shape than other areas they searched, securing them was still a lengthy process. One wrong step or a missed closet could lead to a bad situation.

"We've located two locations with possible supplies we can use, right?" Rowan said.

"Three if you count that small bookstore we came across not long ago," Spence replied.

"Books, huh, that would be a waste of time," Rook replied.

"True, she'd burn them," Spence added. "Maybe not the kids' books, they have pretty pictures," Spence said, getting a small chuckle from the group.

Al's voice cut through the biting wind, his words mirroring Rowan's unspoken thoughts. "Time's running short. The sun's dipping fast, and this storm's only getting fiercer by the minute. Let's hunker down and make camp. That structure with the circular entryway looks like our best bet."

"Agreed," Val replied. "We would have to backtrack a few blocks if we wanted to find some decent shelter that doesn't leave us vulnerable."

A fierce gust of wind roared through the icy landscape,

sending snow swirling in chaotic eddies that stung exposed skin. In its wake, Rowan's gaze was drawn to a looming silhouette cloaked in shadows atop a crumbling building nearby. Straining his eyes against the biting cold, he cautiously advanced, his breath forming frosty clouds in the air. Just as he thought he could make out distinct features, a sudden blast of wind obscured his view, and when the snow settled, the figure had melted back into the bleak scenery, leaving only an eerie emptiness behind.

Rowan stood still, his gaze fixed on the vacant expanse, his hand unconsciously reaching for the hilt of his rifle. Uncertainty gnawed at him, questioning if his vision was deceiving him or if the desolate surroundings were beginning to play tricks on his mind. In a moment of quiet contemplation, he stared intently at the spot where the mysterious figure had been, almost urging its reappearance before a sudden jolt interrupted his focus—a firm grip seizing his shoulder.

"Hey, you zoning out on us?" Spence inquired. "Val's been calling you."

Rowan gave a subtle nod. "I believe I saw movement on that rooftop," he mentioned, gesturing towards it.

"What, have you been getting into Larissa's secret stash?" Spence asked, looking in the direction. "There's nothing out there, brother."

"No way, I wouldn't touch Fluke's brew even if you paid me. Must be the snow messing with my vision. Forget it. Let's head indoors," he dismissed casually, then took one last look before retracing his steps to rejoin the group, Spence tagging along closely.

"Val, you and Mia take the lead, secure the entrance. Keep your head on a swivel. You sense or see anything odd, fall back, and we'll find another place," Rowan instructed.

Val and Mia exchanged silent nods, dropping their heavier gear, leaving it behind with the team so that they could move quicker.

"We'll join and do a room-by-room search to clear the building." Rowan continued.

Mia and Val, known for their unparalleled scouting skills honed in the wilderness, took point as the team's expert infiltrators. Their lithe figures allowed them to slip unnoticed towards the looming structure ahead, blending seamlessly with the shadows. The remaining members of the squad lingered cautiously behind, keeping a watchful eye on their surroundings as they advanced methodically. From a distance of just half a block, the faint figures of Mia and Val disappeared into the building, their movements swift and silent against the backdrop of desolation.

At the back of the group, Rowan couldn't shake the image of the enigmatic silhouette he had glimpsed. The feeling of being under surveillance intensified with every step, prompting him to fixate his gaze on the rooftops ahead.

Chapter 4

In the heart of their makeshift camp, Larissa and her bandit crew sought shelter within a decrepit warehouse as the impending snowstorm loomed over them. The structure, a relic of Old London's architecture, stood tall with its two stories of weathered brick and mortar. Among the group, someone recognized the abandoned machines in the workshop area as once used for crafting shoes.

A glimmer of hope sparked briefly at the prospect of salvaging useful components, only to fade as they found little that remained intact. Despite this setback, Larissa swiftly commanded the dismantling of the machines; her belief being that idle hands invited chaos. She trusted in her people's resourcefulness to repurpose the scraps into something valuable, no matter how rugged it may turn out to be.

In the expansive delivery area, all the vehicles were neatly parked. Before heading out to recon, Rook carefully maneuvered the Scorpion into a separated designated spot, distinct from the other vehicles, a precautionary measure for a swift getaway if needed. Larissa often found amusement in this habit, jokingly suggesting that Rowan and his team were always planning to go AWOL.

"*Silly grunts,*" she thought as she led the group through the building. "Show them you are not afraid, and they will learn to fear your courage," she continued with whispered in a chant.

Bones marched stoically alongside her, seemingly unaffected by her words and showing minimal interest in acknowledging them. With her Winchester rifle at the ready, Larissa exuded someone who had come to understand the state of the world. Despite the absence of any immediate threats, she scanned the surroundings with unwavering focus. To her mild disappointment, the warehouse was devoid of any adversaries.

The ground floor was once dominated by the bustling production area, while a modest office nestled in a corner. Upstairs, a larger office bore the title "manager" on its door. Further beyond lay another section, now in ruins due to the passage of time and erosion.

Commanding the upstairs domain as her own, Larissa directed her companions to establish their base in the bustling production zone below. The office bore marks of neglect, yet she noted with satisfaction its dry interior and a window that opened without protest. Anticipating only a temporary stay, she eyed the worn manager's quarters, where a resilient crimson sofa beckoned from its quiet corner. Scant furnishings met her discerning gaze; nothing within stirred her interest beyond the comfort promised by the solitary couch.

Sinking into the sofa, she shifted uncomfortably, noting its lumpy surface that barely passed for comfort. As she adjusted to her makeshift bed, a hulking silhouette loomed in the doorway. Among Rowan and his companions, only Bones dared to enter Larissa's domain uninvited. His imposing presence conveyed an unspoken understanding of who held authority within those walls, silently assuring Larissa of his unwavering allegiance.

"We should locate one of those five-star hotels to establish our headquarters. Their furnishings are sure to surpass what we have here," she remarked, clutching the sofa's arm as its fabric emitted a puff of dust.

Bones shrugged, "I always enjoyed those pay by the hour joints myself."

"I am sure you have some fond memories." She replied as she watched a smile form on his face. "You need to think bigger, Bones. This is our world now. I want a place to call my own. Something which symbolizes...," she paused, taking the time to run her hand over the dusty material, "me."

"In that case, why not choose a castle? I mean, we are in fucking England."

Larissa scoffed but then looked at Bones with a new perspective. "I like your thinking. Find me one, and I'll give you your own room."

Bones chuckles at the comment. "Make it an ocean view, and I will get you the biggest castle that's still standing." As if a deal had been struck, Bones closed the door and proceeded down the hall.

"Oh, and Bones! Bring me a drink after setting up camp," she yelled leaning back on the couch.

Imagining residing in a fortress brought a grin to her face. She held her rifle with care, as if it were a precious infant, readjusting its position to ensure swift access in case an unwelcome visitor dared to intrude. The 1873 Winchester rifle had been discovered in Germany, unearthed from the rubble of a mansion.

Digging through the rubble, she spotted the safe protruding from a mound of rocks. With painstaking effort, she spent hours clearing away debris and finally managed to pry the safe open with a torch. Inside, gleaming in pristine condition, was a lever-action rifle that bore an uncanny resemblance to the ones she had admired in the classic western movies she cherished from her childhood days spent watching with her family.

Inspecting the rifle never failed to immerse her in memories that lingered like shadows. Curiously, those recollections were the only fragments she retained of them. It was a silent confession she kept to herself, finding solace in these thoughts not for their warmth but for the stark reminder of her profound sacrifices. The weight of her bereavement stoked the fires of her beliefs, propelling her forward with unwavering resolve.

The Winchester was perfect in her hand, and it felt like it was made specifically for her. It was the symbol of her power — power she achieved through force and will. Cracking the safe and taking the gun was her way of giving a middle finger to the world. A world which had screwed her over, keeping her from the authority she was born to have.

She paused for a moment and took in the room. The smile on her face grew more prominent as she started laughing.

"I have my own *Excalibur*."

That castle was sounding more as a necessity with each passing second.

$$\Omega \cdot \Omega \cdot \Omega \cdot \Omega$$

As twilight descended, the members of Larissa's group kindled a jubilant atmosphere. Crackling fires encircled their makeshift camp, casting flickering light to push back the shadows. What was once a desolate factory had transformed into a lively campground through their efforts. A handful of sentries stood vigilant while the majority reveled in merriment. Laughter, spirited cheers, the rhythmic clinking of bottles, and the lively tunes of various instruments crescendoed as night unfurled its dark veil. The stern air of military discipline that had hung over the camp dissipated swiftly, replaced by the vibrant energy akin to a boisterous college gathering within a span of mere hours.

Amidst the bustling activity of the manufacturing floor, Bones navigated through the throngs of people. In the heart of the space blazed a towering fire drum, casting flickering shadows across the makeshift structures. Around the fiery centerpiece, women swayed gracefully to an unheard rhythm, their movements both mesmerizing and fluid. Whistles and cheers filled the air as men watched with admiration.

The scene was alive with a sense of celebration and unity, each individual fully immersed in the moment. The crackling flames illuminated faces etched with stories of survival, their eyes reflecting a mix of weariness and fleeting joy. Laughter intertwined with the crackling of burning wood, creating a symphony of sounds that echoed through the repurposed buildings.

Bones observed this display of communal revelry, his weathered features softening imperceptibly at the sight. There was an unspoken understanding among them all - in this unforgiving world where danger lurked beyond every corner, these moments of respite were rare treasures to be cherished. Each smile shared and every dance step taken symbolized defiance against the bleakness that surrounded them, a testament to their resilience in the face of uncertainty.

Bones maintained a vigilant watch over the group, ensuring strict adherence to the settlement's regulations. Those who deviated from these rules were assigned arduous tasks that spanned several days. Attire was a matter of personal choice, rest was unrestricted, and revelry was a reward reserved for those who upheld their responsibilities diligently.

On this current trek around the party grounds, Bones had a purpose. He had left his men to carry on their duties as he headed towards a mound of wriggling blankets.

"At least he covered himself this time," Bones thought as he approached the blanket.

The room's tense silence shattered as Bones's rough hands seized the sheets, ripping them away with a violent flourish. The fabric tore through the air, a sudden gust of aggression that made the two women huddle closer in fear. Their startled gasps mingled with a chorus of shrill screams that reverberated off the walls, echoing the chaos unfurling before them.

Caught off guard by Bones's abrupt intrusion, the man beside the women faltered, his eyes widening in confusion and alarm. His expression mirrored their shock, a mirror reflecting shared bewilderment at the unexpected and forceful display of dominance.

As Bones loomed over them, his presence suffocating in its intensity, the women recoiled instinctively. Their bodies tensed, muscles coiled like springs ready to snap as they scrambled away from him, driven by primal fear and an urgent need for distance from this rugged figure whose actions spoke louder than any words could convey.

"Wha-, what? Wait. Come back!" The man yelled as he fell face-first on the floor reaching for the fleeing women. He stood and greeted Bones with a middle finger. "Why the hell did you do that?"

Flukes was a plump fellow with round cheeks. How someone

kept that much fat on them with so little food even bewildered a man like Bones. In the world before, Flukes taught chemistry, but in this new reality, he held a prominent role in Larissa's group due to his exceptional talent for creating alcohol from unconventional sources.

"Why the hell did you do that?" Flukes asked again.

The brew master went on a rant, his eyes focused the whole time on the women walking away.

"Do you have any idea, what those two are good at? I'll answer for you. Let me just say, they can make any man weep in pleasure," he continued, oblivious to Bones fleeting patience.

Bones focused intently on tuning out the man's ceaseless grumblings, the passing time feeling interminable.

"Flukes," he said louder.

The man kept talking, looking away from the brute.

"Flukes," he shouted at the half-naked chemist to get his attention. Yet, no response.

His patience worn thin, he seized the rotund man's shoulder and spun him around forcefully.

"Dammit! What do you want moron?" Flukes barked.

"The only thing keeping you off constant watch duty is Larissa's reliance on your unique abilities," Bones remarked, the distinct metallic click of a blade being unsheathed echoing around them.

Flukes let out a strained breath as the razor-sharp edge made contact with his manly bits.

"Your prowess doesn't hinge on your anatomy. Push me further, and I'll serve you a meal of your own defiance," Bones declared, fixing his gaze on the chemist. The realization dawned on the chemist, evident in his expression. Bones emphasized his threat by twisting the knife in a menacing manner. "Raw," he emphasized coldly.

Flukes nervously swallowed, his hands raised in a gesture of apology, "Geez, alright," he sighed. "You do know how to interrupt a man when he's on top of the world."

"Well right now that world is a frozen popsicle," Bones said.

"Seems Larissa's after her custom blend," Flukes remarked, prompting Bones to nod in confirmation as he stepped back and sheathed his weapon. "Alright, I have it over here," he continued, wobbling to a stack of weapon cases.

Bones pried open the lid of a container, revealing an assortment of glass bottles nestled inside. Each bottle held a different shape and size, standing in neat rows like soldiers awaiting orders.

"Probably just as dangerous as the weapons once found in the crate," Bones thought.

Bones remained steadfast in his distrust of the chemist, always avoiding sampling his concoctions. Just as Flukes reached out to offer him the bottle, a piercing shriek pierced through the festive chatter around them.

The entire camp froze in unison, a collective breath held as if time itself had stalled. Whether under the influence or not, a sudden sobriety gripped them all. Every eye was fixed on the vehicle lot, now bathed in flickering firelight from scattered barrels. A tense silence enveloped the scene, halting movement and speech alike. It wasn't until the distinct sound of gun mechanisms being readied pierced the stillness that Bones jolted back to awareness, a chilling realization dawning upon him.

"Where's the patrols?" Bones thought as he peered out into the darkness.

A chilling screech pierced the air, echoing like a desperate creature's final agony. Moments later, a member of Bones' patrol emerged, his face twisted in pain, a crimson stain spreading across his midsection. With trembling hands, he dragged a gleaming blade through the snow, each rasping sound heightening the tension. His faltering steps took him past an abandoned car, the shadows seeming to elongate and clutch at him as he staggered towards the looming building, a silent witness to his ordeal.

"Help me," the patrolman sputtered, his fearful eyes falling on Bones.

Bones remained passive, showing no inclination to assist, and the rest of the group followed suit.

In the flickering glow of the fire, Bones's heart clenched at the sight of a dark shape slinking through the darkness. It darted with eerie grace across the rooftop of an abandoned vehicle, sending shivers down his spine. His gaze snapped back to the wretched man beside him just in time to witness the shadowy form descend behind him. The movements were a blur, a silent dance of death unfolding in the night. All that confirmed its presence was the sudden absence of the limping man's head. A chilling silence settled as the headless body staggered a few paces before crumbling to its knees. For a haunting moment, as if defying gravity itself, the torso swayed in macabre harmony with the howling wind before finally succumbing to stillness on the frozen ground.

A single droplet of sweat traced a path down Bones' weathered cheek, glistening in the dim light. Startled by the sound of water dripping onto the ground nearby, Bones swiveled to find Flukes trembling, his nerves betraying him as a substantial puddle collected at his boots. In usual times, Bones might have derided or belittled Flukes without hesitation, but this moment was different.

Flukes' voice trembled as he whispered, "What in blazes was that?"

"I'm not sure," Bones answered, unfastening his pistol holster.

With all gazes fixated on him, seeking guidance. Bones having a surge of determination, cautiously strode purposefully towards the entrance. Surveying the chamber, he noticed a handful of daring or perhaps reckless individuals following suit. Conversely, some opted for caution, pressing themselves closer to the safety of the walls.

Debris crumbled underfoot with each step, the fire's crackle punctuating the eerie silence that enveloped them. Whimpers of fear and uncertainty echoed through the building, setting Bones' nerves on edge. Just moments ago, his voice had to compete with the howling wind to be heard above a whisper.

Two of Rowan's seasoned mercenaries surged ahead, their weapons raised and sweeping the bleak expanse outside. Bones froze mid-step, his heart racing as he caught a glimpse of shifting silhouettes looming over the entrance, a flicker of movement that sent a jolt of fear down his spine.

"Above you!" his voice echoed through the icy silence.

Eerie silence enveloped the men as a chilling shadow loomed over them. Without warning, elongated hands descended like tendrils of darkness, seizing their heads in a merciless grip. Bones shuddered at the gut-wrenching symphony of agony that echoed through the desolate streets. The metallic scent of blood tainted the air as razor-sharp claws tore into flesh and sinew, rending skin with savage precision.

Helpless against the monstrous force, they were hoisted into the frigid night sky, their anguished cries piercing the stillness.

Upwards they ascended, towards the roof where oblivion awaited. In an instant, silence devoured their screams, leaving only a haunting void in its wake. Then came the sickening descent - bodies plummeting to earth with a sickening crack that reverberated through the frozen wasteland.

Lifeless forms lay sprawled on the unforgiving ground, severed heads resting grotesquely apart from their vessels. The macabre scene unfolded amidst a backdrop of terror-stricken onlookers whose horrified gasps mingled with the howling winds. In that moment of gruesome revelation, chaos erupted like wildfire, consuming all semblance of order in a frenzy of fear and despair.

Chapter 5

Shattered windows echoed with the sound of splintering glass as twisted claws snaked in, seizing unsuspecting victims who had sought refuge within. Pulling out into the darkness not to be seen again. Amidst the chaos, a guard's finger tightened on the trigger, igniting their assault rifle and sparking a frenzy of panicked gunfire from the rest.

Swiftly, those with their senses sharp retreated away from the window establish a protective line further inside. Once the first barrage vanished into the darkness, there was a frantic exchange of magazines, with fresh ones clumsily inserted into weapons.

As the echoes of gunfire faded into the icy night, a haunting silence settled over the desolate landscape. The stillness was shattered by the return of that bone-chilling shriek, now multiplied in a cacophony of eerie wails that seemed to reverberate through the frozen air. A tremor ran through one of the battered vehicles outside, its metal frame protesting as a solitary figure landed on its roof, bathed in an ominous glow from the smoldering barrel nearby.

Time hung suspended for a heartbeat before the creature unleashed another shrill cry, a primal sound that stirred the darkness with an unmistakable call to arms. In response, a horde of these grotesque beings emerged from the shadows like twisted specters materializing out of nightmares, their beastly forms illuminated by flickering flames. They surged towards the camp entrances from all directions, their movements frenzied and malevolent as they overturned fire barrels, sending sparks dancing into the frigid air like fiery omens of impending chaos.

The scene unfolded in a nightmarish frenzy, a twisted ballet of terror and bloodshed. The crowd, consumed by primal fear, tripped over their own feet in a frantic attempt to escape the oncoming horror. Gunfire echoed through the air as the charging beasts closed in, their movements fluid and deadly. Each desperate shot seemed futile as the monsters pounced on their prey with savage precision.

The creatures' fangs tore through flesh like hot knives through butter, crimson streams painting the ground beneath them in a macabre dance. The metallic tang of blood mingled with the acrid scent of fear, creating a sickening symphony that filled the air. In the dim light, shadows danced grotesquely against walls slick with gore, emphasizing the brutality of the scene playing out before them.

Fear clawed at Flukes as he sprinted, his heart pounding in his chest like a war drum. Just as hope flickered, a shadow pounced from a shattered window, hurling him into a stack of alcohol crates. Glass and liquid exploded around him, but amidst the chaos, pain seared through him, its source a cruel mystery in the frenzy. The creature's jaws loomed wide, a gaping maw of terror descending towards, chomping down on his neck, nearly decapitating him.

Amidst the chaos, Bones sprinted towards the manager's office, abandoning Flukes to his fate. He clung to a sliver of hope that Larissa might offer salvation or guidance in this dire situation. A sudden rush of air accompanied by a chilling cry caught his attention. Glancing back, he witnessed a toppled barrel meeting the pooled alcohol, igniting into a blaze that consumed both Flukes' lifeless body and the creature feasting on him.

Momentum carried Bones forward, his body crashing to the icy ground. As he scrambled up, a lifeless figure lay behind him, a grim reminder of the dangers lurking in the frozen wasteland. But ahead, bathed in flickering light, stood his salvation - the stairs to the manager's office beckoning just fifteen feet away.

Suddenly, a chilling presence landed before him, its back turned as if mocking his escape. In the dim illumination, Bones discerned its pallid skin and muscular form, sending shivers down his spine. He remained prone, heart hammering in his chest as he raised his weapon with trembling hands. Each movement deliberate yet fraught with dread, he aimed and pulled the trigger.

The shot echoed through the desolate landscape as it struck true, piercing the creature's back. A guttural cry filled the air as the beast writhed in agony on the frozen ground. Seizing this fleeting moment of vulnerability, Bones pushed himself to his feet and sprinted towards the sanctuary of the stairs, fear fueling every step taken away from the wounded monstrosity.

"Fuck you, you ugly ass bitch," he shouted, firing one last shot into the creature's skull, ending its movement as he passed.

Bones stood amidst the chaos, as he surveyed the scene. His eyes darted from one harrowing sight to another, each detail etching itself into his memory. To his left, shadowy figures moved with eerie grace among his crew, their movements swift and deadly as they attacked with savage precision. The air was thick with the scent of blood and the sounds of desperate cries.

In the opposite direction, bodies writhed beneath the weight of monstrous forms, limbs jerking in futile attempts to break free. The ground trembled with each impact, a grim symphony of pain and struggle echoing through the building. Bones could feel the tension in the air, a palpable fear that fueled both his enemies and his allies.

Despite the overwhelming odds, only a small group of Bones' crew managed to stand their ground against the relentless onslaught. Their faces were etched with grim determination as they fought back, their weapons flashing in sporadic bursts of light against the encroaching darkness. Each shot fired was a desperate plea for survival, a defiance against the nightmarish creatures that outnumbered them.

Through it all, Bones told himself to remain resolute. In this moment of chaos and terror, he had to embodied strength and resilience, in a sea swirling with madness threatening to consume them all.

A sudden, thunderous bang echoed from the manager's office, drawing his focus back.

"Larissa," he thought.

Blood and unidentifiable gore painted the stairway to the office, creating a treacherous path that sent shivers down his spine. With each step he took, the slickness threatened to send him tumbling into the macabre mess below. Ignoring the gruesome sight, he pushed himself to ascend faster, heart pounding in his chest.

Bounding up two steps at a time, a sudden explosion beneath him ripped through the wood, launching him into the air. The world spun around him as he crashed back onto the floor below with a sickening crunch, agony shooting through his body like fiery tendrils. Gasping for breath, he struggled to focus his blurred vision.

As clarity slowly returned, dread gripped him when he saw a monstrous creature looming over him, its form as massive as his own. Crouched and ready to strike, it exuded an aura of primal menace that made every nerve in his body scream with fear.

The creature's claws arched menacingly in the air before descending with a terrifying swiftness. Bones was engulfed in searing agony as his chest and abdomen erupted in torment. His gaze fell upon the gory sight of his body laid bare, akin to a brutal dissection. Each throb of pain hammered home the grim certainty of his demise.

A haunting cry of "Larissa!" tore from his lips, echoing despair as darkness encroached, the monster's talons piercing through his skull.

Ω▪Ω▪Ω▪Ω

Awakening abruptly in the manager's office, Larissa was startled. The flickering light from the fires below shined through the large window overlooking the first floor, helping to illuminate the room and allowing her to survey the room. Everything appeared undisturbed. She blinked, hoping to sharpen her sight, yet in this unforgiving world, clarity remained elusive.

Adjusting her posture on the edge of the couch, her boot nudged an object nearby. Glancing down, she retrieved the bottle. "Cheap shit," she muttered disdainfully at the depleted vessel.

Recollection struck her suddenly - Bones had been dispatched to retrieve Fluke's potent drink. A moment of hesitation gripped her as she struggled to gauge the passage of time. How extensive was her slumber? Had the revelry concluded? The absence of familiar sounds was conspicuous: no echoes of passion, no triumphant shouts marking conquests, no vulgarities from her loyal entourage.

That is when it hit her. It was not something that woke her up — it was the lack thereof. The change from drunken revelry to absolute silence put her on edge. That silence was quickly broken by the screams of her people, prompting her to grab her rifle — her Excalibur. The absence of sound jolted her awake, a stark contrast to the prior revelry. The abrupt shift to eerie quietness set her nerves on edge. Before she could fully grasp the situation, the piercing cries of her comrades shattered the stillness, compelling her to reach for her weapon — her trusted Excalibur.

"Fucking pansies. What the hell are they scared of now?" she questioned, patting Excalibur in her hand as if it solved problems.

Moving in the direction of the door, her steps faltered as she accidentally nudged the bottle that lay forgotten on the ground, briefly loosing her balance.

"That might have been a bit stronger than I thought. Flukes continues to outdo himself," she mused, a grin slowly spreading across her features.

The cacophony of screams reverberated through the air, mingling with the sharp shatter of glass. The haze induced by alcohol dissipated swiftly as her innate survival reflexes surged to the forefront. The realization dawned upon her that they were under attack, and she needed to take charge, to guide them through this turmoil. A barrage of deafening gunfire erupted, harmonizing with the symphony of terrified cries that echoed in unison. Racing towards the window that offered a view of the chaos below, she found herself struck dumb for the very first time in a long time.

The unexpected sight unfolded before her, a chaotic dance of muzzle flashes and flames casting eerie shadows as her comrades were mercilessly ripped apart by an unfathomable force. The sheer number of assailants overwhelmed her senses. Before she could turn for the door, the window shattered with a deafening crash, a stray bullet piercing through the exact spot where her head had lingered mere moments ago.

Backpedaling, Larissa shielded her eyes from the glass fragments cascading around her. Anger surged within her, propelling her upright. When a dark silhouette had already descended onto the window ledge, eclipsing the light below. In the dimness, only a vague outline was visible to Larissa. The creature's monstrous, otherworldly traits pulsed with each shallow inhale in the scant illumination. Time hung suspended as their gazes intertwined, primal instincts clashing silently between them. And then it sprang forth.

In the frigid, unforgiving world that had claimed so many lives, Larissa's survival was no fluke. Her every move spoke of a lifetime spent mastering combat skills, honing them to lethal precision. As she faced off against the creature, her sinewy muscles rippled under scars etched by countless battles, a testament to her enduring resilience.

The clash between predator and prey unfolded with primal intensity. In a swift and calculated maneuver, Larissa intercepted the creature mid-leap. Her grip was unyielding, fingers closing around its arm and throat like steel vices. The sheer force of the beast's momentum forced her back a step, but she held fast, unflinching in the face of adversity as she always had.

Turning swiftly, she propelled the creature against the wall, sending cracks spider-webbing through its surface. As it crumpled to the ground, she unleashed a powerful dropkick straight to its face, driving its head deeper into the fractured wall. Despite its harrowing shriek, the creature remained alive. Assessing her injury, she inspected her right arm where the beast's claws had torn through her shoulder. With a slight tilt of her head, a grin spread across her face at the surge of pain coursing through her. Months of pent-up combat hunger surged within her veins as the reminder of her vitality pulsed alongside the exhilaration of battle-ready adrenaline.

Her focus snapped back to her prey, its claws swiping towards her midsection. Larissa, swift and agile, evaded the attack with a deft leap, anticipating the imminent counter-strike. The creature reared up on its hind legs, revealing its towering form that matched her own height. Its sinewy build hinted at power and speed. Despite its rapid assaults, Larissa danced away from each strike, maneuvering skillfully. As she retreated, she found herself backed into the corner farthest from the office's entrance. To her right, a door marked "Fire Exit" caught her eye as a potential escape route. Yet, before considering retreat, she silently vowed to vanquish whatever stood in front of her.

Larissa danced within the beast's reach, a whirlwind of strikes that missed their mark. As the creature lunged, she weaved through its claws, countering with a swift punch to its jaw that sent its head reeling. Seizing the moment, she unleashed a barrage of blows, each one landing with precision on the monster's chest. With a final flourish, she delivered a powerful kick to its wolf-like knee, giving a sickening crunch, toppling the beast to the ground in defeat.

Larissa's grin widened as she lunged into action. With a swift motion, she seized the monstrous creature by the mane running along its spine, feeling its weight press down on her muscles more than she had anticipated. Struggling slightly, she staggered backward towards the flickering light of the fire exit before regaining her footing. Giving it all she had, she hoisted the beast above her head and emitted a primal roar that echoed through the chamber. Like an ancient gladiator, she readied herself to shatter the creature's spine by driving it down onto her knee.

The door behind her burst open with a deafening crash, sending wooden splinters flying like shrapnel. The impact slammed into her, stealing the breath from her lungs and leaving her reeling. In an instant, she abandoned her prey, feeling a surge of searing pain shoot through her neck and shoulder, spreading like wildfire down her chest.

Reacting on pure instinct, she hurled herself backward, crashing against the wall with a bone-jarring thud. The weight on her back shifted as she pushed off the wall again and again, each forceful movement propelling her closer to the office door. Each push was a battle against pain and panic, every muscle in her body straining to break free from whatever unseen adversary clung to her back.

The creature that had clung to her back suddenly let go, crashing to the ground. Dropping to her knees, she gasped for breath, each inhale a struggle against the searing pain coursing through her. She could feel the blook streaming down her back, a grim reminder of the wounds she couldn't even fully see. The vicious gash across her chest hinted at the devastation elsewhere on her body. With no other choice but to fight, her eyes flared with anger, as she pushed past the agony, every movement a battle against impending darkness. As she crawled towards safety, her hand brushed against something cold and unyielding — Excalibur!

Grabbing the gun, Larissa sprang to her feet, her muscles protesting against the pain attempting to take hold of her. She swiftly aimed at one of the two beasts lurking at the far end of the office. Struggling to control the tremors wracking her body, she focused all her resolve on steadying the weapon. As she prepared to squeeze the trigger, a sudden jolt reverberated from behind, likely near the staircase.

Startled, she jerked her aim off-target, causing her shot to go wide. The unexpected movement sent her tumbling backward just as two monstrous forms lunged towards her. The combined force of their weight crashing down caused the office floor to shatter beneath them in a deafening collapse.

Tumbling backwIn the heart of their makeshift camp, Larissa and her bandit crew sought shelter within a decrepit warehouse as the impending snowstorm loomed over them. The structure, a relic of Old London's architecture, stood tall with its two stories of weathered brick and mortar. Among the group, someone recognized the abandoned machines in the workshop area as once used for crafting shoes.

A glimmer of hope sparked briefly at the prospect of salvaging useful components, only to fade as they found little that remained intact. Despite this setback, Larissa swiftly commanded the dismantling of the machines; she believes that idle hands invite chaos. She trusted in her people's resourcefulness to repurpose the scraps into something valuable, no matter how rugged it may turn out to be.

In the expansive delivery area, all the vehicles were neatly parked. Before heading out to recon, Rook carefully maneuvered the Scorpion into a separate designated spot, distinct from the other vehicles, a precautionary measure for a swift getaway if needed. Larissa often found amusement in this habit, jokingly suggesting that Rowan and his team were always planning to go AWOL.

"*Silly grunts,*" she thought as she led the group through the building. "Show them you are not afraid, and they will learn to fear your courage," she continued, whispering in a chant.

Bones marched stoically alongside her, seemingly unaffected by her words and showing minimal interest in acknowledging them. With her Winchester rifle at the ready, Larissa exuded someone who had come to understand the state of the world. Despite the absence of any immediate threats, she scanned the surroundings with unwavering focus. To her mild disappointment, the warehouse was devoid of any adversaries.

The ground floor was once dominated by the bustling production area, while a modest office nestled in a corner. Upstairs, a larger office bore the title "manager" on its door. Further beyond lay another section, now in ruins due to the passage of time and erosion.

Commanding the upstairs domain as her own, Larissa directed her companions to establish their base in the bustling production zone below. The office bore marks of neglect, yet she noted with satisfaction its dry interior and a window that opened without protest. Anticipating only a temporary stay, she eyed the worn manager's quarters, where a resilient crimson sofa beckoned from its quiet corner. Scant furnishings met her discerning gaze; nothing within stirred her interest beyond the comfort promised by the solitary couch.

Sinking into the sofa, she shifted uncomfortably, noting its lumpy surface that barely passed for comfort. As she adjusted to her makeshift bed, a hulking silhouette loomed in the doorway. Among Rowan and his companions, only Bones dared to enter Larissa's domain uninvited. His imposing presence conveyed an unspoken understanding of who held authority within those walls, silently assuring Larissa of his unwavering allegiance.

"We should locate one of those five-star hotels to establish our headquarters. Their furnishings are sure to surpass what we have here," she remarked, clutching the sofa's arm as its fabric emitted a puff of dust.

Bones shrugged, "I always enjoyed those pay by the hour joints myself."

"I am sure you have some fond memories." She replied as she watched a smile form on his face. "You need to think bigger, Bones. This is our world now. I want a place to call my own. Something which symbolizes...," she paused, taking the time to run her hand over the dusty material, "me."

"In that case, why not choose a castle? I mean, we are in fucking England."

Larissa scoffed but then looked at Bones with a new perspective. "I like your thinking. Find me one, and I'll give you your own room."

Bones chuckles at the comment. "Make it an ocean view, and I will get you the biggest castle that's still standing." As if a deal had been struck, Bones closed the door and proceeded down the hall.

"Oh, and Bones! Bring me a drink after setting up camp," she yelled, leaning back on the couch.

Imagining residing in a fortress brought a grin to her face. She held her rifle with care, as if it were a precious infant, readjusting its position to ensure swift access in case an unwelcome visitor dared to intrude. The 1873 Winchester rifle had been discovered in Germany, unearthed from the rubble of a mansion.

Digging through the rubble, she spotted the safe protruding from a mound of rocks. With painstaking effort, she spent hours clearing away debris and finally managed to pry the safe open with a torch. Inside, gleaming in pristine condition, was a lever-action rifle that bore an uncanny resemblance to the ones she had admired in the classic western movies she cherished from her childhood days spent watching with her family.

Inspecting the rifle never failed to immerse her in memories that lingered like shadows. Curiously, those recollections were the only fragments she retained of them. It was a silent confession she kept to herself, finding solace in these thoughts not for their warmth but for the stark reminder of her profound sacrifices. The weight of her bereavement stoked the fires of her beliefs, propelling her forward with unwavering resolve.

The Winchester was perfect in her hand, and it felt like it was made specifically for her. It was the symbol of her power, power she achieved through force and will. Cracking the safe and taking the gun was her way of giving a middle finger to the world. A world which had screwed her over, keeping her from the authority she was born to have.

She paused for a moment and took in the room. The smile on her face grew more prominent as she started laughing.

"I have my own *Excalibur*."

That castle was sounding more like a necessity with each

passing second.

Ω▪Ω▪Ω▪Ω

As twilight descended, the members of Larissa's group kindled a jubilant atmosphere. Crackling fires encircled their makeshift camp, casting flickering light to push back the shadows. What was once a desolate factory had transformed into a lively campground through their efforts. A handful of sentries stood vigilant while the majority reveled in merriment. Laughter, spirited cheers, the rhythmic clinking of bottles, and the lively tunes of various instruments crescendoed as night unfurled its dark veil. The stern air of military discipline that had hung over the camp dissipated swiftly, replaced by the vibrant energy akin to a boisterous college gathering within a span of mere hours.

Amidst the bustling activity of the manufacturing floor, Bones navigated through the throngs of people. In the heart of the space, a towering fire drum blazed, casting flickering shadows across the makeshift structures. Around the fiery centerpiece, women swayed gracefully to an unheard rhythm, their movements both mesmerizing and fluid. Whistles and cheers filled the air as men watched with admiration.

The scene was alive with a sense of celebration and unity, each individual fully immersed in the moment. The crackling flames illuminated faces etched with stories of survival, their eyes reflecting a mix of weariness and fleeting joy. Laughter intertwined with the crackling of burning wood, creating a symphony of sounds that echoed through the repurposed buildings.

Bones observed this display of communal revelry, his weath–

ered features softening imperceptibly at the sight. There was an unspoken understanding among them all - in this unforgiving world where danger lurked beyond every corner, these moments of respite were rare treasures to be cherished. Each smile shared and every dance step taken symbolized defiance against the bleakness that surrounded them, a testament to their resilience in the face of uncertainty.

Bones maintained a vigilant watch over the group, ensuring strict adherence to the settlement's regulations. Those who deviated from these rules were assigned arduous tasks that spanned several days. Attire was a matter of personal choice, rest was unrestricted, and revelry was a reward reserved for those who upheld their responsibilities diligently.

On this current trek around the party grounds, Bones had a purpose. He had left his men to carry on their duties as he headed towards a mound of wriggling blankets.

"*At least he covered himself this time*," Bones thought as he approached the blanket.

The room's tense silence shattered as Bones's rough hands seized the sheets, ripping them away with a violent flourish. The fabric tore through the air, a sudden gust of aggression that made the two women huddle closer in fear. Their startled gasps mingled with a chorus of shrill screams that reverberated off the walls, echoing the chaos unfurling before them.

Caught off guard by Bones's abrupt intrusion, the man beside the women faltered, his eyes widening in confusion and alarm. His expression mirrored their shock, a mirror reflecting shared bewilderment at the unexpected and forceful display of dominance.

As Bones loomed over them, his presence suffocating in its intensity, the women recoiled instinctively. Their bodies tensed, muscles coiled like springs ready to snap as they scrambled away from him, driven by primal fear and an urgent need for distance from this rugged figure whose actions spoke louder than any words could convey.

"Wha-, what? Wait. Come back!" The man yelled as he fell face-first on the floor, reaching for the fleeing women. He stood and greeted Bones with a middle finger. "Why the hell did you do that?"

Flukes was a plump fellow with round cheeks. How someone kept that much fat on them with so little food even bewildered a man like Bones. In the world before, Flukes taught chemistry, but in this new reality, he held a prominent role in Larissa's group due to his exceptional talent for creating alcohol from unconventional sources.

"Why the hell did you do that?" Flukes asked again.

The brew master went on a rant, his eyes focused the whole time on the women walking away.

"Do you have any idea what those two are good at? I'll answer for you. Let me just say, they can make any man weep in pleasure," he continued, oblivious to Bones' fleeting patience.

Bones focused intently on tuning out the man's ceaseless grumblings, the passing time feeling interminable.

"Flukes," he said louder.

The man kept talking, looking away from the brute.

"Flukes," he shouted at the half-naked chemist to get his attention. Yet, no response.

His patience worn thin, he seized the rotund man's shoulder and spun him around forcefully.

"Dammit! What do you want moron?" Flukes barked.

"The only thing keeping you off constant watch duty is Larissa's reliance on your unique abilities," Bones remarked, the distinct metallic click of a blade being unsheathed echoing around them.

Flukes let out a strained breath as the razor-sharp edge made contact with his manly bits.

"Your prowess doesn't hinge on your anatomy. Push me further, and I'll serve you a meal of your own defiance," Bones declared, fixing his gaze on the chemist. The realization dawned on the chemist, evident in his expression. Bones emphasized his threat by twisting the knife in a menacing manner. "Raw," he emphasized coldly.

Flukes nervously swallowed, his hands raised in a gesture of apology, "Geez, alright," he sighed. "You do know how to interrupt a man when he's on top of the world."

"Well, right now that world is a frozen popsicle," Bones said.

"Seems Larissa's after her custom blend," Flukes remarked, prompting Bones to nod in confirmation as he stepped back and sheathed his weapon. "Alright, I have it over here," he continued, wobbling to a stack of weapon cases.

Bones pried open the lid of a container, revealing an assortment of glass bottles nestled inside. Each bottle held a different shape and size, standing in neat rows like soldiers awaiting orders.

"Probably just as dangerous as the weapons once found in the crate," Bones thought.

Bones remained steadfast in his distrust of the chemist, always avoiding sampling his concoctions. Just as Flukes reached out to offer him the bottle, a piercing shriek pierced through the festive chatter around them.

The entire camp froze in unison, a collective breath held as if time itself had stalled. Whether under the influence or not, a sudden sobriety gripped them all. Every eye was fixed on the vehicle lot, now bathed in flickering firelight from scattered barrels. A tense silence enveloped the scene, halting movement and speech alike. It wasn't until the distinct sound of gun mechanisms being readied pierced the stillness that Bones jolted back to awareness, a chilling realization dawning upon him.

"Where's the patrol?" Bones thought as he peered out into the darkness.

A chilling screech pierced the air, echoing like a desperate creature's final agony. Moments later, a member of Bones' patrol emerged, his face twisted in pain, a crimson stain spreading across his midsection. With trembling hands, he dragged a gleaming blade through the snow, each rasping sound heightening the tension. His faltering steps took him past an abandoned car, the shadows seeming to elongate and clutch at him as he staggered towards the looming building, a silent witness to his ordeal.

"Help me," the patrolman sputtered, his fearful eyes falling on Bones.

Bones remained passive, showing no inclination to assist, and the rest of the group followed suit.

In the flickering glow of the fire, Bones's heart clenched at the sight of a dark shape slinking through the darkness. It darted with eerie grace across the rooftop of an abandoned vehicle, sending shivers down his spine. His gaze snapped back to the wretched man beside him just in time to witness the shadowy form descend behind him. The movements were a blur, a silent dance of death unfolding in the night. All that confirmed its presence was the sudden absence of the limping man's head. A chilling silence settled as the headless body staggered a few paces before crumbling to its knees. For a haunting moment, as if defying gravity itself, the torso swayed in macabre harmony with the howling wind before finally succumbing to stillness on the frozen ground.

A single droplet of sweat traced a path down Bones' weathered cheek, glistening in the dim light. Startled by the sound of water dripping onto the ground nearby, Bones swiveled to find Flukes trembling, his nerves betraying him as a substantial puddle collected at his boots. In usual times, Bones might have derided or belittled Flukes without hesitation, but this moment was different.

Flukes' voice trembled as he whispered, "What in blazes was that?"

"I'm not sure," Bones answered, unfastening his pistol holster.

With all gazes fixated on him, seeking guidance. Bones, having a surge of determination, cautiously strode purposefully towards the entrance. Surveying the chamber, he noticed a handful of daring or perhaps reckless individuals following suit. Conversely, some opted for caution, pressing themselves closer to the safety of the walls.

Debris crumbled underfoot with each step, the fire's crackle punctuating the eerie silence that enveloped them. Whimpers of fear and uncertainty echoed through the building, setting Bones' nerves on edge. Just moments ago, his voice had to compete with the howling wind to be heard above a whisper.

Two of Rowan's seasoned mercenaries surged ahead, their weapons raised and sweeping the bleak expanse outside. Bones froze mid-step, his heart racing as he caught a glimpse of shifting silhouettes looming over the entrance, a flicker of movement that sent a jolt of fear down his spine.

"Above you!" his voice echoed through the icy silence.

Eerie silence enveloped the men as a chilling shadow loomed over them. Without warning, elongated hands descended like tendrils of darkness, seizing their heads in a merciless grip. Bones shuddered at the gut-wrenching symphony of agony that echoed through the desolate streets. The metallic scent of blood tainted the air as razor-sharp claws tore into flesh and sinew, rending skin with savage precision.

Helpless against the monstrous force, they were hoisted into the frigid night sky, their anguished cries piercing the stillness. Upwards they ascended, towards the roof where oblivion awaited. In an instant, silence devoured their screams, leaving only a haunting void in its wake. Then came the sickening descent - bodies plummeting to earth with a sickening crack that reverberated through the frozen wasteland.

Lifeless forms lay sprawled on the unforgiving ground, severed heads resting grotesquely apart from their vessels. The macabre scene unfolded amidst a backdrop of terror-stricken onlookers whose horrified gasps mingled with the howling winds. In that moment of gruesome revelation, chaos erupted like wildfire, consuming all semblance of order in a frenzy of fear and despair.

Chapter 6

Shattered windows echoed with the sound of splintering glass as twisted claws snaked in, seizing unsuspecting victims who had sought refuge within. Pulling out into the darkness not to be seen again. Amidst the chaos, a guard's finger tightened on the trigger, igniting their assault rifle and sparking a frenzy of panicked gunfire from the rest.

Swiftly, those with their senses sharp retreated away from the window and established a protective line further inside. Once the first barrage vanished into the darkness, there was a frantic exchange of magazines, with fresh ones clumsily inserted into weapons.

As the echoes of gunfire faded into the icy night, a haunting silence settled over the desolate landscape. The stillness was shattered by the return of that bone-chilling shriek, now multiplied in a cacophony of eerie wails that seemed to reverberate through the frozen air. A tremor ran through one of the battered vehicles outside, its metal frame protesting as a solitary figure landed on its roof, bathed in an ominous glow from the smoldering barrel nearby.

Time hung suspended for a heartbeat before the creature unleashed another shrill cry, a primal sound that stirred the darkness with an unmistakable call to arms. In response, a horde of these grotesque beings emerged from the shadows like twisted specters materializing out of nightmares, their beastly forms illuminated by flickering flames. They surged towards the camp entrances from all directions, their movements frenzied and malevolent as they overturned fire barrels, sending sparks dancing into the frigid air like fiery omens of impending chaos.

The scene unfolded in a nightmarish frenzy, a twisted ballet of terror and bloodshed. The crowd, consumed by primal fear, tripped over their own feet in a frantic attempt to escape the oncoming horror. Gunfire echoed through the air as the charging beasts closed in, their movements fluid and deadly. Each desperate shot seemed futile as the monsters pounced on their prey with savage precision.

The creatures' fangs tore through flesh like hot knives through butter, crimson streams painting the ground beneath them in a macabre dance. The metallic tang of blood mingled with the acrid scent of fear, creating a sickening symphony that filled the air. In the dim light, shadows danced grotesquely against walls slick with gore, emphasizing the brutality of the scene playing out before them.

Fear clawed at Flukes as he sprinted, his heart pounding in his chest like a war drum. Just as hope flickered, a shadow pounced from a shattered window, hurling him into a stack of alcohol crates. Glass and liquid exploded around him, but amidst the chaos, pain seared through him, its source a cruel mystery in the frenzy. The creature's jaws loomed wide, a gaping maw of terror descending towards, chomping down on his neck, nearly decapitating him.

Amidst the chaos, Bones sprinted towards the manager's office, abandoning Flukes to his fate. He clung to a sliver of hope that Larissa might offer salvation or guidance in this dire situation. A sudden rush of air accompanied by a chilling cry caught his attention. Glancing back, he witnessed a toppled barrel meeting the pooled alcohol, igniting into a blaze that consumed both Flukes' lifeless body and the creature feasting on him.

Momentum carried Bones forward, his body crashing to the icy ground. As he scrambled up, a lifeless figure lay behind him, a grim reminder of the dangers lurking in the frozen wasteland. But ahead, bathed in flickering light, stood his salvation - the stairs to the manager's office beckoning just fifteen feet away.

Suddenly, a chilling presence landed before him, its back turned as if mocking his escape. In the dim illumination, Bones discerned its pallid skin and muscular form, sending shivers down his spine. He remained prone, heart hammering in his chest as he raised his weapon with trembling hands. Each movement deliberate yet fraught with dread, he aimed and pulled the trigger.

The shot echoed through the desolate landscape as it struck true, piercing the creature's back. A guttural cry filled the air as the beast writhed in agony on the frozen ground. Seizing this fleeting moment of vulnerability, Bones pushed himself to his feet and sprinted towards the sanctuary of the stairs, fear fueling every step taken away from the wounded monstrosity.

"Fuck you, you ugly ass bitch," he shouted, firing one last shot into the creature's skull, ending its movement as he passed.

Bones stood amidst the chaos as he surveyed the scene. His eyes darted from one harrowing sight to another, each detail etching itself into his memory. To his left, shadowy figures moved with eerie grace among his crew, their movements swift and deadly as they attacked with savage precision. The air was thick with the scent of blood and the sounds of desperate cries.

In the opposite direction, bodies writhed beneath the weight of monstrous forms, limbs jerking in futile attempts to break free. The ground trembled with each impact, a grim symphony of pain and struggle echoing through the building. Bones could feel the tension in the air, a palpable fear that fueled both his enemies and his allies.

Despite the overwhelming odds, only a small group of Bones' crew managed to stand their ground against the relentless onslaught. Their faces were etched with grim determination as they fought back, their weapons flashing in sporadic bursts of light against the encroaching darkness. Each shot fired was a desperate plea for survival, a defiance against the nightmarish creatures that outnumbered them.

Through it all, Bones told himself to remain resolute. In this moment of chaos and terror, he had to embody strength and resilience in a sea swirling with madness threatening to consume them all.

A sudden, thunderous bang echoed from the manager's office, drawing his focus back.

"*Larissa,*" he thought.

Blood and unidentifiable gore painted the stairway to the office, creating a treacherous path that sent shivers down his spine. With each step he took, the slickness threatened to send him tumbling into the macabre mess below. Ignoring the gruesome sight, he pushed himself to ascend faster, heart pounding in his chest.

Bounding up two steps at a time, a sudden explosion beneath him ripped through the wood, launching him into the air. The world spun around him as he crashed back onto the floor below with a sickening crunch, agony shooting through his body like fiery tendrils. Gasping for breath, he struggled to focus his blurred vision.

As clarity slowly returned, dread gripped him when he saw a monstrous creature looming over him, its form as massive as his own. Crouched and ready to strike, it exuded an aura of primal menace that made every nerve in his body scream with fear.

The creature's claws arched menacingly in the air before descending with a terrifying swiftness. Bones was engulfed in searing agony as his chest and abdomen erupted in torment. His gaze fell upon the gory sight of his body laid bare, akin to a brutal dissection. Each throb of pain hammered home the grim certainty of his demise.

A haunting cry of "Larissa!" tore from his lips, echoing despair as darkness encroached, the monster's talons piercing through his skull.

Ω▪Ω▪Ω▪Ω

Awakening abruptly in the manager's office, Larissa was startled. The flickering light from the fires below shone through the large window overlooking the first floor, helping to illuminate the room and allowing her to survey the room. Everything appeared undisturbed. She blinked, hoping to sharpen her sight, yet in this unforgiving world, clarity remained elusive.

Adjusting her posture on the edge of the couch, her boot nudged an object nearby. Glancing down, she retrieved the bottle. "Cheap shit," she muttered disdainfully at the depleted vessel.

Recollection struck her suddenly - Bones had been dispatched to retrieve Fluke's potent drink. A moment of hesitation gripped her as she struggled to gauge the passage of time. How extensive was her slumber? Had the revelry concluded? The absence of familiar sounds was conspicuous: no echoes of passion, no triumphant shouts marking conquests, no vulgarities from her loyal entourage.

That is when it hit her. It was not something that woke her up — it was the lack thereof. The change from drunken revelry to absolute silence put her on edge. That silence was quickly broken by the screams of her people, prompting her to grab her rifle — her Excalibur. The absence of sound jolted her awake, a stark contrast to the prior revelry. The abrupt shift to eerie quietness set her nerves on edge. Before she could fully grasp the situation, the piercing cries of her comrades shattered the stillness, compelling her to reach for her weapon — her trusted Excalibur.

"Fucking pansies. What the hell are they scared of now?" she questioned, patting Excalibur in her hand as if it solved problems.

Moving in the direction of the door, her steps faltered as she accidentally nudged the bottle that lay forgotten on the ground, briefly losing her balance.

"That might have been a bit stronger than I thought. Flukes continues to outdo himself," she mused, a grin slowly spreading across her features.

The cacophony of screams reverberated through the air, mingling with the sharp shatter of glass. The haze induced by alcohol dissipated swiftly as her innate survival reflexes surged to the forefront. The realization dawned upon her that they were under attack, and she needed to take charge, to guide them through this turmoil. A barrage of deafening gunfire erupted, harmonizing with the symphony of terrified cries that echoed in unison. Racing towards the window that offered a view of the chaos below, she found herself struck dumb for the very first time in a long time.

The unexpected sight unfolded before her, a chaotic dance of muzzle flashes and flames casting eerie shadows as her comrades were mercilessly ripped apart by an unfathomable force. The sheer number of assailants overwhelmed her senses. Before she could turn for the door, the window shattered with a deafening crash, a stray bullet piercing through the exact spot where her head had lingered mere moments ago.

Backpedaling, Larissa shielded her eyes from the glass fragments cascading around her. Anger surged within her, propelling her upright. When a dark silhouette had already descended onto the window ledge, eclipsing the light below. In the dimness, only a vague outline was visible to Larissa. The creature's monstrous, otherworldly traits pulsed with each shallow inhale in the scant illumination. Time hung suspended as their gazes intertwined, primal instincts clashing silently between them. And then it sprang forth.

In the frigid, unforgiving world that had claimed so many lives, Larissa's survival was no fluke. Her every move spoke of a lifetime spent mastering combat skills, honing them to lethal precision. As she faced off against the creature, her sinewy muscles rippled under scars etched by countless battles, a testament to her enduring resilience.

The clash between predator and prey unfolded with primal intensity. In a swift and calculated maneuver, Larissa intercepted the creature mid-leap. Her grip was unyielding, fingers closing around its arm and throat like steel vices. The sheer force of the beast's momentum forced her back a step, but she held fast, unflinching in the face of adversity as she always had.

Turning swiftly, she propelled the creature against the wall, sending cracks spider-webbing through its surface. As it crumpled to the ground, she unleashed a powerful dropkick straight to its face, driving its head deeper into the fractured wall. Despite its harrowing shriek, the creature remained alive. Assessing her injury, she inspected her right arm where the beast's claws had torn through her shoulder. With a slight tilt of her head, a grin spread across her face at the surge of pain coursing through her. Months of pent-up combat hunger surged within her veins as the reminder of her vitality pulsed alongside the exhilaration of battle-ready adrenaline.

Her focus snapped back to her prey, its claws swiping towards her midsection. Larissa, swift and agile, evaded the attack with a deft leap, anticipating the imminent counter-strike. The creature reared up on its hind legs, revealing its towering form that matched her own height. Its sinewy build hinted at power and speed. Despite its rapid assaults, Larissa danced away from each strike, maneuvering skillfully. As she retreated, she found herself backed into the corner farthest from the office's entrance. To her right, a door marked "Fire Exit" caught her eye as a potential escape route. Yet, before considering retreat, she silently vowed to vanquish whatever stood in front of her.

Larissa danced within the beast's reach, a whirlwind of strikes that missed their mark. As the creature lunged, she weaved through its claws, countering with a swift punch to its jaw that sent its head reeling. Seizing the moment, she unleashed a barrage of blows, each one landing with precision on the monster's chest. With a final flourish, she delivered a powerful kick to its wolf-like knee, giving a sickening crunch, toppling the beast to the ground in defeat.

Larissa's grin widened as she lunged into action. With a swift motion, she seized the monstrous creature by the mane running along its spine, feeling its weight press down on her muscles more than she had anticipated. Struggling slightly, she staggered backward towards the flickering light of the fire exit before regaining her footing. Giving it all she had, she hoisted the beast above her head and emitted a primal roar that echoed through the chamber. Like an ancient gladiator, she readied herself to shatter the creature's spine by driving it down onto her knee.

The door behind her burst open with a deafening crash, sending wooden splinters flying like shrapnel. The impact slammed into her, stealing the breath from her lungs and leaving her reeling. In an instant, she abandoned her prey, feeling a surge of searing pain shoot through her neck and shoulder, spreading like wildfire down her chest.

Reacting on pure instinct, she hurled herself backward, crashing against the wall with a bone-jarring thud. The weight on her back shifted as she pushed off the wall again and again, each forceful movement propelling her closer to the office door. Each push was a battle against pain and panic, every muscle in her body straining to break free from whatever unseen adversary clung to her back.

The creature that had clung to her back suddenly let go, crashing to the ground. Dropping to her knees, she gasped for breath, each inhale a struggle against the searing pain coursing through her. She could feel the blood streaming down her back, a grim reminder of the wounds she couldn't even fully see. The vicious gash across her chest hinted at the devastation elsewhere on her body. With no other choice but to fight, her eyes flared with anger as she pushed past the agony, every movement a battle against impending darkness. As she crawled towards safety, her hand brushed against something cold and unyielding — Excalibur!

Grabbing the gun, Larissa sprang to her feet, her muscles protesting against the pain, attempting to take hold of her. She swiftly aimed at one of the two beasts lurking at the far end of the office. Struggling to control the tremors wracking her body she focused all her resolve on steadying the weapon. As she prepared to squeeze the trigger, a sudden jolt reverberated from behind, likely near the staircase.

Startled, she jerked her aim off-target, causing her shot to go wide. The unexpected movement sent her tumbling backward just as two monstrous forms lunged towards her. The combined force of their weight crashing down caused the office floor to shatter beneath them in a deafening collapse.

Tumbling backward, the force of the fall brought down a cascade of debris from above, burying her beneath the crumbling ceiling and roof. The monsters descended upon her with a vicious fury, their claws tearing through her midsection. In the chaos, her belt and shreds of flesh were scattered around her. The debris had blocked out her vision, but not her sense of pain.ard, the force of the fall brought down a cascade of debris from above, burying her beneath the crumbling ceiling and roof. The monsters descended upon her with a vicious fury, their claws tearing through her midsection. In the chaos, her belt and shreds of flesh scattered around her. The debris had blocked out her vision but not her sense of pain.

Chapter 7

The structure Rowan and his team had selected for their temporary shelter appeared much larger on the inside than it did from the outside. They spent nearly three hours navigating through its expanse to make it safe and habitable. This former corporate building, standing at almost twelve stories high, had once been a hub for various businesses. Fortunately, a significant part of the building had crumbled in the past, reducing the time needed to secure it. However, the surviving floors were a maze of unique office setups, prolonging the clearing process on each level. After confirming its safety, they established their camp on the sixth floor, where a half-collapsed room provided the perfect view of the city.

The collapsed segments restricted upper access to the level. They settled on a roomy office, strategically chosen for defensibility against ground-level threats, with windows for both repelling invaders and making a swift exit if necessary. This kind of "real estate" selection, as Spence humorously dubbed it, was a familiar routine for Rowan's team. Through repeated practice, they had honed their ability to identify ideal defensive positions and escape routes. While experience had streamlined the process of pinpointing optimal spots, they understood the importance of thoroughness, especially when exploring unfamiliar territory.

Arrangements were swiftly made for shifts and alternating responsibilities, allowing them precious moments to unwind and replenish their energy. The constant vigilance required at every turn, the biting cold's relentless assault, and the burden of their equipment could drain even the most resilient warrior of vitality.

Perched on a sturdy table by a weathered window that offered a glimpse of the desolate cityscape, Rowan observed the sky as dusk gradually enveloped the remnants of daylight. Though the tempest had subsided, a thick layer of clouds lingered overhead, shrouding any hint of moonlight. Despite the darkness cloaking their surroundings, Rowan and his team remained vigilant, their senses attuned to the subtlest shifts in their environment. In this world devoid of electricity, they had learned to rely on more than just sight. With Mia's unparalleled tracking expertise and her guidance, even in the absence of traditional light sources, Rowan's team navigated the shadows with ease and confidence.

Rowan's hand instinctively closed around the hilt of his knife. Not driven by fear or discomfort, but by a simmering rage. His gaze remained fixed on the solitary beacon of light in the desolate expanse – a sector of the city, four blocks distant, glowing like a crimson ember amidst shadow.

"Stupid," he mumbled to himself.

He knew Larissa was going to throw a celebration of some sort after they arrived. She always did to bring up the morale of her followers after such a long trip. However, she usually waited until Rowan's team had time to establish a perimeter and return. If she did not, at least she had Rowan's team there to patrol. They never partied with the others, favoring the joy of obliterating anything that attempted to enter the camp.

During those moments, Rowan often confronted Larissa about her rash choices, aware that his opinions held little weight with her. He imagined countless scenarios where he contemplated ending her and her crew. However, deep down, he feared retaliation and that some lucky fool would manage to reach Larissa's device and might trigger the collar bombs, dooming his team in return.

As Rowan adjusted his stance, Rook drew near. "Larissa's having another hoot-nanny, I see," the big man said without surprise.

"Yeah, I hear they have fish and chips," Rowan replied.

"Think we'll be lucky enough for Larissa to choke on a fishbone?" Rook questioned.

"Doubt it. That woman would survive —" Rowan paused before finishing.

"Were you going to say 'survive the apocalypse'? Cause I think we're all doing that," Rook joked.

Rowan chuckled, "Yeah, I guess some old sayings no longer apply."

Mia's silhouette slipped soundlessly through the creaking doorway, a shadow against the eerie ruin's darkness. With a subtle gesture, she beckoned for Rowan and Rook to trail behind her. Without a word, Rowan motioned for Al to take over his watchful position. In this desolate landscape where danger lurked in every shadow.

Approaching Mia's patrol zone, she began gesturing silently. Rook almost cautioned her about the near darkness and urged her to proceed cautiously when he noticed her sudden alertness outside. Rowan also caught sight of it. Though subtle, it was unmistakable. Far in the distance, several miles away, a glowing dome pierced the night sky on the horizon. This familiar light had not escaped any of them before.

"Seems like we are not the only residents. Looks like we know where to find power," Rowan commented.

"I've seen one place that large before, and they didn't have a friendly disposition," Rook added.

In the sprawling urban expanse of Old London, encountering the resident population was inevitable. The discovery of such a substantial stronghold would undoubtedly alter Larissa's strategic approach. Moreover, with a significant population illuminating the night, it signaled the presence of smaller neighboring communities without a doubt.

"To survive the White with this sizable presence means resources and firepower," Rowan commented. For a moment, he remained silent as he took in his newfound knowledge. "Let's tell the others."

On their way back, Al met up with them. "There is trouble at the caravan. Not sure how bad, but we heard faint gunfire."

"You sure it's not her drunk lackies firing into the night?" Rowan asked.

"It could be," he shrugged.

"Val, see what you can find out. If something happens to the caravan, it's on them," Rowan said. *Maybe Larissa's luck had finally run out*, he happily thought to himself. But then there was the nagging thought in the back of his mind, reminding him they needed those people. Also, there was the constant irritation around his neck, which foreboded to him the possible outcome if they did not return.

"Alright, break time's over. Pack up. Looks like we're heading back regardless if we're needed or not."

Ω▪Ω▪Ω▪Ω

"It was definitely gunfire coming from the camp, but it has died down," Val reported when she returned to the group, as the others finished up their packing

"Maybe it's our friends out yonder, scavenging for resources," Rook said.

"What is he talking about, Rowan?" asked Spence.

"Right before you guys told us about the gunfire back at camp, Mia showed us some light coming from a settlement a few miles from here. But they had to be too far to know we entered the city. Either way, we take caution heading back. Okay, Mia, Val, you two scout ahead. Be our eyes and ears, keeping an eye out for patrols. If need be, neutralize, but don't take any risks. At this point, our goal is to save as many as possible. If we can't achieve that, then we will follow the bastards back to their base recon and return the favor. Understood?"

Exchanges of grunts and affirmative nods conveyed their unanimous consent.

"Let's go!" Rowan ordered.

The atmosphere shifted instantly. Ease and laughter gave way to a disciplined demeanor honed by years of training, each action purposeful and efficient.

Between watching for attackers, the darkness, and the snow, navigation had been slow. Rowan and his team were now a hundred feet from the shoe warehouse where they had left Larissa, and all was silent. This was expected.

"Fucking stupid, Larissa. You knew we were not there to cover your ass, and Bones is not worth his weight in shit. And now you jeopardize all our resources," Rowan kept repeating in his head

as they closed in on the camp.

Honestly, he did not give a crap about Larissa or her goons, but only for those who pulled their weight for the caravan. As Rook put it one time: *"They are surviving just like us. They're just doing it differently."* That was the argument Rook had made when Spence offered to kill a lot of them. In which Rowan had to agree. He had met good people in the camp who only wanted to blend in and survive.

His main focus remained on the collar's controller held by Larissa. Any interference with it would lead to dire consequences for him and his team. Getting to Larissa was imperative regardless of any obstacles in their path, a sentiment shared by his team. Observing each member maneuvering through the streets - adeptly handling the landscape, protecting each other's vulnerable points, he pondered the profound thoughts concealed within each of them.

Rowan felt the weight of the world pushing him into roles he never chose. Despite his mercenary days with Triple Top, he refused to sink to the levels demanded post-Impact. He quickly gestured to Mia, directing her to shift towards the back of the warehouse for a strategic advantage, scouting for potential threats.

Rowan's senses prickled with unease as the eerie silence enveloped them, amplifying every creak and rustle in the desolate alley. As he cautiously neared the bend that opened into the warehouse, a shadowy figure emerged – Mia, her form blending seamlessly with the darkness. Knowing the dangers lurking in the shadows, she refrained from venturing closer to the camp alone, her instincts sharp in the oppressive blackness.

Within sight of the warehouse, remnants of chaos littered

the parking area; overturned barrels spilling their fiery contents onto the frozen ground, wisps of steam rising eerily. Without uttering a word, Mia conveyed to their team through swift gestures that she too had found no one.

"What's the play?" whispered Al.

Rowan bit his lip as he ran through the possibilities. "Rook and Val, head to the Scarecrow, and be ready for a quick escape. Val, while Rook preps our ride, you watch the roofs. Al, Spence, and Mia, follow me inside. We need to locate the collar remote."

"Survivors?" Spence asked.

"Secondary to finding the collar. We cannot help them with someone controlling these," Rowan replied, pointing to the bomb collar around his neck. "Stack up and watch your corners."

Splitting into two columns, the team positioned itself on either side of the narrow alley. Rook and Val held back, ready to secure their armored vehicle before regrouping. Advancing cautiously, they scanned every nook and cranny, their weapons sweeping across every possible hiding spot for any lurking danger.

Moving into the parking lot, they stuck close to the walls, utilizing shadows to conceal their advance. The absence of any sentries stood out as unusual. There were no bandits conducting a cleanup operation, no sounds of groaning wounded, not a single lifeless body in sight. Only the dwindling fires offered any hint that this location had once been occupied.

Rowan reassured himself that the shifting shadows were merely deceiving his vision, knowing that once they stepped inside the building, the grim discovery of bodies would explain the quietness.

"No team is capable of clearing out this many bodies so quickly," he told himself.

Rowan and Mia positioned themselves diagonally across from the collapsed side, with Spence and Al standing adjacent to it on the other end.

Rowan scanned the area, checking for Val and Rook's positions, only to have his line of sight obstructed by Larissa's haphazardly parked vehicles. A curious realization dawned on him – her vehicles remained untouched, unchanged since his departure. If bandits had been involved, signs of looting would have been evident by now. It wasn't a trick of his eyes after all.

Movement grabbed his attention, and he turned swiftly as Spence motioned for him to inspect the ground. Following Spence's indication, Rowan's gaze landed on dark puddles staining the snow, unmistakably blood. Tracing the gruesome trail, his eyes widened at the sight of what seemed to be entrails. Initially thinking of cannibals, a curse forming in his mind, Mia's subtle Morse code communication shifted his perspective. With precise clicks and touches on his shoulder, she spelled out "B" in Morse code. Rowan's pulse quickened as Mia continued to convey "E-A-S-T," hinting at a non-human origin for the horror before them. Trusting Mia's instincts without question, he relayed the message to Spence with a series of hand signals spelling out B-E-A-S-T.

With practiced ease, Spence allowed his rifle to rest against his vest before deftly unsheathing his Shillelagh from the holster on his back. Rowan caught a glimpse of what seemed like a muttered curse from the Irishman as Spence silently readied his cherished Hercules shotgun.

Surveying the vast chamber, amidst the flickering flames

and strewn wreckage, Rowan struggled to discern what really had happened.

Across from where the cars were parked, Rook and Val reached the Scarecrow. The flickering flames cast a glow on the vehicles in the darkness, but Rook could identify his prized possession in any situation. Having meticulously tailored the advanced APC they had salvaged from a military installation over numerous years, he had transformed it into a mobile sanctuary for the team, complete with sleeping provisions, attire, a modest food reserve, and armaments.

Val's foot caught on a hidden obstacle near the side door, almost causing her to stumble. With practiced efficiency, she unearthed the buried item from the snow, revealing an assault rifle. After a swift inspection, she cast a brief glance at the magazine before bringing the barrel up to her nose for a quick sniff.

"This gun has not been fired in a while. The guard was dead before he could use it," she whispered. Rook promptly nodded as if giving his full attention, but Val knew he was focused on his baby, the APC. "Did you hear me?"

"Yeah, I heard you. The gun wasn't fired," he whispered back, maneuvering around the vehicle, checking the treads and tires. Seeing nothing out of place, "I don't understand. She's in the same condition I left her. Whoever did this to the camp, why would they leave the best hardware behind? Doesn't make sense."

"Assuming whoever did this was rational," she whispered back.

"In any case, this shit's not good," Whispering under his breath, he navigated towards the passenger's side door with caution. With his weapon raised, he reached for the handle and pulled the door open. Finding the vehicle clear, he signaled to Val with a subtle thumbs-up. In response, Val began her silent ascent up the side of the vehicle.

Val inched along, hugging the roof of the vehicle as she moved into position. Her gaze lifted upwards, sweeping for any hint of activity. Finally positioned, she peered through her rifle scope to keep watch over Al and Spence stationed by the entrance. The line of vehicles obstructed her view inside the building, yet what caught her eye sent a jolt of shock through her. A solitary forearm rested on the ground just a short distance from the entry — perhaps a grim message left by scavengers.

"This ain't good. I hope you're ready to haul-ass out of here when the time calls," Val said, peering down on Rook.

"Sure enough," Rook reassured as he continued to work.

While the Scorpion boasted impressive strength, stealth was not its forte. Opening the ramp at this moment would undoubtedly alert anything within a half-mile radius. The vehicle's primary purpose was to safeguard them, ensuring that if danger loomed, they could defend their position from within the Scorpion until the threat passed.

Val activated the laser, signaling Al through Morse code that she had taken her position. She felt assured that only Al would catch her rapid flashes since he was on the lookout for them. In response, he gestured a thumbs-up.

"Ok, they're going in," Val informed Rook.

"Roger," he replied, his hand gripping the handle a bit tighter.

Al, positioned at the entrance, gave a subtle hand signal to indicate Val's readiness. Mia conveyed her preparedness by giving Rowan's shoulder a reassuring squeeze. Meanwhile,

Spence initiated a silent countdown with his fingers. As he reached the final count of one, the team swiftly moved into the building, smoothly spreading out to cover the expansive open area before them.

The pungent scent of blood, stale liquor, and smoldering refuse assaulted Mia's senses, making her gut twist uneasily. Despite the overwhelming odors, she stayed alert. This grim scene wasn't unfamiliar to her, though usually on a smaller scale. In the flickering light of the flames, the walls bore macabre patterns of dried blood like shadows in the night. Moving cautiously through the room, she navigated around scattered debris, mindful that even the faintest sound could betray their presence. Each footfall created a sickening squelch as her boots met sticky puddles of crimson on the floor.

Mia glided alongside her companions through the tumult, her movements fluid and silent. Amidst the disorder, Al's hand abruptly halted their progress. His gesture directed her attention to a spot on the ground just ahead, partially obscured by a barrel. With a subtle motion, he indicated the metal collar encircling his neck. A surge of relief flooded Mia as she comprehended that they had located Larissa's control mechanism. The prospect of shedding this oppressive device filled her with elation. Initially touted by Rowan as state-of-the-art armor upon her enlistment in his team, Mia later discerned that his words were meant to pacify rather than inform. The unspoken truth lingered - living with an explosive collar was preferable to a swift death without one.

"Al, secure the remote," Rowan ordered.

As Al headed towards the remote area, Mia remained vigilant, scanning the room for any signs of activity. Her focus shifted to the section of the second floor that had crumbled down.

In the glow of the fires, she observed what appeared to be a former office space; its shattered wooden walls now formed a heap of rubble behind Al.

In the wavering glow, Mia's sharp eyes caught a subtle movement. Camouflaged within the dimness, a figure with a human-like form skulked in the shadows above. Its predatory posture hinted at imminent danger to Al. Without hesitation, Mia's bow rose, her fingers finding their mark on her cheek while she readied the arrow for flight. Just before she let it loose, a chilling realization dawned — there were others lurking unseen around them, poised to strike.

Ω▪Ω▪Ω▪Ω

Their luck seemed almost unbelievable to Al. Within mere minutes of their arrival and entry, perched atop a heap lay the remote control for the collars. With a directive from Rowan, he reached for the device. Pausing briefly with his back pressed against the entrance wall, he gazed at the abandoned remote, pondering the mystery behind its neglect.

While in his thoughts, he glanced at Spence, who had a look on his face as if saying, *What are you waiting for?* And if that was what he was getting at, he had the right. The entire squad has had their collars on for years, and this was their moment to be free of them.

Receiving a low whistle from Rowan, Al filed the thought away and entered the room; his weapon up, swaying in all directions. He reached for the controller and was now capable of fully taking in the pile it lay upon. He paused. The controller lay, not only atop a pile of collapsed debris, but on a heap of flesh as well? If the situation were not serious, he would call for Spence and ask the Irishman to pick it up simply to watch him puke out his guts. Though Spence played hardball and was tough as nails with the living, he did his best to steer clear of corpses.

Not long after, he heard a whistle as an object flew over him, followed by screeching and the snapping of wood as a towering figure crashed into the debris. All three men snapped their guns in the direction of the crash. The scene before them was surreal. Waiting on the edge of the light, outlined in flickering orange hues, were beasts. The shadows masked their features, yet large, smoke-like puffs of warm breath helped to reveal their locations. Low growls and hisses signaled that danger was imminent. Al made out three of them on the upper floor of the broken office.

"Movement, outside the windows. Al, grab it and be ready." Rowan ordered with a whisper; his weapon locked in their direction.

Al, needing not to be told twice, scooped up the controller with a squish of the flesh it rested on. "Got it!" he said, repositioning his weapon at the creatures.

His gaze remained fixed on the monstrous creatures ahead, their forms shrouded in an eerie ambiguity that defied easy classification. Though obscured by shadows, a feline essence seemed to emanate from their sleek outlines, accentuated by the glint of predatory eyes that mirrored the dim illumination around them. Momentarily shifting his focus, Rowan's attention drifted to the fallen beast struck by Mia's arrow. Despite its motionless state, a sense of unease crept over him, prompting Al to subtly retreat towards Spence as a precautionary measure. "What are we waiting for?" he asked.

"Hey Rowan, are we waiting on a phone call?" Spence added.

"Mia signaled wait, so we wait," Rowan stated. "Hold position until she gives the go."

Spence shifted his gaze to Mia, observing her vigilant scan of their surroundings. While Spence excelled in combat against humans, Mia's expertise lay in understanding animals. Her focused stance signaled a purpose behind her watchful wait.

Weapons in hand, the team's aim darted between beast and shadow, their movements swift and calculated. Time stretched endlessly until Mia's sharp whistle pierced the air, a prelude to the whoosh of her arrow soaring just inches over Al's head. The projectile struck true, embedding itself squarely in the monstrous face before it crumpled to the ground, a limp heap of defeated terror.

As the creature drew its last breath, a sudden stillness enveloped the room. Everything seemed to freeze in time — the monster's exhale, the gentle draft of air. Despite the eerie quiet, Rowan sensed a palpable surge of tension that gripped the entire building.

"Oh, we're fucked!" That was all Spence could muster as all hell broke loose.

The piercing shrieks of the beasts shattered the eerie silence, their cries echoing through the frozen wasteland like a chilling call to battle.

Chapter 8

"Drop 'em!" Rowan's command echoed, punctuated by the sharp crack of his rifle coming to life.

Al swiftly joined the fray, his rifle cracking against the skull of a creature skittering down the rubble-strewn path. With a deft flick to the right, he unleashed a precise three-round volley into the next approaching threat. Swiveling his weapon back to the center, he brought down another adversary with lethal accuracy. The creatures' erratic movements tested his aim as he struggled to anticipate their agile dodges—his shots veering to the right, then left, and back to the right in rapid succession. Though each bullet found its mark, hitting them squarely grew increasingly challenging. A momentary miscalculation caused him to fire prematurely, the rounds veering wide of an oncoming monstrosity's charge.

A deafening explosion shattered the icy silence, sending the monstrous creature hurtling towards Al's right, crashing into a pile of rubble. The sharp crack of gunfire echoed through the desolate landscape as a bullet severed another beast's leg, followed by a third shot that made its head thud onto the frozen ground. Al swiftly pivoted to identify his savior amidst the chaos.

"Get behind me and reload!" Spence yelled as he moved in, his Herakles shotgun letting the monsters know they were not the only ones in town who could tear shit up.

Spence's keen eye caught the momentary calm amidst the chaos, but his focus shifted back to the imminent threat of two approaching figures. With precision, he steadied his shotgun and unleashed a thunderous blast. The shot found its mark, tearing through the neck and shoulder of one creature as it attempted to evade. The impact was devastating, nearly severing the creature's head, causing it to wobble precariously before tumbling down a heap of wooden debris.

Reacting swiftly to Spence's deadly accuracy, the remaining stalker sprang into action, leaping towards the wall and clinging on with unnatural agility. The sudden move threw off Spence's aim, forcing him to lose his lead. "Duck!" he yelled.

Spence and Al swiftly dove to the icy ground as the monstrous creature lunged towards them. With Spence leading the charge, the abomination locked onto him with chilling precision, its claws aiming for his skull. Yet, before it could reach its target, a deafening gunshot erupted mere inches away, striking the beast square in the chest. The creature crumpled to the frozen earth with a thunderous crash, its momentum carrying it forward to collide forcefully with Spence and Al, sending them sprawling.

The creature exuded a putrid stench that seeped into their senses like a noxious fog, overpowering even the acridness of any sewer they had ever encountered. Its weight pressed down on them like an avalanche of despair, a tangible burden that threatened to crush their very spirits beneath its grotesque mass.

They each knew lying down might be a luxury, but it also meant their deaths. The two immediately began pushing against the creature's weight, taking them several seconds to roll the damn thing off them.

Being the more agile one, Al managed to make it to his feet first and was already scanning the area. "No contacts," he yelled, helping Spence to his feet.

Rowan glanced at Mia, who gave a single wave in front of her eyes, "No contact," Rowan repeated, confirming Mia's clearing of enemies.

With a second breath, Spence grabbed ammo shells from his reserve pouch and reloaded his shotgun.

"Get to the Scorpion, now," Rowan shouted as he and Mia joined the other two.

Spence was not sure how many they had killed, but looking at Mia's half-empty quiver gave him an idea. She was good for an average of two per target. "I hope Rook has that baby started."

"I can hear it," Al stated.

"Enough small chat. Sights up and move." Rowan continued, heading for the exit. Rowan strode at the forefront, Spence guarding their rear, while Mia and Al flanked him. The piercing beams of the APC illuminated their way but obscured their advance towards the vehicle. Barely a couple of strides beyond the building's threshold, a gunshot shattered the air, and a lifeless form tumbled to the icy ground just a stone's throw from Rowan. Val's voice attempted to pierce through the chaos, but her urgent words were drowned out by the rumbling engine of the APC.

"They're on the walls!" Al yelled.

Rowan's gaze lifted, catching sight of a dozen shadowy figures darting agilely along the walls, their movements reminiscent of insects scurrying for cover. Like a cunning pack of predators, the creatures swiftly divided their forces —

some slinking along the sides with eerie grace, while the rest leaped back over the edge and vanished through the gaping maw of the skylight above.

"Contact Right!" Spence yelled as his shotgun made mincemeat out of one of the creature's arms, blasting it off.

In the icy silence, Rowan's sharp eyes caught sight of two twisted figures dropping to his left, their eerie howls fading into the wind. A third creature skittered along the frost-covered wall, its elongated limbs a grotesque dance of death. With instinctive precision, he smoothly raised his weapon in a fluid motion as he moved, each movement a testament of honing his reflexes. The gun roared to life, sending three rounds tearing through the frigid air with deadly accuracy. Two shots found their mark dead center on the creature's mutated form, while the third pierced its skull with chilling finality.

Before the echoes of gunfire could fade, Val's lethal shots came into play. Her sniper rifle cracked like thunder in the stillness as she swiftly eliminated another threat, forcing the remaining abominations to scatter in disarray. Rowan observed their calculated retreat behind abandoned vehicles for makeshift cover, their glowing eyes betraying a primal fear that echoed through the desolate landscape. Meanwhile, a few daring creatures continued their relentless advance up the icy wall, claws scraping against frozen metal in a macabre symphony of impending danger.

"They are going for Val," he thought. "Cover your section, and double time!" Rowan yelled, pushing his team harder forward.

He cursed Larissa's goons, parking the vehicles to close together, giving the creatures cover to maneuver undetected, at least until they were right on top of them.

Al and Spence locked their gaze on a pack of twisted figures rounding the bend. With a swift motion, Spence slung his Herakles across his back and deftly swapped to his rifle, ready to engage the approaching threat. In unison, they pinpointed their marks, each shot a calculated dance of precision and deadly intent. The crack of gunfire echoed through the desolate streets as they aimed to cripple or eliminate their adversaries, aiming for fatal blows with every pull of the trigger.

"Spence, how's Mia?" Al asked during the lull.

Spence turned to find Mia had downed two in front of her; her arrows in vital spots.

"She's good," Spence reported.

"Figured as much."

Navigating the clearing, the team edged closer to the abandoned vehicles, their presence a stark contrast against the desolate backdrop. Val's watchful gaze darted between her companions and the looming threat surrounding them. Amidst the chaos, she managed to spot a menacing beast that lurked within the vehicle cluster, while others skulked across. Swiftly transitioning from her magnified scope to the crimson dot sight perched atop her weapon, Val tracked their movements. As one agile adversary vaulted from a wall onto a car roof, then bounded from vehicle to vehicle like a sinister dance, Val stayed steps ahead, predicting its trajectory before unleashing a well-aimed shot that sent it tumbling over the edge.

Repositioning herself swiftly, her focus unwavering, Val locked onto the next assailant hurtling towards her with relentless speed. In a heartbeat, as she aligned her sights, the creature closed in rapidly. Without faltering, she squeezed the trigger without hesitation. The creature staggered backward violently as her shot found its mark, splitting its skull in a gruesome display of finality.

"Not on my watch," Exhaling sharply, she caught the faint sound of Rook's rhythmic thumps from inside the APC amid the chaotic gunfire. Reacting swiftly, she gripped a sturdy roof rail as the vehicle jolted into motion.

The swirling snow danced in protest as the massive wheels of the vehicle finally caught traction on the slick surface, propelling it forward with a growl. Rook's hands, weathered from years of toil, gripped the wheel with a seasoned confidence. Today, finesse took a backseat to urgency as he guided the vehicle towards his comrades with a raw determination etched on his face.

Positioning the armored APC strategically near the entrance, Rook awaited the arrival of his team, every muscle in his body poised for action. Val, her eyes sharp and unwavering, swiftly slung her rifle across her back, opting for a secondary weapon that promised a rapid barrage of firepower.

Rook expertly maneuvered the vehicle, aligning it for a swift entry through the rear ramp. Rowan signaled for the team to ease their pace as they approached the final stretch towards the APC. Drawing closer together, they formed a protective barrier amidst the scattered vehicles, strategically shielding each other. This tactic not only disrupted the beasts' advance but also thwarted their attempts to overwhelm them in a frenzied attack.

From the shadows, a creature slinked out on Rowan's right, its form silhouetted against the remnants of a rusted car. Rowan's steps never faltered as he swiftly raised his weapon and unleashed a precise shot. The creature convulsed as the bullet ripped through its hide, collapsing onto the hood. As if summoned by some unseen malevolence, two more of the nightmarish beings materialized. Rowan's mind raced with disbelief at their relentless onslaught even as he took down one with deadly accuracy. Val's sniper rifle echoed his shot, felling the second assailant. However, a third abomination leaped from the darkness and charged towards Rowan on all fours, hunger for blood gleaming in its eyes.

Rowan could not resist being intimidated by its size. Illuminated by the APC's light, its grotesque humanoid traits became clearer, but its feline-like agility was unnerving. With each step, its muscles rippled beneath its skin, giving it an unsettling grace as it prowled forward.

"Ugly!" Rowan said to no one in particular.

Squeezing the trigger, he unleashed a rapid burst, the shots grazing past the creature's flank. Undeterred by the minor injury, the beast surged forward relentlessly. Rowan recalibrated his aim swiftly and pulled the trigger once more. The bullet struck true this time, shattering the monster's femur with a resounding crack. As its balance faltered, inertia propelled it forward, crashing face-first onto the icy terrain and skidding several feet in a gruesome display. Unfazed by the chaos around him, Rowan matched strides with his comrades, seamlessly overtaking the fallen foe. In a swift motion, he ensured its demise by dispatching two final rounds into its skull before swiftly moving on.

"Reloading!" he yelled.

Al and Spence found themselves in the midst of a fresh wave of creatures that descended upon them. Unlike the initial surge that swarmed in, these new assailants leaped from crumbling walls to rusted vehicles, their razor-sharp claws seeking purchase on anything they could grasp. Al's senses sharpened, and anticipated their landing spots and unleashing precise shots towards their torsos. Each bullet, even if non-lethal, acted as a temporary barrier impeding their advance through the chaos of the battleground.

The next twisted form lunged towards Al, aiming to tear into his flesh, but it met a hail of bullets ten feet away. The gunman's finger tightened on the trigger, expecting the creature's head to snap back from the impact. Yet, there was no reaction.

"*Fuck, empty!*" Al cursed at himself.

The creature must have expected something similar, for it paused momentarily. Al's hand instinctively went for his weapon, but the creature swiftly veered to his right with uncanny speed. Trying to keep up with its agile form was akin to tracing the path of lightning, yet Al persisted, guiding his aim and unleashing two rapid shots towards its anticipated trajectory.

As the elusive creature darted around, Al swiftly secured his sidearm and deftly loaded a fresh magazine into his rifle. It was a risky move, but in a situation such as this, power and rate of fire were needed.

Al's heart raced as the creature lunged towards him, its monstrous form hurtling through the air. Reacting swiftly, he raised his rifle just in time before the impact sent him crashing to the ground. With a desperate maneuver, he wedged the barrel of his weapon into the creature's gaping maw, preventing its razor-sharp teeth from tearing into his flesh. The beast snarled and gnashed its jaws against the unyielding steel, hungry for a fatal bite. Locked in a fierce struggle, Al met the creature's coal-black eyes, each push testing his resolve as he fought to keep himself from becoming its next meal.

Al strained against the weight of the beast bearing down on him, muscles trembling with effort. The creature loomed over him, its hot breath reeking of decay washing over his face. Saliva dripped from its jagged teeth, a vile concoction pooling near Al's cheek. As he fought the urge to retch, the monster shifted its weight, forcing the gun closer to his chest with a deliberate nudge of its chin. Like a predator ready to strike, it arched forward, jaws gaping wide in a menacing display of imminent danger.

Al's survival instincts kicked in as he evaded the creature's snapping jaws, causing them to crunch down on the compacted snow instead. Undeterred by the failed attack, the beast adjusted its position, getting closer to Al with a menacing intent. In a swift motion, Al lowered his rifle and drew his combat knife from its sheath secured on his chest. With his blade in hand, he sliced upwards, carving a deep gash across the creature's face as it mirrored his movements in a chilling mimicry of aggression.

The blade sliced across the beast's eye, eliciting a piercing howl that echoed through the icy air. The creature thrashed in agony, its claws tearing Al's pants and drawing blood along his hip. Gritting his teeth against the pain, Al didn't falter. Driven by adrenaline, he swiftly somersaulted away from the wounded creature, determined not to let this confrontation be his last stand.

The one-eyed creature barreled towards him, its sinewy muscles rippling with ferocity. Suddenly, two arrows materialized in its flank, causing it to pivot sharply towards the unseen attackers. Before it could react, an ax swiftly found its mark, sinking into the beast's skull with a sickening thud.

It collapsed soundlessly to the ground, convulsing in its final moments.

By the time Al realized what had happened, and that he was still alive, Mia had already yanked her throwing axe and arrows out of the monster. Al slung his rifle over his back and took hold of his pistol. Transformed into a plaything for the creatures, he hesitated, uncertain if the rifle would fire, realizing that the battlefield was not the ideal setting to test a weapon.

Mia pointed at his leg when she saw he was favoring it. "I'll be fine," he growled through gritted teeth. She made a gesture to lead on, as he turned back and whistled to Spence, who was already heading their way.

"Not the time for a rest, you two," Spence said exhaustedly as he moved past them. Mia and Al took after him, only making it a few steps before Al tripped and fell.

Mia whistles, getting Spence to stop and his tracks.

"Rowan, Al needs help. Cover us," Spence yelled, but their leader was already on top of it, his gun covering the roofs of the vehicles. As Spence reached Al, he looked at Mia.

"I got him; you cover the rear."

Mia responded by showing him her empty quiver. He went to ask her about her sidearm, but knowing she had not practiced with it as told, she would probably go through half the magazine before hitting one. "Then go, I've got the rear," Spence added as he spun around.

Mia took Al's arm and threw it over her shoulder, grabbing the opposite side of his gear for more support, and began making for the Scorpion. "*Man, this girl can hold her own,*" Al thought as she dragged him through the snow.

Gunfire crackled in the air, punctuating the chaos as creatures vanished from the vehicle rooftops like elusive shadows.

The fate of these foes – whether wounded, lifeless, or cunningly evading capture – hung in uncertainty. As another adversary succumbed, Spence swiftly regrouped, seamlessly synchronizing with Rowan in a dynamic leapfrog to rejoin their comrades.

"Spence, seven o'clock!" Rowan yelled, catching up with Al to support him with the other arm. "Have to say, this is not the best neighborhood for you to be jogging," he quipped, dragging him along.

Without missing a beat, Spence snapped around, took down the creatures, and went back to running for the vehicle. He could make out Val's figure on top of the APC with each flash of her rifle, it was followed by a whistle and thud as a round sizzled by him. With a quick look over his shoulder, to find another lifeless creature on the ground with its head missing.

"*Now I am going to have to play nice with her for sure,*" he thought.

"Spence, get your ass moving," Rowan shouted, reaching out for his brother in arms.

With Al being hauled up the ramp and into the APC, Val jumped from the roof and landed as Spence approached.

"Ladies first," Val whispered as Spence passed by.

"Oh, now you want to flirt," he smiled.

"A little encouragement shouldn't hurt," she smiled and followed suit. Inside, she hit the button, closing the ramp.

"Rook, someplace else would be nice," Rowan yelled.

The APC quickly lurched forward as the ramp door continued to close. Rook glanced at his side mirror, finding a large number of them perched on roofs and cars like gargoyles protecting the night.

"And I was told Notre Dame is not creepy," Rook replied to

no one in particular.

"Val, toss me that med-kit behind you," Al said, looking at his leg.

Snatching the kit by the exit, a Stalker sprang into the narrowing ramp, aiming for Val's head. As the closing mechanism restricted its advance, trapping its upper body, it thrashed wildly but failed to reach her. In a synchronized move, Val and Rowan swiftly drew their sidearms and fired at the creature. The bullets found their mark on the Stalker's skull, halting its movements abruptly as it slumped lifeless against the metal confines of the ramp.

For a minute, the hum of the diesel engine was all they heard as the team studied the corpse.

"So, are we just going to leave it there? You know, looking at us?" Al asked, breaking the silence. "It's bleeding on the floor."

"If you're making a mess back there, better make sure to clean it up," Rook shouted.

"Just keep your eyes on the road, Rook, we got this," Rowan replied. "You ready, Spence?"

"As I'll ever be."

Rowan pressed the release button for the ramp, and together they pushed the body out. It rolled off the ramp and onto the empty street.

"Does anyone find it odd they're not giving chase?" Val chimed in, no longer seeing the creatures pursuing them.

As soon as the sentence came from her mouth, the roof of the APC started to thud with massive objects landing on top. Spence and Rowan looked to Val.

"Why you put that shit out in the universe? Now you have to fix it," Spence said.

A faint bestial cry could be heard beneath the engine. "Front," Rowan warned, grabbing an SMG off the APC's wall.

"I got the back," Spence said, double-checking his sidearm. He takes a step next to Val, "Watch my six."

"I always do for the team," Val replied.

"For the team," Spence confirmed, then opened the swing door within the ramp and started to climb the ladder. "The things I do for these people," he said, glancing down at the ground speeding past.

Rook had painstakingly tweaked the APC for icy terrain, but the vehicle's adaptations struggled on the uneven London streets. Each collision with a car either sent it careening aside or flattened it like a discarded rug. The jolting ride felt to Spence like scaling a cliff face during a seismic upheaval.

"He has to be aiming for shit to hit," Spence said through clenched teeth, while holding on for dear life. At their current speeds, the fall would not be life-threatening, but the moving shadows behind them would. "I need whiskey for this shit," he muttered.

The biting cold gnawed at his exposed skin as he cautiously rose above the armored vehicle, spying the distorted shapes of two creatures viciously scraping at its metal frame. Balancing carefully, he took another step and steadied his grip on the pistol. His breath forming mist in the icy air, he aimed to draw their focus. Aiming with precision, he squeezed the trigger, the gunshot drowned by a piercing shriek that followed as one of the beasts convulsed in agony, its twisted form contorting against the backdrop of frozen ruins.

"Why, thank you. I would like a larger mass to shoot at," Spence thought, squeezing the trigger the moment Rook side swiped

another vehicle, causing his next shot to go wide as he slipped on the rung, nearly falling from the APC. "GOT! DAMN! ROOK!" He grunted, managing to hold onto the rung while his body dangled and banged against the side like a flag in the wind.

Ice clung to the ladder, forming a treacherous layer that hindered his ascent. He wedged the pistol's grip onto a rung, seeking a firmer hold. At that moment, Val emerged from the doorway, her strong fingers grasping his tactical vest firmly, effortlessly hoisting him back up to safety on the ladder.

"I knew you loved me," Spence quipped, only to get her usual emotionless stare.

Planting his feet firmly, Spence began his ascent. As he reached for the next rung, a grotesque face crept into view over the rooftop's edge, its eyes glinting in the dim light. Without warning, the creature lunged, its jaws gaping wide to expose rows of razor-sharp teeth aimed at Spence's face. In a swift motion, Spence deftly maneuvered his weapon beneath the beast's chin. A spray of brains and blood erupted from the top of its head before it collapsed lifeless onto the roof, leaving a chilling silence in its wake.

"Sorry, no kisses on the first date. Unless—," Spence said, before glancing down at Val. His thoughts were interrupted as more shots shattered the eerie silence, echoing through the frozen wasteland. A ghastly figure, twisted and contorted, tumbled along the icy roof of the vehicle before disappearing into the darkness at the rear.

Chapter 9

Sliding into the front seat of the armored personnel carrier, Rowan observed the monstrous claws relentlessly striking the reinforced windows. He had faith in the glass's durability, knowing it was crafted to resist nearly all assaults except for a fifty-caliber anti-tank round, according to Rook's assurances. However, as he witnessed the scratches deepening with each impact, doubts crept into Rowan's mind about the window's true strength.

"They're making it hard to see," Rook said, his eyes focused on the road. His point was punctuated by the jolt of the vehicle as it bounced off another object.

"Try using wipers?" Rowan said in question form.

"Sorry, I had to skimp on luxury. Freezing planets tend to have that effect," Rook replied, trying not to let his tension show. But navigating obstacles as claws constantly slammed into the windows proved challenging.

A gunshot pierced the air, followed by a chilling scream echoing from the shadows above. Rowan's muscles tensed as he instinctively headed towards the door. With Spence drawing the creatures' attention, he saw a chance to act. As the relentless assault on the windows subsided, Rowan swiftly swung open the door, he hoisted his SMG overhead. Without hesitation, he unleashed a barrage of blind shots towards their known positions, each round aimed to disrupt and disable.

BAM!

The armored vehicle collided with a car, jolting Rowan off his seat, sending him hurtling through the open door.

"Shit! Shit! Shit!" Rowan yelled, losing his weapon.

Assisted by gravity's gentle pull, he maneuvered his way back to the APC. Fortunately, the SMG's strap secured around his shoulder prevented him from completely losing hold of the weapon. After a moment of searching, he located the grip and prepared himself once more.

Another gunshot echoed from the APC's rear, drawing Rowan's attention. He scanned the scene and spotted a lifeless monster sprawled on the rooftop while another creature poised to attack. With swift precision, Rowan raised his SMG and unleashed a barrage of bullets at the approaching menace. The rounds ripped through its side and leg, propelling it over the roof's edge in a chaotic descent. The monster plummeted headfirst to the ground below, a crumpled heap of twisted limbs and shattered bones.

"What are you doing? Mind coming in and closing the door? My mom always said Close the door behind yourself," Rook smiled.

Rowan climbed in and closed the door with an emphasized slam. "Happy?"

"Quiet," Rook replied, focusing back on the road. "I'm getting the feeling something is not right. I mean, look at the road."

"This was intentional; this was planned," Rowan thought, his sharp gaze swept over the road ahead, noting the unusual arrangement of vehicles. Unlike the scattered remnants of

abandoned cars they were used to encountering, these vehicles were strategically positioned at awkward angles, forming a barricade that blocked all passage. Rook's apprehension was warranted; their path was obstructed deliberately. The APC, typically adept at plowing through obstacles, faced a challenge on the icy terrain with the vehicles intentionally placed to impede their progress. The reduced speed due to the treacherous conditions added an extra layer of difficulty to what would have been a straightforward task.

Whether it was the creatures or someone else, he did not know. If the creatures were responsible, it meant something far worse — that they were capable of planning and evaluating. If humans were responsible, they were organized. Also, not good.

After clearing the barrier of vehicles, Rook was able to bring the Scorpion up to speed. "Okay, maybe we are good," Rook informed with little confidence.

Rowan's skepticism lingered as he scanned the path ahead, alert for any lurking dangers. His suspicions seemed validated when his gaze landed on a suspicious sight. Just at the fringes of the illumination, they encountered a mound of debris clustered against a dilapidated structure. The jumbled wreckage stretched across half of the thoroughfare. Following the stack upwards, Rowan noticed sizable fragments of the wall standing precariously to the left. Upon closer scrutiny, he discerned eerie movements within the shadows dancing along the exterior surface.

"Shit," Rowan whispered as the realization set in. "Rook, veer right now!"

Rook yanked the steering wheel sharply to the right, his actions mirroring Rowan's concern. The vehicle juddered in response to the sudden maneuver, colliding with the strategically positioned delivery truck.

"Brace for impact!" Rook yelled while the Scorpion shifted to one side.

Unsecured items careened wildly inside the APC, causing chaos as they ricocheted off surfaces, jostling the team members. Positioned at the front, Rowan swiftly seized the sturdy handle fixed to the dashboard, humorously labeled the *Oh Shit!* handle.

Rook's calloused hands clenched the worn steering wheel, his gaze fixed on the obstacle-strewn path ahead. The Scorpion rumbled over the treacherous terrain, each jolt sending vibrations through Rook's sturdy frame. As a cascade of rubble cascaded down the mound of debris, the vehicle lurched to the right, responding to Rook's expert maneuvers just as Rowan had anticipated. Yet, what awaited beyond the obstruction was hidden from view: a blockade of vehicles tightly packed together, a menacing barrier daring them to find a way through.

The weight of the debris, reinforced by the cars, nearly caused the APC to tip over and roll end over end with the pile. If anything, it did the opposite by propelling it over the barricade of vehicles and through the front of a building.

Rook managed as best he could, but the APC's momentum and size were too much. Coming to a halt inside the building, a section of the ceiling collapsed, partially burying the Scorpion.

"Oh, thank the Lord! Wasn't sure if the ol' girl was going to see another day," Rook sighed in relief as he looked to his right to find Rowan still holding onto the *Oh Shit* handle.

"Let's not do that again," he murmured, facing those in the back. "Everyone okay?"

"Spence and I are good," Val reported.

"Of course, you're good; you landed on me," Spence replied.

"I had a box of MREs on my head, but I am good," Al replied.

Lastly, Mia lifted her arm from the floor to give a thumbs-up.

"Ok, grab your weapons and some ammo," Rowan ordered. A smile came across his face as he took pleasure in saying his next words. "Al, get these goddamn collars off before we do anything else."

"So, apparently...," Al stammered, as he patted his pockets.

"Apparently what?" Rowan demanded, sensing the change of tone in his voice.

"Apparently, when the beast clawed through the pocket I put it in," presenting his shredded pants leg. "It's still back at the camp."

Immediately, the APC was filled with *"Hell Nahs"*, *"How Could This"*, and Mia's rapidly moving fingers.

"Hold your horses. You're fucking telling me, I nearly had this beautiful face of mine ripped off, on several occasions, for nothing?" Spence chimed in.

"I'm sorry, Rowan," Al continued, studying the disappointment on everyone's faces. Knowing this was the moment they were all waiting for, and yet somehow, he dropped the ball.

In disbelief, Rowan wiped beads of sweat from his face before resting his head against the bulkhead, "It's not your fault. Who could have expected that engagement? You did what any of us would have done — survive."

Just when Rowan thought he was about to have his break, this wretched existence he called life threw another wrench into it.

"We can always go back for it," Rook added.

"I don't think I can go back there," Spence shouted, taking

a seat. "I mean, we barely made it out as is."

"First, we need to survive this night, then we can go back," Val added as she loaded a fresh mag into her pistol.

"This vehicle is tough. It's designed to survive all we went through, and then some," Rook boasted, "but we won't be going anywhere until she's wedged free."

As if given an order, Mia and Val stood up and made for the rear door. Al looked at them and back at Rowan. Val turned to Rowan.

"The night's still young," she shrugged.

"So it is," Rowan responded.

Then out of the quietness came a *BANG* as something smashed into the rear of the vehicle, joined by claws scraping against the metal hull.

Spence took a step away from the door as the beast's screams drowned out any other sounds of the night. "How's the front looking?"

"On it," Al responded, stumbling to his feet.

"Gotcha," Spence said, aiding Al to his feet. "You alright?"

Al nodded, "Didn't get patched up much. Bumpy ride."

"Quit your whining," Spence replied, giving him a firm pat on the back.

A different sound rang out. Al's attention immediately went towards the end of the APC, "Did you hear that?" he asked.

"Shh, it sounded like gunfire," Val confirmed.

A cacophony of gunfire erupted outside, diverting the creature's attention from the Scorpion. The haunting cries of the beasts were abruptly halted by the relentless barrage of bullets. Time seemed to stretch as the shots continued, until a solitary screech pierced through, feeble and stifled. Its eerie sound lingered briefly before being extinguished by a lone gunshot that reverberated through the air, resonating for what felt like an endless moment.

A chilling hush descended upon the group, each member tensing as they pivoted towards the rear ramp, their weapons poised for action. The air was filled with the eerie symphony of icy gusts swirling outside, wrapping the vehicle in a cocoon of isolation. Suddenly, a series of deliberate knocks reverberated through the metal door at the back, resonating like ominous drumbeats in the frozen wasteland beyond.

"You're in the wrong part of town, my friends," a voice boomed from the outside.

Chapter 10

"What the hell? Who in their right mind would be out there?" Spence whispered.

"*Someone familiar with the area*," Rowan thought.

"I know you're in there. We witnessed the crash. We can promise your safety as long as you leave your weapons inside and exit the vehicle with your hands up," the husky voice shouted.

"*Who are these guys? Can't be survivors from the camp. They would have recognized the Scorpion*," Rowan thought, moving to one of the small rear panel windows to get a peek at the mystery figure.

"What are you doing? You're not considering talking to these folks, are you? Right now, we're sitting ducks. Hell, for all we know, they could be cannibals ready for leftovers," Spence added, seeing Rowan making his way to the rear.

As he reached the rear panel, Rowan turned and looked at Spence with a contorted face that suggested one thing — "*shut the hell up.*" Seeing that his point was received, he opened the panel.

"Let's be civil," the voice continued, receiving no response from inside. "There are other means to go about this. We all had a rough day. What do you say, we talk face to face? Before more of them return. Which I guarantee is bound to happen. I can also guarantee we will not be here to keep them from finding a way into that APC. So, what's it going to be?"

The small panel creaked open, unleashing a blinding cascade of light that engulfed the Scorpion's cramped confines. Rowan instinctively raised his arm to shield his eyes, allowing them a moment to acclimate to the sudden brilliance spilling in from outside. Gradually, as his vision cleared, the stark scene before him materialized — the lifeless forms of the creatures sprawled motionless in the snowy expanse encircling the Scorpion. Amidst the stark illumination cast by the floodlights, a solitary figure loomed tall and ominous, its silhouette commanding attention against the icy backdrop.

Observing the silhouette before him and the dire circumstances they found themselves in, Rowan couldn't shake off the feeling that fate had a cruel way of twisting his path. Despite surviving a world-altering cataclysm, he now found himself at the beck and call of a power-hungry despot. Just when a glimmer of hope emerged to rid them of their cursed collars, the means to freedom slipped through their fingers. Now confined within a steel enclosure with a solitary exit, the air thick with uncertainty, surrounded by unseen adversaries armed to the teeth.

"What's our move?" Val asked, seeing Rowan grasping his weapon a little tighter.

His initial instinct urged him to swiftly aim, fire, and bring down the silhouette in its tracks. However, he understood that resorting to gunfire immediately wasn't always the most strategic choice. Occasionally, it was imperative to assess the situation thoroughly beforehand. How many adversaries lurked nearby? Which paths offered the safest retreat options?

"I need to find out what we are dealing with. It's clear that they've crossed paths with these beasts before," he whispered back.

"How about I help to speed up your decision process?" the figure interrupted. "Being that you're unwilling to talk, they say actions speak louder than words. To get your attention...," the man raised his hand to someone Rowan could not see, "do me the honor, please?"

Taking his words as a threat, Rowan raised his weapon in the small window, and before he could pull the trigger, a red light flashed around his neck. Settling back into the APC, he glanced around at his team's collars as one by one they began to flash and become armed.

"*Fuck! This can't be happening*," Rowan thought.

"If that didn't get your attention, I'm not sure what will." Seconds later, the collars deactivated. "Come to think about it, if I meant any of you harm, I could detonate those. Look, I just want to talk. I don't care about what you did or who you are."

"I say we drop this wanker where he stands, while the collars are down, take the remote from his body, and boom; we are free citizens," Spence said.

Facing the teams, "That would work if he were alone. But clearly, he's not. For all we know, we could be surrounded. If we dropped him, we could quickly follow," Rowan said, rubbing his head. "This is how we are going to handle this, Spence, you come with me, everyone else provide cover. Val, you know what to do if this goes south." Stepping back to the small window, "What do you want?"

"So, there's life in there after all," the voice boomed from the blinding light. "How many in the APC?"

"Show your face and your numbers. And I'll think about

telling you," Rowan replied.

There was a slight hesitation before the lights died on the two subordinates' shoulder mount. Rowan's eyes took several seconds to adjust, revealing a three-person team. *Oh, I like these odds.*

The strangers outside were well equipped for extreme conditions. Two were dressed in winter Parkas, while the last wore a *Hijab Shemagh* headdress protecting him from the elements. Peering through his scope, Rowan noticed that their winter gear appeared near pristine, a stark contrast to their own patched and weathered clothing that had seen countless repairs in the past.

"You guys have clear shots?" Rowan asked, quickly getting confirmation from the remaining four, he hit the latch, unlocking the rear hatch door. With his rifle up, he leaps from the APC, landing in the snow with a crunch, his gun already trained on the mysterious figure. After a few steps, Spence followed.

"Besides the two of you, how many of you are inside?" the man asked again, while the other two stood only feet away at his sides, their assault rifles trained on them. The air became silent as the figure waited for a response.

Obscured from view, Rowan observed the mist of their exhalations crystallizing in the frigid air. The quickened puffs hinted at a mix of anticipation and unease; he silently wished for the latter. Such emotions could trigger hasty decisions or paralyzing hesitation, potentially offering him an opening crucial for his survival in this tense moment. Yet, their breaths flowed evenly, betraying seasoned composure and readiness. Their posture echoed this assessment, speaking volumes without a word.

"Why should we share anything?" Rowan asked.

The leader's silence lingered, his gaze shifting towards a subordinate whose action revealed a sleek device snug on his wrist. With a subtle press, the device's blue screen flickered to life casting a soft glow on the youthful face of its wearer, barely twenty years old. Skillfully navigating the compact five-inch screen like a virtuoso pianist, the light on Rowan and Spence's collars transitioned from a steady blue to an erratic flashing accompanied by urgent beeping, indicating the activation of their explosive collars. A series of precise taps on the device restored the collars to their tranquil blue glow.

"I'm not much for words, but one thing is for sure: I keep my word. Our device has already informed us that there are six collars, which include both of you. I just need to know, are there any additions to that? We don't mean any harm, but we will protect ourselves by any means. Even if it means initiating your collars. What you did to receive those collars is of no concern to us. However, this is how this is going to work. As a result of our vehicle breaking down, using your APC, you're going to come with us and assist us with getting some cargo back to our base a few kilometers from our current location. Afterward, we take you back out into the white, deactivate your collars, and set you free. It's a win–win scenario," the leader continued, lowering his weapon.

"Damn if I'm tired of being herded around like cattle," Rowan thought.

"Hell, if we're going anywhere with you. I'd rather shoot this out like men. Leaving the chance of taking that pretty bracelet of his," Spence chimed in.

"Before you even get close, it will be lights out. You see, the moment I initiated your collar, I installed a program. That if I didn't enter a code every fifteen minutes, they would detonate. So, think twice," the young soldier said, taking a step forward, his weapon up. Spence grimaced, challenging him with his own step forward.

"Jasper, that's not necessary. Lower your weapon," the leader suggested with his hands. "Do we have a deal?" he asked, maintaining his attention on Rowan.

"Spence, lower your weapon," Rowan ordered.

"What?"

"Lower your weapon," he repeated, cutting an eye at him.

"We can't allow ourselves to be brought under another when we're so close to being our own," Spence continued, grasping his weapon tightly.

Grabbing the top of Spence's barrel, "You damn well know I feel the same," Rowan growled through clench teeth. "But damn if I'm going to put the rest of the squad in jeopardy. Lower your damn weapon!"

"This is bullshit," he whispered, as he lowered his weapon, and gave the young soldier a death-dealing stare.

"It looks like we have a deal then," the leader added, signaling the last soldier to lower his weapon.

"Just know I'm also a man of my word, and I will do everything in my power to keep my team alive. Including putting an end to you and your men if you even think about crossing us."

"I'll be sure to keep that in mind. In the meantime, what can we do to help before more show up? And the name's Buirke," he said, approaching Rowan, his hand extended.

Rowan eyeballed the man's hand, "You did enough already with fighting off the beast. I can get it from here," Rowan ended before walking back to the vehicle. "Rook, get some line and the crank. Let's get the old girl out of this rubble and onto her feet."

"On it," Rook replied, standing just inside the vehicle.

Moments lingered before Rook emerged from the rear hatch, his hands gripping a thick rope coiled around a heavy-duty winch. Stepping past the scattered remains of the fallen creatures, he meticulously secured the winch to a robust post and fastened the other end to the vehicle's sturdy rear hitch. Each turn of the winch handle tugged the armored personnel carrier inch by inch out of the debris-laden ruins. While Rook deftly tinkered with the Scorpion, his companions stood vigilant, their gazes darting between lurking shadows for any sign of movement and the watchful soldiers stationed nearby.

Returning to Buirke, "Where is your vehicle?" Rowan asked, as Spence stood there keeping an eye on Buirke's two men.

"We've been stranded out here for several hours now. Just before sundown. Our vehicle broke an axle beyond that building there. We were working on a solution when we heard the gunfire and crash. With your vehicle on all four, we're going to go there, transfer the load, then it's a short ride to the base," he said, adjusting the rifle slung across his shoulder.

"Sounds like a well-thought-out plan," Rowan commented.

"Well, a plan is only as good as its execution," Buirke answered, hearing a crash.

Both men turned to see the Scorpion freed from its brick and concrete prison. "Be ready to move out in fifteen," Rowan finished, leaving to check on the Scorpion's condition.

"You sure this is a good idea? Trusting them?" Val asked Rowan, upon his reaching the Scorpion.

"Val, you know I don't trust anyone I've haven't bled with. The fact is, they primed our collars using some device on their wrist. And if a code is not entered every fifteen minutes, it's lights out for all of us. How they did it, I'm not sure. If anything, I'm curious where they got the tech from. Haven't seen anything like it since the NWF."

"You think they're NWF soldiers?" Val questioned, keeping pace with him.

"Not sure, but tech like that could go a long way nowadays."

"What's your angle?" Val continued, stopping in her tracks; Rowan with her.

"No angle on this one. Keeping it basic. Check out their base, and have these damn collars removed for good."

"It may not be that simple, Rowan."

"It never is," he concluded before leaving her to check Rook's progress.

Minutes ticked by as Rook meticulously inspected every cog and bolt of the Scorpion, his weathered hands deftly maneuvering over its metal frame. Meanwhile, the team tended to their injuries, wrapping bandages tightly around cuts and bruises. Satisfied that the APC was undamaged, they all climbed aboard, each member finding a seat as they ensured the doors were firmly locked. The journey to the rendezvous point unfolded in silence, filled with glances heavy with unsaid disapproval passing between them like unspoken judgments in a court of shadows.

Val settled into the driver's seat, the worn leather creaking softly under her weight as she waited for Rook to recover from his thorough examination of the APC. The vehicle bore scars of past battles, each dent and scratch a testament to their survival in this unforgiving world. Behind the wheel, Val felt a sense of control amidst the chaos that surrounded them.

Navigating through the shadows became a less daunting task

without the looming threat of ravenous creatures lurking in the darkness. The absence of those flesh-eating monsters offered a temporary reprieve, casting a fragile veil of tranquility over their journey through the treacherous night.

The path to the stranger's vehicles was brief, yet they encountered a labyrinth of charred cars stretching out from the shadows. These remnants stood as a haunting testament to the celestial inferno that had engulfed the world a decade prior, forcing people to forsake their means of travel and causing urban areas to become paralyzed in traffic jams.

Being guided to the location by their leader, Buirke, Val parked at the small side street entrance. The APC's headlights immediately illuminated the dark corridor, revealing a medium-sized truck thirty yards down.

"That's us," Buirke reported from the passenger seat so all could hear. "The package is on the rear. With one of your men, the four of us will haul it back here and head for the base. Ten minutes tops."

"Not a problem. I'll go, but one of my own will be joining," Rowan answered. With a nod, Buirke agrees, opens the door, and steps out into the cold. "Keep the engine running," he whispered to Val before releasing the rear ramp.

Down the sloping ramp, they emerged, Rowan leading the way with Spence and Buirke's seasoned soldiers by his side. The trio approached the abandoned vehicle, a relic of the past left to rust in the icy desolation. Rowan, ever watchful, allowed the newcomers to take point while he lingered at the rear, his gaze scanning their surroundings with a soldier's precision.

As they neared the truck, Buirke's deliberate steps slowed to a cautious advance, his rifle-mounted flashlight casting an eerie glow into the darkness of the cab. Without a word spoken,

Spence and Rowan seamlessly secured the front of the vehicle, their movements practiced and swift. This intricate dance of survival was one that only seasoned scavengers could execute flawlessly.

Following Buirke's lead, his two soldiers positioned themselves at the rear, their senses heightened in anticipation of any threat. Their eyes darted from shadow to shadow as they stood guard, ready to react at a moment's notice, while Buirke meticulously inspected every corner of the abandoned vehicle for signs of danger or opportunity.

"Clear," Buirke whispered loudly. Turning to the flatbed of the truck, he opened the bed's door. Sitting there was a large object wrapped beneath a thick green canvas dusted with snow.

"What's that?" Rowan asked, seeing only four metal handles emerge from beneath the canvas.

"It's the package. And knowing what it is was not part of the agreement," Buirke stated, not taking his eyes off the object. "Jasper, Haider, circle up and get this out of here."

This marked the pivotal instant for Rowan, the revelation of the identities of the remaining two soldiers. Names held the power to anchor a person in reality, turning a face from a mere specter into a tangible entity. With their names in hand, the missing puzzle pieces were their purpose for being out and the precise whereabouts of their encampment.

The pair of soldiers positioned themselves, each grasping a handle, leaving only a single handle unclaimed. Rowan glanced back to check the delay and saw Buirke's gaze fixed on him, silently requesting to grab the remaining handle.

"Spence, grab the handle. I'll keep watch."

Reluctantly, Spence assumed his place as the four men lifted the cumbersome load from the truck's cargo area, setting off once more towards the Scorpion.

Within moments, the precious cargo was securely stowed in their vehicle, and they were en route to Buirke's stronghold nestled deep within the city ruins. Buirke extended his arm, a sophisticated wristband encircling it flickered to life, casting a holographic map of the post-apocalyptic London into the frosty air. Their path was traced by a solid line of luminescent amber; their position marked by a pulsating sapphire speck.

He manipulated his wristband with practiced ease, "Tower, Devil Squad on approach, ETA ten," he announced.

"Good to hear your voice, Devils. We feared you'd been claimed by The White," came the anxious reply from an unseen operator. "Everything intact?"

An uneasy silence descended as Buirke surveyed his companions, locking eyes with Rowan, who stood poised at the cockpit entrance. "Just a minor hiccup - axle issue. Inform gate control, we'll be arriving in an unregistered vehicle?"

"Understood about the untagged vehicle. Welcome back, Devils." The operator signed off.

"Devils? What's this all about?" Al murmured to Mia, who remained stoic and alert, her hand never straying far from her weapon.

Buirke deactivated his comm channel and turned towards them. "My people aren't exactly trusting of outsiders... especially bandits. But what they don't know won't hurt them."

"And how do we know this isn't some elaborate ambush?" Val queried.

"You don't," Buirke admitted bluntly. "I understand your skepticism, but believe me when I say there are still good souls left out here."

"In our world, seeing is believing," Val retorted coolly.

"We're nearing our destination; you'll see soon enough," he replied with a cryptic smile before refocusing on the map. "Slow down as we approach the gates and whatever you do, stay on this path."

"Or else?" Rowan challenged.

Buirke gestured to the hologram. "See this amber line? It's our safe route. Beyond the gates, anything outside of it is a minefield. For all our sakes, stick to the path."

"Message received," Rowan confirmed as they continued their journey through the bleak landscape now devoid of abandoned vehicles and debris.

Suddenly, twin beams of light pierced the darkness enveloping their vehicle - the Scorpion. Val instinctively reached for her weapon as she hit the brakes.

"We've got company!" Rowan warned.

"Hold your fire," Buirke interjected, "Bring the vehicle to a stop ahead," he gestured with a nod.

Doing as instructed, the vehicle came to a stop several feet later, and Buirke stepped out into the spotlight before quickly reboarding. The spotlights dimmed, revealing a towering fence materializing from the darkness as its gates creaked open.

Rowan squinted into the gloom, hoping to discern those manning these colossal barriers, but was met with nothing but shadowy voids.

Pass the towers, lights flickered on illuminating a pathway leading them further along in the darkness.

"We're not in Kansas anymore," Rowan muttered under his breath.

The path led them straight to an imposing hangar door which began grating open at Buirke's command, revealing a figure silhouetted against the interior light.

"Not again," Rook sighed under his breath.

"That's Mitch," Buirke reassured him before reaching for the door handle, only to be halted by six soldiers emerging from shadows dressed in white camouflage gear with weapons trained on them and faces obscured by gas masks.

"You betrayed us!" Rowan accused, pressing his sidearm against Buirke's temple while Jasper and Haider leapt into action, aiming their rifles at Rowan's crew.

"The moment you pull that trigger is your last," Jasper threatened through gritted teeth.

"I knew we shouldn't have trusted you!" Spence exclaimed while Al tried to calm him.

"What's the situation back there? And what do we do about them?" Val demanded, eyeing the soldiers outside warily.

"I swear if your men don't stand down, I'll paint this vehicle with your brains," Rowan threatened Buirke, jabbing his weapon harder against his temple.

"You follow suit if you pull that trigger," Haider warned, his own weapon trained on Rowan.

Buirke raised his hands in surrender. "There seems to be a misunderstanding. Let me speak to them and clear this up. I assure you, I haven't crossed you."

As he spoke, two soldiers moved in and attached a magnetic bar lock across the driver and passenger doors, effectively disabling their escape route while simultaneously emitting an electromagnetic pulse that killed the vehicle's power, trapping them inside.

While their transport came to a halt, the soldiers hastily

fell back, each extracting a sleek cylinder from their vests. With a unified motion, they hurled the canisters under the immobilized Scorpion. Almost instantly, an ethereal plume of emerald smoke began to billow outwards, blanketing the vehicle in its toxic grasp.

The verdant mist slithered its way into every crevice of the Scorpion, infiltrating through vents and seams like a silent predator. Inside, the occupants scrambled in desperation. Hands fumbled over latches and handles as panic clawed at their throats. Their frantic efforts echoed hollowly against the cold metal interior, doors that once offered protection now held them captive as they wrestled with unyielding locks. But it was too late; the emerald fog had already claimed them, rendering them all unconscious in seconds.

Chapter 11

Rowan jolted awake in a sweltering chamber, clad in worn cargo pants and a simple tee. Blinding light from an overhead fixture seared his eyes, and his skull pounded as if a war drum beat inside; the gas was wreaking havoc on his senses.

"Damn it," he spat bitterly. How long had he been out? The thought churned in his mind as he shook his head in disbelief, clinging to a fragile grip on the situation.

Sitting bound to a chair in a stark room was a harbinger of grim trouble. His eyes darted around the space, noting its unnervingly pristine condition—a meticulousness he hadn't seen since the Impact. The brick walls gleamed with a fresh coat of paint, and white floor tiles shimmered beneath the harsh glare of the lamp. Apart from the solitary chair he was anchored to, the room was barren of all other furniture. The most jarring detail was the pair of menacing, black-painted steel bars looming before him.

Cannibals weren't part of his calculation; he had long dismissed them as sub-human savages incapable of executing such meticulous care. They wouldn't have bothered cleaning him up, let alone allowed him to wake with every limb intact. He had seen with his own eyes how cannibals treated their victims like mere cattle, dismembering them without remorse.

This cold, clinical space defied anything cannibals could conceive—too immaculate, far too calculated. But before he could settle on any conclusion, his priority was to locate his team, retrieve their gear, and escape this wretched place, whatever this hellhole was.

Another bandit camp, perhaps? He mused grimly. "No, they'd be celebrating over this idiot by now. Better a bandit camp than a cannibal lair," he whispered hoarsely.

Desperation overrode his pain as he tried to rub his neck, only to realize his collar had been removed. A flicker of relief surged through him, swiftly extinguished when he discovered his right wrist was shackled to the cold steel arm of the chair.

"Apologies for the restraints," a stern, shadowed voice declared from behind him. "But surely you understand—no one's too careful these days. Besides the shackles, how might I make your stay more... accommodating? I am your concierge, after all."

Before Rowan could process the words, movement at his left snapped his attention away. Two hulking figures in black military gear emerged from the darkness. One seized his free hand while the other unleashed a crushing blow upon his gut, sending a shockwave of agony as air exploded from his lungs. Bent in pain, the soldiers forced him back into the unforgiving chair. In a heartbeat, his other wrist was trapped by another cuff clamped to the rigid armrest. Coarse duct tape was slapped over his mouth, smothering his protests before a swift, savage punch slammed into his face.

Dazed yet defiant, he strained to listen as heavy, deliberate boot steps advanced from behind. One of the soldiers meticulously placed a chair before him as a middle-aged man in blue overalls limped into view. His dark brown hair, steely blue eyes, and graying sideburns burned into Rowan's mind—a face to remember when gathering intelligence.

Silence, grunts, and murderous glares were all the responses he received. For every sound exchanged, Rowan absorbed brutal blows to his face and body from shadowed assailants. As he gurgled blood, the man raised a hand, halting further punishment. "Enough—I need him to talk. Don't you understand?" The soldier's tone was icy. "Now, can you fix that?" he demanded, nodding at the peeling tape dangling from Rowan's mouth.

Gritting through the pain, Rowan locked eyes on the shadowed figure as they re-secured the tape shut.

"Listen carefully," the figure continued, his voice dripping with cold amusement. "This man was honed in relentless combat—days of punishment lie ahead for someone like you, who can only earn Triple-Top tattoos with a history steeped in the grisly. Breaking you will be like squeezing bread from cement—impossible without a new approach."

What the hell was this place? Where was his team? How did this man know so much about him, to even mention his tattoo, needed intimate knowledge of Triple Top? But none of that mattered now. Right now, escape was his only focus.

"Don't worry; there's no exit here," the man sneered. "I can practically see your training kicking in, scanning for a way out. Let me assure you: there are absolutely no escapes. But there is a little twist." He extracted a controller from his overall pocket. "I also know that while you're tough, you care for your people—a bandit might only think of himself. Look at your face; you know exactly what this is." He flicked a switch, activating one of the ominous collars, and began counting slowly. "Ten, nine... which one shall go first?" He tapped his chin mockingly. "Maybe the Irish prick who makes me question if the Irish are even worth a damn?"

Rowan tried to croak out a response, but only mumbled incoherently beneath the tape.

"Give me a moment," the man said, raising a single finger as if granting a brief reprieve. "Let me give you the chance to speak. Where was I? Yes—eight, seven... or your sniper? The one my men managed to cuff before she even stirred awake. Oh, the look in her eyes..."

Summoning every ounce of strength, Rowan lunged towards the man in the chair, but two iron hands gripped his shoulders, pinning him and the chair to the floor. Sweat trickled painfully into his eyes, merging with the blood and grime from his earlier injuries.

"Six, five... maybe the castle-like brute? You call him Rook, don't you? Four, three... and don't forget the unhinged Brazilian! To simplify matters, I might as well press this button now. That would eliminate one of the two."

Every muffled number was a searing blow to Rowan's pride as he forced his gaze to track the man's finger tapping cheaply on the button.

"Two, one... or the young girl. The one who, even while bound, managed to overpower one of my best soldiers."

Veins contorted in Rowan's forehead as he gnashed his teeth, desperate to break free of the tape.

"Zero," the man declared, slamming the button with finality.

"No!" Rowan roared, managing to break the tape free from his lips—his voice a raw scream of fury and despair—uttered a heartbeat too late.

Chapter 12

Rowan's mind ached with disbelief as he surveyed the shattered remnants of the world he once knew—its contours twisted and contorted beyond recognition—and now, with his team gone, the few souls he respected as family had vanished into memory. Locked into a fevered stare with the man holding him captive, Rowan spat through gritted teeth, "Consider yourself the walking dead," even as he twisted against the cold, unforgiving metal of his restraints. His defiance was met with a swift, brutal gut punch from a nearby guard—the sound of bone crunching and his own ragged breath mingling with the metallic tang of fear.

A man, eyes hardened as he looked at the guard and murmured, "I don't think he's going anywhere." The guard merely shrugged, as if the strike was nothing more than an everyday inconvenience. The man's voice dropped to a low, dangerous tone, each word weighed with finality as he gave his attention back to Rowan: "I need you to listen very carefully, my friend. Out there in the White, your words might have carried a little weight, but here they are nothing more than a soft whisper lost in a storm. Here, my word is law—especially when it comes to dealing with the scavengers from the wastelands." As he spoke, he roughly propped Rowan's head upward, "And know this: as long as you remain here, you, and the few you cling to, are alive solely by my decree."

With the mingled taste of saliva and blood coating his tongue, a grim reminder of his defiance. Rowan's eyes widened in horror, his heart pounding against his ribcage as the implications sank in.

"Yes, all your people are still alive," the man continued, his voice deliberately slow, "for this remote isn't connected to their collars. For now, they're safe—as long as you cooperate."

Catching his breath, Rowan's tone sharpened, "The fact we're all still alive means one thing. So, who exactly are you, and what do you want from us?"

The man smirked, methodically peeling off his worn work glove to reveal calloused hands. "Name's Mitch. You're stuck here because you trespassed on our land—a trespass that makes me naturally wary. When you and your crew rolled through the checkpoint in that clunky APC, the array of unrecognizable heat-signatures had me checking every angle to ensure Devil's Squad wasn't compromised." He dabbed the sweat on his forehead with a stained handkerchief before continuing. "And where are we? We're at Haven. The most secure place for a thousand miles—no one enters without my say, and no one leaves without it either."

Rowan's anger simmered as he pressed for answers, "Again, what do you want with us?"

Mitch's gaze grew calculating as he leaned back in his creaking chair, crossing one leg casually. "I admire a man who cuts straight to the chase. Buirke mentioned how your team held back the beasts, despite the odds. Tell me, how do you justify that?"

Rowan's eyes remained unyielding, "I call it surviving."

A chuckle escaped Mitch. "Surviving, huh? Well then, tell me—what the hell do you want with us?" His voice hardened. "I'm essentially what you might call an overseer. As Haven's overseer, it's my duty to sniff out bandits, even the ones hiding behind slick smiles and polished words. It only takes a single self-centered soul to gamble on their own survival. So, what do I want? This purple scarf came from one of your people. It means one thing: you're pillagers preying on the weak. And trust me, you have no idea what we do to people like you in here. This isn't a lawless wasteland; it's civilization."

Rowan's voice thundered, "Where are my people? I don't have time for your games!"

Mitch, seemingly undisturbed, slid a worn cigar from his breast pocket and lit it with a practiced flick of his lighter. The glowing ember danced across his weathered face, casting long shadows that only amplified his air of authority. "I know who you are—ex-Triple Top Mercenaries," he drawled with an almost lazy confidence. Inhaling deeply, he exhaled a plume of smoke as if it were an unspoken confession. "Your silence only confirms it. And those coal-black knives clutched by you and a few of your men? It gave the game away—the signature TM etched along their blades. But make no mistake, that changes nothing between us." He let the smoke swell into a ring that slowly dissolved into the stale air. "There's nothing quite like a fresh Cuban these days. I recall stumbling across a rare box of these fine cigars a few years back—they're delicate treasures, once taken for granted."

Rowan's retort cut through the thick haze, "I frankly don't give a damn about your cigars. All I care about is you getting my people out of here!"

Mitch's expression softened into an amused apology as he

leaned forward slightly. "Relax, Mr.—oh, pardon me, I never caught your name. It's been a long day."

Silence hung between them for a heartbeat before Rowan finally spoke, "The name's Rowan."

Mitch inclined his head, "The way I see it, Mr. Rowan..."

"Just Rowan," he snapped, his tone slicing through the air like a serrated blade.

Mitch shrugged, taking a leisurely drag on his cigar. "Alright, Rowan. I'm not particularly fond of your kind, and let's be honest, you're clinging to life solely because you helped out my team. Now, we have a choice: either we assist each other through these trying circumstances, or we part ways right here."

Rowan's muscles tensed, and he said, "I'm listening."

Mitch's voice dropped as he spilled new information. "Our newly installed surveillance caught your caravan entering Old London, though you vanished shortly after. Yet somehow, Devil Squad was fortunate enough to arrive on time. Had they not, the relentless Stalkers would have come back for you."

"Stalkers?" Rowan echoed, a tremor edging into his tone.

Mitch nodded gravely. "Yes, the monsters now haunt the ruins of Old London. But let's not dwell on that now. I propose a sanctuary for you and your people. And since none of your bandit caravan followed, I must assume they've been snared by those very Stalkers."

Rowan's eyes narrowed. "Under what conditions?"

"Simple," Mitch replied, exhaling a swirl of smoke. "You and your squad join my forces. Fight alongside us, train hard, and support our expeditions. Refuse, and you'll continue to be treated like the lowlife bandits you are. And believe me, I don't fancy the thought of your caravan left to fend for itself out there. Especially at this late hour."

Rowan's anger flared. "If you're hoping for forced labor, you should've left those stupid collars on."

A wry smile crept over Mitch's face as he tapped the ash from his cigar. "I removed the collars at a friend's request. He promised that if you helped bring him back here, he'd free you all. But make no mistake, the idea did cross my mind."

At the mention of the promise, Rowan's whisper was hoarse, "Buirke."

Mitch's eyes softened slightly. "Yes, Buirke. Without his word, we wouldn't even be having this conversation. I'm offering gratitude for his help—and for yours—by freeing you and even the possibility of joining us. Quite against my better judgment, I know, but such is the offer before you."

Frustration roiled within Rowan as he struggled to reconcile the crumbling world with the new chains that bound him. "What exactly does this training entail? I saw your forces in action—they're far from a ragtag bunch," he challenged.

Mitch's tone held no hint of compromise. "Don't misunderstand me. I can't keep Haven secure if every soldier is unfit to repel external foes. My soldiers are too valuable to pull away for mass training missions. If you're unwilling to endure this, then I find no purpose in keeping you around—and our negotiations end here."

"And if I refuse?" Rowan retorted, the tension snapping like a taut wire.

Mitch leaned back, a mirthless laugh rumbling from his throat. "That's typical of your sort. I lay out an ultimatum, and you question it. Think of it this way: refuse, and you remain a mere bandit—treated as such. I won't let you run wild like stray dogs, but I would simply expel you from Haven's inner circle and leave you to scavenge on the outskirts. With your caravan decimated, I doubt you'd fare much better." He took another languid pull on his cigar before continuing, "Rowan, the choice is crystal clear: join us, as Buirke suggested, and in return, we offer shelter, food, and protection—as long as you prove you're worth it."

Rowan's eyes burned with conflicted resolve as he studied Mitch's weathered yet unyielding face. He understood the brutal reality all too well—his squad's survival against the relentless Stalker onslaught was nothing but mere luck. "Before I decide anything, I need to see my team," he declared, his voice rough with urgency.

A heavy silence settled over the room as Mitch considered the request. Finally, he nodded, rising slowly from his creaking chair. "That won't be an issue, Mr. Rowan. You'll be taken to your team promptly." With a swift wave of his hand, the cell's metallic locks disengaged with a resounding bang, and the heavy door creaked open on well-oiled hinges, revealing a long corridor dimly lit by flickering overhead lights. "Welcome to Haven, Mr. Rowan. My men will escort you to your team. I suggest you come to a decision quickly."

Rowan's voice was low and determined as he responded, "Once I see my squad, the pleasure will be all mine." He rose unsteadily from the chair, his eyes flicking toward the two guards before striding past Mitch's outstretched hand and into the stark, echoing corridor beyond.

Mitch's parting words were barely a whisper as he lowered his hand, a final reminder echoing in the silence, "We'll see soon enough."

Chapter 13

Rowan stepped into the corridor and was immediately greeted by elegant light fixtures that hung from the high ceilings like sparkling chandeliers, transforming his grim prison into an almost enchanted space. His footsteps clapped sharply against the white, polished marble flooring, and each echo seemed to resonate with the heartbeat of the mysterious building.

"What the hell did I get us into?" Rowan wondered, his eyes darting toward Mitch's two guards. Both stood imposing and alert, each wielding the NWF's standard Enfield SN-1 assault rifle slung across their shoulders. The weapon itself was a masterpiece of deadly engineering—its sleek design masking a formidable killing range of five hundred meters and the unsettling ability to pierce even the toughest body armor.

The first guard, a stern, middle-aged man with the resolute gaze of someone who'd seen countless battles, exuded an aura of expertise that made him the most dangerous among them. The second, not more than twenty-five and still burning with the impetuosity of youth, seemed less battle-hardened and perhaps more vulnerable—a fact that Rowan mentally noted might work to his advantage, if ever the need arose. Still, these tactical thoughts he shoved to the back of his mind until his team was safely in sight.

After several minutes of silent, measured walking along the quiet corridors, the two sentinels finally led him to a massive cast-iron door adorned with thick iron bands and rugged rivets. "Your friends are inside," the young soldier said, nodding toward the door with a clipped firmness.

Rowan's pulse quickened as he cautiously scanned both guards before stepping closer. The older guard leaned forward and, with a swift swipe of his card, the lock emitted a series of beeps, and the heavy door swung open on mechanized hinges, revealing an expansive cafeteria bathed in soft, ambient light. The room was mostly empty except for several long rectangular tables arranged with meticulous order, and in the center sat five individuals. The moment they heard the door's mechanical whisper, every face snapped in unison toward the entrance, eyes wide with anticipation.

"Rowan!" Spence's voice burst out in a mix of relief and excitement as he threw his hands up in welcome.

"We will leave you to your people. Will be outside when you're ready to see Mitch again," the young soldier stated flatly as Rowan stepped inside and the door clanged shut behind him, sealing him into a new chapter of uncertainty.

A haze of relief mingled with apprehension washed over Rowan as he surveyed the familiar faces. He navigated through the long arrangement of tables toward his squad. "Rowan, what the hell is going on?" Spence blurted, his voice a cocktail of worry and incredulity. "We didn't know what happened to you. When we came to, you were the only one missing." At that moment, Mia rushed forward, wrapping him in a warm, tight hug.

"Miss you too, Mia," he murmured, returning her embrace as if to stitch together the frayed edges of their separation.

"Everyone, are you alright?" he continued, shaking hands and making quick, visual checks of their conditions. "Al, how's the ankle?"

"As good as new," Al replied with a light chuckle, giving a small bounce to his foot to prove his claim. "I don't really know what to make of it, but I feel fantastic."

"Based on how you couldn't walk on it, I was bracing for a disaster," another quip filled the air.

"Tell me about it," Al added with a rueful smile.

Rowan turned his attentive gaze toward Val. "And you, Val?"

"I agree with Al. It's so bizarre—it feels as though nothing ever happened. Not a trace of the battle fatigue we should've all been feeling," Val said, his voice laced with an eerie calm.

His eyes then shifted between Rook and Mia. "What about you two?"

Rook's face hardened as he responded, "Physically, I'm intact, but mentally, I'm mad as hell." Mia punctuated his words with a definitive hand gesture—a 'Y' shape with her pinky and thumb—while her steely expression said it all. Rowan knew she never tolerated being caged, and he silently vowed that he would do everything in his power to keep her free.

"I hear you," Rowan conceded, his voice low but earnest.

"You're all fretting about us. The real question should be, How are you doing?" Rook asked.

"Understood, I did just appear with a face full of bruises—a small price, you know." Rowan flashed a wry smile. "I'm fine. Since when did a few bruises ever slow me down?"

"Never," Spence agreed with a light laugh. Then, hopping onto the table, he continued, "So what's our plan? We call in the guards, seize their weapons from these fools, locate the Scorpion, and then bust out of this joint. Surely, you all agree?”

“That might sound like a solid plan, Spence, but consider this: we have two guards, which means two guns, facing who knows how many adversaries. More pressingly, we need to figure out exactly where we are in this forsaken labyrinth before making our move. On the other hand, they offered us asylum,” Rowan continued, settling next to Spence.

“On what grounds?” Rook quickly probed, leaning forward with interest.

“On the grounds that our unique skill set can bolster their forces,” Rowan explained coolly.

“In other words, they want us to become their hired guns. Just like with Larissa—down with one problem and in comes another,” Spence remarked with a tone of weary sarcasm.

“In a way. Buirke kept his promise, and he vouched for how we handled ourselves and dispatched those creatures to his leader. With that endorsement, they now expect us to train their forces so they can better defend themselves,” Rowan recounted with deliberate calm.

“And if we refuse?” Al ventured, his voice edged with doubt.

“If we say no, they’ll cast us out to the wolves, no questions asked,” Rowan replied gravely, letting the silence that followed hang thickly in the air.

“Do you trust them?” Spence asked the question, hanging like a dark cloud.

“Honestly, the only ones I trust are those right here beside me,” Rowan declared. “And to answer ... no, I don’t trust them.”

“With the collars off. I say we stay here a while, gather whatever resources we can, and then carry on south as originally planned," Val suggested, his tone even yet tentative.

"That crossed my mind, too," Rowan admitted, "but we need a unified decision: we either all stay, or we all leave together. And before you decide, notice that none of us is wearing thermal gear right now. Ask yourself—when was the last time you felt the comforting heat of proper indoor warmth? Don't worry about answering that—it's been years."

"Whoa, speak of gear—where is our shit anyways?" Al interjected, his concern shifting from the abstract to the immediate.

"I'm sure Mitch has them," Rowan responded matter-of-factly.

"Who the hell is Mitch?" Rook demanded, leaning forward on his elbows with genuine curiosity.

"Mitch—or should I say General Mitch—is the man running this entire operation," Rowan clarified, his voice both respectful and wary.

"Hold on! General Mitch of the Congo Rebellion? I heard he was killed in action, that he once dismantled an entire rebel force by himself," Al blurted out, his disbelief mingling with awe.

"What does he even look like? I've heard he stands at least seven feet tall," Rook mused, his expression a mixture of wonder and skepticism.

"I don't know exactly how, but it's him—trust me. And he's well aware of our past as Triple Top," Rowan said, a knowing gleam in his eye.

"How so?" Spence prompted, eager for the explanation.

"The etching on my blade tells that story. But it changes nothing—right now, he remains ignorant of our awareness of who he is, and for now, it's best to leave it that way. I propose we accept his offer. Once the situation stabilizes, I'll see if we can swing back to retrieve more weapons from the Mammoth," Rowan suggested with cautious optimism.

"You sure you want to take this route, mate? I'm not certain we should. The promise of food and a warm place might seem appealing, but it comes with a load of terrifying, monstrous baggage," Spence continued, running his fingers through his hair as if trying to compute the risk.

"They're called Stalkers," Rowan stated bluntly.

"Stalkers?" Val echoed, the name heavy with foreboding.

"Yes—Stalkers. Beyond that, Mitch didn't share any additional intel. I'm not sure how you guys feel, but I'm dying to uncover the truth about what really happened at camp. I want to understand where everyone vanished and where these creatures truly come from. And to reveal that mystery, we'll need much more than just the five of us. So, you know where I stand—what about all of you?" Rowan concluded, his gaze sweeping across the room and settling on each face that reflected a mix of resolve and uncertainty.

Chapter 14

Sometime later, a deep, resonant knock came at the door, echoing through the quiet room. Before anyone could muster a reply, a young soldier pushed the door open with purposeful haste and stepped inside. His clear, steady voice filled the space, "So, have we come to an arrangement?" He eyed the room with cautious optimism.

Rowan, his eyes darting to his companions clustered around him, spoke with controlled resolve, "We have. Inform Mitch that if he grants us asylum, we accept his terms." The hushed murmurs of agreement danced in the air like a fragile promise.

"Splendid!" the soldier exclaimed, his bright enthusiasm cutting through the tension. "Now, follow me," he ordered, and without a pause, he strode from the room, leaving behind a trail of echoing footsteps.

As they stepped out into the corridor, they met the gaze of five more soldiers, each one standing alert and armed with their sleek Enfield SN-1 rifles. The metallic glint of the rifles and the resolute expressions on their faces heightened the sense of urgency. Spence's voice came out in a quiet, nervous whisper as he surveyed the armed line, "What if we had said no?" His words trembled in the charged atmosphere.

Al, leaning in with a mix of exasperation and relief, retorted,

"At this point, I'm trying not to think about what would have happened if we'd listened to you." The dim light of uncertainty flickered briefly in his eyes.

Rowan's brow furrowed as he looked between the soldiers and his own team. "What is this? And where's Mitch?" he demanded, his tone mingling confusion with underlying tension.

The young soldier, unfaltering in his stance, replied, "You agreed to Mitch's terms, correct?"

Rowan confirmed, "Yes, we did."

A subtle smile crept onto the soldier's face. "Well, upon your agreement, Mitch ordered that all of you be escorted to your quarters for the evening. Mitch himself has other pressing matters and will regroup with you tomorrow. Now, if there are no further questions, please, come with us."

Mia's sharp eyes met Rook's for a brief, resigned moment—a silent commentary on the disappearance of any pretense of friendliness. Rowan offered a quiet reassurance, "That's it for now."

Before they moved off, Rowan reminded everyone with clinical precision, "Before we set out, be sure to grab your winter gear from the chest behind you. It's below zero outside." The frigid air seemed to seep through his words, emphasizing the urgency.

Val's voice cut through the murmuring group as she asked, "Where the hell is the rest of our gear?" Her gaze wandered over the meager pile of clothing they had on.

"The remainder of your gear remains with the vehicle, which will all be returned to you shortly," came the measured response.

Once every soldier was buckled in with additional winter

gear, the six accompanying soldiers split into two separate groups, flanking Rowan and his team like sentinels as the young soldier guided them through the somber corridor. The cold walls and harsh lighting amplified the sense of foreboding.

Their short journey culminated at another heavy steel door. The young soldier produced an access key; its metallic glimmer was briefly visible as he waved it in front of a sleek card reader. A robotic beep resonated, and the ensuing clatter of unlocking mechanisms reverberated down the hall. With a firm tug on the lever, the door swung open, and a gust of frosty wind burst forth, playfully rustling their clothes as if whispering secrets of the outside world.

Beyond the threshold, the temperature plunged drastically to below freezing. The soldiers found themselves wading through shin-deep, pristine snow. One of the soldiers, with a final stern look, closed the door behind them, sealing off the harsh exterior. As the corridor led them further from the comforting building, a white haze gradually parted to reveal three vast, rectangular structures emerging like silent titans from within the blizzard.

Each structure, uniformly one story high and built of cold, gray stone, featured evenly spaced, small square windows that glinted like distant eyes in the dim light. They paused at the central building, where the door was swiftly unlocked and they were ushered inside.

"This is Barrack-B, and it is where Mitch has ordered you to reside until further notice," the young soldier explained as he led them through a stark hallway. The sudden illumination revealed nearly twenty barren military bunk beds, arranged with unyielding precision. "Your tour ends here for the night.

Welcome to Haven. Per Mitch's order, everyone must remain inside the barracks at all times. Should you need anything, relay your message through the soldiers posted outside your door—they will inform me, Trevor."

Rowan's reply held a mixture of resignation and obedience: "I'll be sure to remember that."

A skeptical murmur of protest came from Al. "What, are we on house arrest or something?" he asked, cynical yet curious.

The young soldier's tone remained calm as he explained, "No, you are not prisoners. However, Mitch has placed you all under close observation—a standard procedure for newcomers in Haven. There are showers in the rear; please make thorough use of them."

"And where the hell is Scorpion?" Rook's demanded.

"Scorpion," Trevor questioned.

"That would be the vehicle you gassed us in," Rook answered.

The soldier nodded apologetically, "Ah, yes. Your vehicle was removed to the garage with strict orders that it be repaired for operation."

"Hell nah," Rook snapped, his protective tone unmistakable. "Nobody is allowed to touch my babe."

Rowan intervened calmly, his voice steady as he met Rook's eyes, "Calm down, Rook. They mean no harm." He continued, "Trevor, could you ask Mitch to cancel that repair request? Rook would prefer to handle it himself when he finds the time—he's quite attached to it."

After a moment of thoughtful pause, the young soldier tapped on his Comm-Tec and confirmed, "I'll be sure to pass the message along."

In a low voice almost lost in the ambient silence, Spence

quietly whispered, "It's a rather weird attachment, at that."

Rook, seizing the moment to chide gently, retorted, "Well, you didn't find it weird when I pulled you up and kept your ass from being eaten." His words hung in the air, and Spence's surprise was evident as he registered that his comment had been heard.

"If there's nothing else, I will take my leave now," the soldier announced, his eyes lingering briefly on Mia standing resolutely by Rowan's side. "Oh, and yes, food will be arriving shortly—courtesy of our chef. Be sure to get your rest," he added before turning and exiting the building, his footsteps fading away.

Left with the now quiet barracks, Rowan addressed his team with a somber tone, "Okay, everyone, remember to rest tonight. We haven't the faintest idea of what awaits us tomorrow. Every detail matters now, which means we must cross all our t's and dot our i's... even if that includes some much-needed R&R."

Spence, clutching a small flash adorned with a Black Widow etched on its front, grinned as he flopped onto the nearest bed. He twisted off the cap and took a massive gulp. "My baby and I are going to have a nice night together," he declared with a laugh.

Al, shaking his head in disbelief, added with a wry smile, "I'm not even going to ask where he hid that, lest it gets confiscated."

"Family secret, ol' boy," Spence whispered conspiratorially, taking another long drink. "Don't tell anyone."

Grinning broadly, Al chimed in, "I'm all good for a bite before calling it quits for the night," and Mia nodded in agreement with a cheerful thumbs up.

As Mia, Rook, and Al moved off in one direction to settle in, Val silently headed the opposite way toward a vacant bed. Left momentarily alone, Rowan took the chance to reflect on the swift and brutal changes that had befallen them. Only days ago, his clan of nearly thirty-five had been busy migrating and scavenging for supplies; now, a grave count of only six survived. Even though those lost weren't necessarily close friends, the brutal reality that no one should perish by being eaten alive pressed heavily on him.

He regarded his remaining squad not merely as soldiers, but as a makeshift family—a fragment of his past life clinging to survival. Rowan's gaze drifted to the small window where delicate frost etched intricate patterns. Outside, a curtain of fresh snow cascaded in shimmering beams from the fog lamps mounted on the building's side. Snowfall had become their relentless companion since the impact, yet in this quiet moment, Rowan felt an unusual sense of ease.

It was strange, almost surreal, to find solace in a fully operational facility. In truth, he was deeply grateful to avoid another night spent in a cramped vehicle or a desolate building. The promise that Haven might provide everything they needed fell like a whispered miracle among them—a tiny break to savor. Still, with comfort came an undercurrent of doubt, for at the moment, all he knew was that the only barrier between them and the relentless Stalkers was an electrical fence and one man's capricious opinion.

"Haven," he murmured softly, a bitter laugh escaping his lips. "We'll see." Turning from the window, his eyes fell upon Val, who was sitting on the edge of a narrow bed. A single tear slipped down her cheek, a quiet token of months spent without sleep, always armed and alert. It had been even longer since she had lost both her baby and her fiancé to an RPG attack—a loss that haunted her like a recurring nightmare.

With trembling fingers, she unclasped the magnetic charm necklace that always rested near her heart, releasing it from its steady position. As the delicate heart-shaped box clicked open, it revealed a faded, cherished photograph of her embracing her lover, Michael Hayes—a bittersweet relic of a life that might have been. Michael, tragically unaware of the impending fatherhood, had been caught in the chaos; neither had she been informed of the pregnancy until she awoke from a coma two weeks later.

The picture recalled a time just two days prior to its capture, when the convoy was on a routine border patrol in Afghanistan. In a moment of horror, an RPG slammed violently into the ground next to their vehicle. Michael's door was struck, and in an instant, he was gone—killed on impact. If Michael had not shielded her by taking the full force of that fatal blow, both of their lives would have been snuffed out. The scene replayed repeatedly in her troubled mind, an endless loop of pain that no variation could ease.

As if it were still yesterday, she vividly remembered the day her eyes fluttered open. The conversation with the doctor played over in her memory with crystalline detail.

"She's waking up. Sergeant Valencia, can you hear me?" a gentle assistant had asked as his voice tried to coax her back from oblivion.

"Take it easy, ok," came another calm, reassuring word.

"Yes... yes. I hear you," Val had murmured, blinking rapidly as her vision adjusted to the harsh, stinging light flooding in through the window. "Close the blinds, please," she requested softly. "Where am I? And where is Mich—Michael?" Her voice wavered, haunted by the name.

"Sergeant, there are a few things you need to know," the doctor had explained carefully. "The first may be hard to accept: for the last two weeks, you have been in a coma."

"A coma? Impossible," Val had whispered, fighting to sit up despite her weakening strength.

"Take it easy. Let me help you," he said while gently lifting her into a sitting position. Then, with a heavy pause, he added, "Now, the second thing might be even harder."

"What can be worse than learning you were nothing more than a vegetable for fourteen days?" she joked, in an attempt to mask her weakened state.

Holding his clipboard protectively under his arm, he delivered the crushing news: "Sergeant, Corporal Hayes did not survive the attack on the Humvee."

"What—what are you trying to say?" she stammered, her voice cracking as she struggled to hold back tears.

"Shrapnel from the RPG penetrated the vehicle exactly where he was seated. He died on impact. I'm truly sorry." The silence that followed was heavy with empathy, as he watched helplessly while she wiped tears from her eyes, knowing words could not mend her shattered world. He continued with deep regret, "Sergeant, I'm sincerely sorry for both of your losses."

"Both my losses? No one else was in there with us," she said, her voice barely a whisper.

"Sergeant, you were three months pregnant at the time of the attack."

She shook her head as if it were rid herself of the thought, pulling her back into the moment. Her reflection was only mere seconds, but in her mind, it could have easily been a lifetime. In the depths of her despair, she allowed herself to drift into a silent reverie—a fantasy of raising her unborn child alongside the only person she had ever truly loved. The gentle warmth of that imagined future wrapped around her heart when suddenly, a soft, reassuring hand rested upon her shoulder.

"Val, you okay?" Rowan asked, his voice fully pulling her back from the fragile dream and grounding her in the stark present. His eyes held a quiet promise. "We'll have your gear back soon. I'll make sure of that."

She quickly brushed away the residue of tears, snapping the charm closed with determination. "I'm fine," she replied, her tone mild as she untied the laces on her worn combat boots. A small, contented sigh escaped her as she flexed her aching feet. "Ah, now that's refreshing."

"Do you mind if I sit with you?" Rowan inquired softly, motioning toward the bed across from her.

With a playful glint in her eyes, she teased, "Asking never stopped you before."

"Val, I know you treasure your solitude," he began earnestly, his gaze locking with hers, "but we've been through so much together since Larissa placed you on my team. In my eyes, that makes us family—even if we're the most dysfunctional kind there is. With that, you don't have to shoulder everything alone. Just as you've always had my back, I've got yours."

"I never questioned that," she said, not taking her eyes from her feet.

"I know that what I'm trying to get at is—if you ever need to talk, I'm here for you." His words, laden with warmth and genuine care, coaxed even the smallest of smiles to light her face. After a moment of silence, Rowan quietly rose and turned away, leaving her with the echo of his promise.

"Why are we doing this?" Val suddenly demanded, halting his retreat. "Why must we continue fighting and cling to a life that might never be ours? Have you ever thought that this world might not be worth saving? It all feels pointless. If it's not bandits killing, then it's cannibals. And if it's not cannibals, then it's the cold. And if it isn't even the cold, it's monsters..." Her voice trailed off in disbelief at the harshness of the words—monsters. "Humans had their chance, and now it feels as if Mother Nature herself is hinting that perhaps it's time to throw in the towel." With deliberate care, she arranged her boots neatly by the bed and stretched out, her hands clasped behind her head in a gesture of weariness and resignation.

Rowan stopped in his tracks, locking his eyes with hers. "C'mon, Val, what are you talking about? I fight every day with the hope of waking up one morning and taking a nice jog, then maybe—even enjoying a beer at the local bar," he said, his tone both sincere and wistful. "And besides, I believe we're doing this for the very reason you hold onto that necklace. We fight not just out of self-preservation but for each other. Even if we've all dirtied our hands along the way. Hell, I did none of that to please Larissa or anyone for that matter—it's about mankind, stepping back up to the plate."

A soft chuckle mixed with melancholy escaped her as she rolled over, "Well, when mankind hits that next home run, let's hope we're still here to see it," she murmured.

"Let's hope," Rowan whispered in return, his tone a blend of optimism and uncertainty, before he respectfully left her alone.

The world was no longer bathed in sunshine and rainbows, but instead filled with bitter hardships. For a fleeting second, he had to summon the strength to believe in his own words—that perhaps, just perhaps, they had a chance to rebuild something here. And like all the others on the team, Val's inner struggle was one he would do his best to help her overcome.

Finding solace in a nearby bed, he sat on its edge and relished in the softness beneath him. It wasn't a Tempur-Pedic masterpiece by any stretch, but it served as a modest sanctuary from the night's chill. After a careful unlacing of his boots, he leaned back and allowed himself to sink into the simple comfort of rest.

The moment his head touched the pillow, memories of his old life—a stark contrast to the countless nights wasted huddled against bitter cold with strangers for warmth—flooded his mind. He closed his eyes, a soft exhale marking his reluctant acceptance of the present.

"Can this be real?" he questioned quietly to himself, the whisper of doubt mingling with the warmth of fleeting hope.

In that quiet moment, he understood that it was not about him helping his team get through another day, but them being there to help each other see another day.

Chapter 15

Rowan awoke to the gentle percussion of small taps on his leg, his eyes fluttering open to see Val patiently standing above him. "Hey," she said, giving him another soft tap, her tone light yet insistent.

"I'm up, I'm up," he mumbled, shielding his eyes from the brilliant rays that slanted through the windows. Although the night had been cloaked in snow, stray beams of sunlight had managed to pierce the lingering, heavy clouds over the city, infusing the early hours with a modest glow that promised a brighter day, if only temporarily.

"Mitch requested us in the south wing, wherever that is at," Val announced casually, her voice carrying both urgency and ease.

"Where's the rest of the squad?" Rowan asked, rising slowly from his bed, each movement heavy with the remnants of sleep.

"Everyone's up and ready. You're the last; figured you could use the extra sleep," she replied, her arm draped over the top bunk as if in a gentle embrace of camaraderie.

"Yeah, a warm bed... It's been years." As he sat upright, rubbing the sleep from his face, he felt the comforting weight of memories and the contrast of years spent in warmth.

"It's been years for us all," Val added with a sly smirk, her eyes twinkling with a sense of gratitude for such a reprieve.

"How'd you sleep?" he asked.

"I got a few good hours," she replied.

"A few good hours," he said with a smirk. "I don't even know why I ask. You're like a vulture, always perched and watching."

Val's half-smile deepened as she shifted her weight. "Anyway, the gang and I will be waiting at the door. There's a sink with running water over in the corner," she explained while walking toward the indicated direction. A few steps later, she paused and tossed him a small silver package. "Oh yeah, here you go," she said playfully, adding, "What, were you expecting a five-course meal?" Rowan glanced down at the MRE with a wry smile, then watched as she continued on her way.

The memory of last night's hot shower clung to him like a cherished secret—more refreshing than simple water, it had felt like a cascade of spring water revitalizing barren life. Slipping into his boots and long-sleeved thermal, Rowan rose and began navigating the narrow aisle between rows of bunk beds. His mind wandered to how many other myriad souls had once walked them. People who had once known a concept he believed was lost—a true home. Maybe, just maybe, they would all come to experience it again.

After a brisk routine at the sink, he made his way to the door. There, Val stood a few feet from the exit, her head casually leaning against the wall with her eyes closed in a moment of quiet reflection. Brooks and Al gathered in a relaxed semi-circle, their conversation low and animated as Mia listened intently. Nearby, Spence sat on a bench, meticulously cleaning beneath his fingernails with his knife as if it were a cherished ritual. When Rowan stepped up, all eyes lifted to greet him.

"Took the old man long enough. I thought I was going to have to come in there and resuscitate your ass," Rook teased as the group converged around him.

Trevor, accompanied by another soldier, stood at the door's threshold, snapping to attention at the sound of Rook's comment, though he had failed to notice Rowan's quiet arrival as his gaze remained fixed on Mia.

"At ease, soldier, I'm no Patton," Rowan instructed kindly yet firmly.

"Who?" Trevor asked, adjusting his stance as Rowan halted before him with an appraising look.

"How old are you?" Rowan inquired, his eyes scrutinizing Trevor as if measuring his worth.

"Twenty-five," the young man replied confidently.

"That explains it," Rowan mused, shaking his head in mild disbelief.

"But I was ordered to respect your rank," Trevor insisted, a note of deference coloring his tone.

"Rank—that was a long time ago, son," Rowan replied, the wistfulness of bygone times lacing his words.

"Man, I thought you were ugly during the day; the mornings aren't any better," Spence interjected with a mischievous grin.

"You wish you were as good-looking as me," Rowan shot back with a teasing smile, then turned to Trevor. "Okay, Trevor, where are we heading?"

"First stop, meet with Mitch. He'll brief you from there," Trevor answered, and as if the words were a cue to action, the other soldier swung open the door.

With everyone now ready, Trevor led them back along the same worn path that had brought them to their bunks. Outside, the winds had calmed, offering Rowan a breathtaking glimpse of Haven and its enduring glory. "Hell, if it isn't Buckingham Palace," he remarked, halting briefly to admire the intricate Victorian architecture towering before him.

"Got damn! The Buckingham Palace," Al exclaimed in awe.

"You can say that again, chief," added Spence with a jovial nod. As they reentered through yesterday's steel door, they continued their march down the lengthy, echoing halls.

"So, what did everyone do before turning in last night? Spence, I know you didn't do much after taking a swallow from the Widow the way you did. Who knows what Flukes made out of it? I'm surprised you're still alive," Rowan joked, eliciting chuckles from the group.

"You haven't learned yet, huh? The Black Widow gives me strength," Spence replied proudly.

"After the meal came, Mia and I hit the bunks for the night. One of the best sleeps of my life," Al said warmly.

"I found the shower, and not willing to pass up the opportunity, I indulged in a long, deserved hot one. And man, it was everything I remembered," added Rook.

"And you? Did you take a shower too, Val?" Spence gleamed at her, sparking light-hearted laughter among the others. Val merely ignored him, eyes fixed forward. "Now, why you gonna act shy?"

"Alright, Spence, keep it civil," Rowan interjected with a calm gesture, his tone both gentle and authoritative.

After a series of brief exchanges and about fifteen minutes of traversing labyrinthine corridors, they reached another door that led into what at first glance appeared to be an airplane hangar. In reality, it was a colossal garage annexed to the south wing. Stretching fifty yards in length, thirty yards in width, and soaring three stories high, it was constructed entirely of reinforced concrete. Massive pipes snaked along the walls, and enormous steel beams supported intricate ductwork and lighting, while expansive catwalks crisscrossed the ceiling overhead.

Every conceivable type of vehicle was stored and organized within: four-wheelers, motorcycles, SUVs, heavy military trucks, and even large construction vehicles all lined the cavernous space, accompanied by an array of specialized tools and machinery to maintain them.

Inside, Rowan's instincts kicked in as he mentally noted the guards patrolling on the catwalks above. There were twelve in total, each one stoically wielding an Enfield SN-1 slung across their shoulders, their presence both reassuring and formidable.

Under orders, Trevor led the group to Mitch, who stood at a large table addressing several soldiers clad in a patchwork of tactical gear. As a chorus of boots soundlessly approached from behind, Mitch straightened and turned, still sporting his worn overalls.

Meeting Rowan and his team halfway, he grinned warmly. "Well, look what the cat dragged out! How was your first night's sleep at Haven?"

"Well, if you don't count sleeping under guard, but I guess it still beats the alternative," Rowan replied.

"I completely understand. I'll be sure to assign you all to a more private area upon your return," Mitch assured him.

"Upon our return?" Rowan echoed, puzzled.

"Don't worry. It will all be explained at the briefing table," Mitch said, leading the group back to join three familiar faces already waiting.

At that table, Jasper, Haider, and Buirke were huddled around a holographic map of London, its designated zones highlighted in pulsating red that seemed to beat like a warning heart.

Before Rowan could speak, Buirke interjected, "My apologies, Rowan. I didn't expect things to fall into place so quickly upon our arrival. My boy decided to send a friendly message to the director without my knowing," he said with a side glance at Jasper, who stood nearby..

"Good thing he did," Mitch chimed in, patting Jasper on the back. "This is a cruel world; one can never be too safe. But enough small talk. Let me properly introduce you to the Devils, whom you're already acquainted with—or what's left of them, at least. When the Devils first started, there were at least twenty-two of them. Eventually, death and injuries took their toll. Today, the only operational members from The Devils are team leader Buirke, his son Jasper, and second-in-command Haidar," Mitch explained as he pointed to each man in turn.

Buirke was a burly man with a head full of silver hair and a neatly boxed gray beard. Though his appearance might have suggested old age at a glance, the way his tactical outfit clung to his broad chest told a different story of one who had experience. During the impact, Buirke had vowed to keep his family safe—and despite the odds, he had upheld that promise.

Buirke's son, Jasper, was a light and wiry contrast to his father, but he made up for his slight frame with an extraordinary intellect. Specializing in technology, Jasper had a reputation for quickly fixing any device on the fly, a talent that proved invaluable beyond Haven's fortified doors. Inheriting his mother's traits, his blond hair, blue eyes, and a delicately shaped snub nose, Jasper came from a lineage of mountaineers and wilderness survivors, making him an ideal tracker and resource hunter.

Then there was Haidar, standing solemnly in his white parka. His long, thick, curly black hair spilled out from beneath his hood and melded into a full, meticulously groomed beard that helped to hide the ghastly scar that ran from his chin down the side of his right arm, lending him an air of hardened survival. An elaborately patterned scarf lay loosely around his neck, and his piercing black eyes studied the newcomers with a measured intensity. Rook returned Haidar's gaze with a respectful nod.

"What is all this?" Al asked with a wry laugh, eyeing the sizable digital map displayed on the table. "What, are we planning the next D-Day or something?"

"I hope not with this legion of soldiers you've got standing here," Spence added, his tone light and teasing.

"Ungrateful," Haidar retorted with a hint of exasperation, taking a step forward—only to be gently halted by a timely gesture from Mitch.

Mitch laughed, then reached into his overalls and produced a cigar. Striking a match, he shielded the flame until his cigar glowed a bright red, casting an orange hue across his face before he took a deep, contemplative pull.

"Please don't misunderstand me," Mitch continued, his smile now soft and sincere. "We have many soldiers here, and even more in training. However, none of them are Devils— not yet, at least. In the old world, you might have labeled The Devils as a special ops unit, as their duty is to venture into this unforgiving city every morning to retrieve supplies that have help to keep Haven alive. The reason we allowed six of you to remain within Haven's gates is solely because of your unique abilities." He exhaled a cloud of smoke, stepping closer and locking eyes with Rowan. "You remember our deal: you stay and train my people. Not just in basic combat—since many of them already have that—but in the harsh art of surviving beyond Haven's protective whiteness."

In that moment, everything became clear to Rowan. Mitch intended to use him and his squad to train recruits in survival tactics, for the Devils' numbers had dwindled dangerously. With scavenging teams so few and far between, Haven's operations hung by a thread. If anyone could instill the necessary resilience in Mitch's men, it was Rowan and his battle-hardened crew. The deal was simple, but as sweet as it sounded, unease gnawed at him. There had to be more to Haven than just soldiers and retrieval missions.

"My conversation with Buirke informed me of what happened to your camp—all the equipment left behind. More importantly, your equipment," Mitch said, tapping the digital map where crimson X's marked crucial locations. "These markers indicate..."

Before he could finish, a commanding female voice sliced through the murmurs behind the table. "Mitch, what's taking The Devils so long to depart?" All eyes turned as Dr. Orion stepped forward, her lab coat open and her gaze unwavering. For a suspended moment, Rowan was struck by the sight of her perfect caramel complexion and the air of assured authority that radiated from her.

"They were supposed to have left an hour ago," she insisted, her tone brisk.

"Dr. Orion, it's a pleasure to see you this morning as well," Mitch welcomed her warmly. "Come join us, I was just explaining the objectives for this excursion."

"You can skip the pleasantries, Mitch. We all know your opinion of me and my work. Do us a favor and cut to the chase," she said firmly as she stepped up to the holographic map, her eyes scanning it with clinical precision.

"I like her," Val murmured quietly to Rowan.

"I can see why," Rowan replied under his breath.

"What was that?" Dr. Orion asked, arching an eyebrow.

"Ah, nothing, just talking with my team," Rowan answered, his cheeks warming slightly.

"Dr. Orion, these are the folks who returned with the Devil Squad. This is Rowan, their squad leader," he gestured to him. Rowan gave a slight nod as Mitch continued, "With their help, we plan to make Christmas come early for the labs," Mitch explained, his tone a blend of humor and determination.

"Let's get to the point. Some of us have other matters that cannot wait," Dr. Orion snapped, her gaze never leaving the pulsating hologram.

Rowan leaned close to Val, whispering with a teasing smile, "I might have to take that back."

Glancing around and then locking his eyes with each of them, Mitch continued, "As Dr. Orion stated, let's keep this simple: as usual, Buirke, you're leading this excursion. Rowan, I need you and your team to follow his orders exactly so that everyone returns safely. Can that be done?"

"As long as we can get our equipment, it shouldn't be an issue," Rowan replied, though his tone carried a hint of reluctance.

"Well, I'm glad. Let's move on, shall we? First, you need to return to your previous camp and grab any useful items, along with any vehicles if they haven't been salvaged already. Once your gear is secured, Buirke will lead everyone to the other sites indicated on the map," he explained, his finger sweeping over markers that denoted old warehouses, electronics stores, and home repair shops where previous teams claimed to have spotted generators.

"Hold on a second. You expect us to risk our lives chasing down some damn generators?" Spence interjected with incredulity.

"Spence, quiet!" Rowan said, raising a calming hand to hush the Irishman. "Mitch, why generators?" turning and facing him.

Mitch replied calmly, "There's no harm in telling you. First, Haven runs entirely on renewable energy, though we still rely on generators for some vital equipment. With such a tremendous amount of power coursing through this facility, generators are always a top priority. Secondly, protocol allows teams one excursion per day, depending on the season. With the generators being located near where Buirke said your initial encounter occurred, we're effectively achieving two objectives in one sweep."

"Mitch, let me please," Dr. Orion said, before facing Rowan. "Rowan, is it?" she said pointedly.

"That's correct, ma'am," he responded, leaning over the map in deference.

"Alright then. Mitch originally promised to send an expedition to locate the generators necessary for my research. Just days ago, a group of Skin-Walkers tried breaching our defenses to get to our livestock, resulting in a section of the fence being completely trashed, along with a generator. Mitch had taken a generator from my lab in the meantime, until the old one was repaired or a new one was locked beforehand. Either my research can't wait. It is taking days to make repair as others are pulled from other critical tasks to help. Mitch told me you'd agreed to help train his men after retrieving your gear. I have no objection to training; my problem is the delay of my work due to missing equipment. So let's work together on this—two birds, one stone," she proposed firmly.

A heavy silence descended around the table as Mitch folded his arms and waited expectantly. Rowan knew that if he was to continue living within Haven's secured walls, he would have to play along. "Okay, we'll get your generator after picking up our supplies. But naturally, I have to ask—what exactly are you researching, and why is it so important that we risk our lives for it?"

Dr. Orion's expression softened slightly. "Sorry, Mr. Rowan, but I can't disclose that level of information to someone so new. I will say, however, that my work benefits everyone here— everyone gets to eat, including you." Turning from Rowan and facing Mitch, she added, "Please keep me informed when they return with the generators."

"Sure will, Doc," Mitch replied with a smile as Dr. Orion exited the garage, leaving every eye tracking her graceful departure. "Words of advice, Rowan: around here, you must learn quickly which trees to bark up. She's definitely not one many chose to get on the wrong side of."

There was a brief silence as they all took in Mitch's words.

"Anyway, let's get back to the task," Mitch continued. "Buirke fill them in."

Over the next several minutes, Buirke methodically brought everyone up to speed, manipulating the briefing table's holographic display to address Rowan's questions about high and low grounds, choke points, and potential evacuation routes. It felt as though he were fighting another man's battle while leading his own team—his new mission was painfully simple yet carried the weight of survival: locate the Mammoth, then hunt down Dr. Orion's elusive generator.

As the debriefing concluded, Mitch led them further into the vast garage. The group passed rows of vehicles that had been meticulously modified to withstand the hostile environment outside—one such marvel being the Boeing 300 VX, code-named The Ghost. Next, Buirke halted at a solitary parking pad where every eye was drawn to the Scorpion. Nearly a day had passed since any of them had last seen it, and its absence was as palpable as the tension in the air.

"So, what do you think about the upgrades?" Buirke asked as he positioned himself beside the Scorpion, his tone both proud and playful.

"What the hell did you all do to my babe?" Rook demanded, his voice thick with anger and affection.

"I had the repair team working around the clock. We added all the bells and whistles—from winter camouflage paint to quarter-inch steel plating on the sides—making her nearly impenetrable. I know you requested no modifications, but knowing what we're up against out there, the Scorpion was simply outdated," Buirke explained, his voice ringing with conviction.

"Outdated? No, no—she's perfect just the way she was!" Rook countered, shaking his head as if in disbelief.

"Mitch even made sure you got bulletproof glass for the windows. And hold onto your hats, because here comes the best part," Buirke said with a flourish.

He opened the driver's door and pressed a button on the dashboard. A low, mechanical hum filled the air as the roof hatch unlocked, revealing a sleek Viper-STG rising from its center mount.

"Yes, your eyes are not deceiving you—this mounted Viper is the only electromagnetic weapon model designed by the NWF. It fires no projectiles, just high-velocity volts capable of tearing through flesh. It took some convincing, but Mitch eventually approved it, and hopefully with this addition, any creature thinking of mounting an attack will think twice," Buirke finished as if delivering a well-rehearsed presentation.

"The good news is our weapon tech is advancing even further. A modified handheld version is in the works, which should reduce our dependence on projectile-based firearms," Mitch added with a confident nod.

"What gives you the right to alter her without our permission? Granted, I'm in love with what's been done," Rook said, running his hands over the smooth, cool metal of the Scorpion's body.

"By agreeing to our terms, I took the necessary steps to ensure every vehicle reaches its full potential. What's the point of venturing out if failure is our only option?" Mitch replied succinctly.

"Anyway," Rowan interjected, nodding approvingly at Buirke while stepping closer to inspect the Scorpion, "we appreciate it all. If she wasn't badass before, she sure is now."

Mitch grinned and sauntered toward the rear of the Scorpion. Pressing the button for the rear hatch, he listened as it hissed open to reveal a weapons chest loaded with the gear that had been taken from them. "As promised, your weapons," he said, his tone casual yet meaningful. "Just remember, Buirke, Jasper, and Haidar will be with you out there as well."

Rowan looked from one man to the next. "Like I said, you hold up your end, and we'll do the same."

"Time will tell," Mitch concluded, clasping his hands behind his back. "I will now leave you in Buirke's hands. We'll have eyes on you out there," he nodded and turned to leave.

After a few seconds of charged silence, Rowan faced his team. "You know the drill. Let's get on it. In and out as always."

Val was the first to head up the ramp, quickly gathering her gear—carefully checking for 'Scott', her trusted Banshee rifle, and 'Charity', her dependable sidearm—breathing a sigh of relief when both were nestled safely within one of the duffle bags inside the chest.

It wasn't long before the rest joined her, extracting their equipment from the weapons crate with a blend of anticipation and routine.

Buirke approached them once more, "Rowan, before I forget, I've got something for you," extending a handful of collar bombs with interconnected mini-charges.

"And why in the world would we want those back?" Rowan replied, a skeptical frown forming as he eyed the array of delicate triggers.

Buirke laughed heartily, retracting his hand. "It's not like that. I had Jasper reconfigure them so that now there are three distinct triggers. The first sets the timer—each press adds a second. The second arms the explosive, and the third arm deactivates it. They're quite handy for opening jammed doors. So, what do you say?" He extended the devices once more.

After a long moment of weighing his options, Rowan took them. "I guess they could come in useful. Thanks."

Buirke grinned. "No problem. The way I see it, your survival boosts our chances of completing this expedition. I had several walkies placed in your vehicle for you and your people."

"It's much appreciated," Rowan said, as they all went back

to making preparations.

With their weapons and attachments collected, Rowan and his team took their seats in the formidable Scorpion, while Buirke, Jasper, and Haidar climbed into a four-passenger all-terrain truck fitted with armored caterpillar tracks. A turn of the ignition key sent both vehicles roaring to life as their engines echoed powerfully throughout the vast open space.

Rook's face lit up like a child with a new toy as he gently pressed the accelerator, making the Scorpion purr with life.

"That's my girl," he whispered, a private declaration of affection.

"The shoe warehouse is only a few kilometers away, so stay close. If you see anything, call it in," Haidar instructed over the walkie, as he maneuvered the truck in front of the Scorpion to lead the way.

With practiced ease, Haidar shifted the gear into drive and delicately massaged the clutch until the large vehicle groaned into motion. They approached the garage's massive hydraulic steel doors, and he deftly guided the truck to within mere inches of the door just as Buirke signaled the operator overhead.

In a small booth, a soldier pulled a lever that released the heavy door's locking mechanism. With a series of metallic clanks and groans, the gigantic thirty-foot steel gates slowly began to part, revealing a narrow gap through which windswept snow tumbled inside. Both vehicles paused within that cavernous doorway for a breathless moment before steadily advancing into the swirling snow dunes of Old London.

Every sound—the roar of engines, the rattle of the closing doors—was a stark reminder that Rowan was now leaving the relative safety of Haven behind, venturing into an unforgiving world of white isolation.

In the desolate, frozen wasteland, Rowan's gaze lingered on the subtle exchange of nods among his companions. Their unspoken communication spoke volumes, a silent language born from shared dangers and battles fought side by side.

Chapter 16

Crossing the London Bridge with the frozen Thames covered in a layer of snow beneath them, the heavy machine roared forward. Their vehicles' caterpillar tracks carved through several feet of snow as if it were soft powder. Beyond their frosted windows, the day had already surrendered to a blinding whiteout, with cold, violent winds whipping tiny shards of ice into a chaotic frenzy. Visibility had plummeted to a mere fifteen feet, leaving the crew feeling both isolated and exposed.

As they ventured on, Rowan replayed every word of his conversation with Mitch over in his head. Amidst the bustling activity at Haven, it really did not make sense to put his faith in strangers. Was he really longing for a place to belong after so many years out in the white? His inner dialogue teemed with doubt: What is driving him to place his trust elsewhere? Or was it something else that was driving him? The question gnawed at him as the bitter wind howled.

Breaking the silence, Val's clear, calm voice came through. "Rowan, since we have a little drive ahead of us and the scenic route is a no-go – how about we pick up some intel from our guides on the Stalkers?" Her tone was measured, yet resolute, the kind that suggested she felt more comfortable gathering facts than blindly charging ahead.

"I agree," Rowan replied, his eyes never leaving the tempest outside. Occasionally, he caught ghostly glimmers of skyscrapers, their outlines distorted by the storm. He reached over, retrieved the handheld walkie-talkie from the dashboard's cup holder, and pressed the button. "Hey Buirke, me and the team need a bit more information," he said, releasing the button.

After a few, Buirke's growly voice rumbled over the channel. "Let it fly," Buirke instructed, his tone rough like gravel yet laced with command.

"What exactly are these Stalkers, and where did they come from?" Rowan asked, as the rest of the crew listened in.

A pause followed, laden with static and uncertain tension, until the reply came. "I don't have clean answers for either, but I can tell you this: you do not—under any circumstances— want to face them head-on. Most of them are strong, agile, and damn near legion in numbers. In my opinion, they're the very embodiment of evil."

"Jesus, isn't this just some insane sh—" started Rook, but before he could finish, Rowan's stern voice cut through the wind.

"Hold on, Rook," he commanded curtly, leaving no room for further protest.

Buirke continued, his words painting a grim picture. "They emerged about twelve years ago. Overnight, they decimated or forced out every other colony in the area, even some of those ragged bandit groups. And, strangely, they favor the night. Spotting one during the day is as rare as seeing a ghost."

"Why only at night?" Rowan pressed, his eyes still scanning the swirling storm.

"We're not entirely sure. Could be instinct—or just the way they are," Buirke answered, his voice fading into the sound of slamming snow.

Just then, Haider said in the background, "Five minutes until we reach the warehouse. What should I be watching for?" he asked, interrupting their discussion with a cautious tone.

Buirke passed the question along, and Rowan answered succinctly, "The clan was holed up in an old, battered shoe warehouse. You'll see the Mammoth parked right out front— a monstrous transport that's part bus, part tractor. It's not subtle looking at all."

"Mammoth?" Jasper interjected, his voice laced with incredulity.

"Exactly. It's the clan's main ride. Our late clan leader, Larissa, once called it home along with our stored weaponry, which is exactly why we're here. With your help, we'll recover every weapon we can and secure the Mammoth, which Val will drive back," Rowan explained, his tone shifting between nostalgia and steely determination.

"Understood," Buirke responded as Haider deftly guided the all-terrain truck through a maze of abandoned cars. As they approached, Haider broke through the veil of snow to reveal the Mammoth and its rugged caravan of vehicles, their exteriors frosted, storm windows barred, and fuel tanks glaring like sentinels.

"Your vehicle looks intact. If any groups were in the area, they would have stripped it in hours. Guess last night's storm was worse than it looked," Haider added.

Slowly, the two vehicles came to a halt. Doors creaked open one by one, and the teams disembarked, weapons slung securely over their shoulders. They quickly surrounded each vehicle, clearing the perimeter with practiced precision. The only sounds were the relentless wind and the soft shifting of snow dunes, as if the world itself was holding its breath.

"Tower, you copy?" Buirke spoke into his Tec-comm, his tone demanding confirmation.

"Tower copies," came the steady reply from a distant voice.

"This is Devil's leader. We've reached our first target. I'll update you again once we hit the second destination."

"Tower copies your arrival. We'll await your next transmission. Tower out."

After Buirke wrapped up his conversation, Rowan's voice rose above the roaring wind. "Aye, Buirke. The warehouse is this way," he called, gesturing with a firm hand for him to follow.

"Lead the way," Buirke replied, nodding subtly as he fell in step behind Rowan.

Assuming the role of seasoned scout, Rowan advanced toward the warehouse with deliberate, measured steps. His eyes darted from corner to corner—ever alert, expecting any sudden movement. He had witnessed too many men fall, too many horrors unfold, yet nothing had ever truly scared him. Today, however, the notion of abominations popping from the white drifts set a cold shiver down his spine. Whether it was the storm's chill or the fear of the unknown, he couldn't dispel the uneasy sensation.

"Something feels off about this place," Spence muttered, keeping his AK-47 pressed tightly against his shoulder, his gaze sweeping the tops of the ice-coated buildings.

"Keep it low, Spence, and keep moving," Val instructed coolly, keeping pace in the middle of their scattered formation.

As the tension built, Spence's nerves seemed to fray. "Honey, any other day, I would ask you to help me out with that, but not today. But has anyone noticed how there are no bodies left? Neither ours nor those damned creatures'—it's like they vanished without a trace."

"What do you mean?" Jasper exploded, his voice echoing off the icy walls.

"I mean, we've taken down a whole swarm of those bastards, yet not a single corpse remains. It's as if we were never here!" Spence exclaimed, his eyes darting away from the snow-smeared rooftops to the red-stained ground.

"Maybe you were never even here," Jasper shot back, a trace of mirth dancing in his tone.

"What's that supposed to mean, you greenhorn? You think we're lying?" Spence growled as he eased his grip on his weapon, pivoting towards Jasper and closing the distance until their breaths mingled.

"No, I'm merely suggesting it might be a setup, you cantankerous old leprechaun," Jasper retorted, standing his ground as he faced Spence directly.

In an instant, before anyone could intervene, Spence snatched Jasper by the collar, shoving him backward hard enough to make him stumble. Jasper recovered swiftly, leveling his weapon at Spence.

Snapping his weapon up as well, "Go ahead and shoot, you little virgin pisser, before I finish you off," Spence sneered, standing toe-to-toe with Jasper.

"You wish you could, old man," Jasper shot back sharply.

Before either could escalate the confrontation further, both Buirke and Rowan stepped into the fray, positioning themselves between the two and their loaded weapons. "Spence, lower your weapon and fall back in formation," Rowan ordered with the calm authority of a battlefield commander.

"That runt just accused me," Spence barked, his face red

with indignation.

"What you need right now is to lower that gun and fall in line. There are bigger targets worth shooting than each other," Rowan insisted, locking eyes with Spence.

"Next time, that little pisser won't be so lucky," Spence warned as he stepped back reluctantly.

Meanwhile, Jasper leaned in close and whispered, almost conspiratorially, "For all we know, Pop, they might be luring us out here to salvage what we have. Why are we trusting outsiders? There are no bodies, and we have no idea if their bandit buddies are lying in wait to ambush us in that warehouse."

Buirke's voice cut through the murmurs. "Quiet down, Jasper. That might be true, which is why I'm carrying a locator—just in case another squad has to find us. Besides, how could they set an ambush if they hadn't known we existed until yesterday night? But isn't that beside the point? Our job is to retrieve what Dr. Orion requested and get back to our families, right?"

As any devoted son would to a grizzled veteran like Buirke, Jasper lowered his rifle without protest.

"So, what I need from you is to focus on the objective. So you can get back to your little girl and stop provoking strangers into fights. Understood, son?" Buirke added with a wry smile.

"Understood," Jasper replied softly before rejoining the line.

Turning his gaze forward, Buirke caught Rowan's eyes. "Everything alright?" he asked quietly.

"We're good on this end," Rowan replied, his tone resolute. "Let's keep moving before we lose any more daylight."

"Agreed," Buirke replied, and together they forged ahead.

A brief shootout had been narrowly averted, and to help ease the tension, the group split up somewhat. Rowan delegated tasks: handing out hand radios to Rook, Spence, and Mia, instructing them to scavenge every bit of usable weaponry and ammunition from the surrounding speeders. Their haul was to be stowed in the Mammoth, and the vehicle was prepped to move out on a moment's notice.

Meanwhile, Rowan, Val, Al, Buirke, Jasper, and Haider began a cautious search of the warehouse, intent on uncovering clues about the mysterious disappearance of the bodies.

Stepping inside the warehouse felt like entering a macabre gallery. Unlike the pristine, snow-covered exterior, the interior bore the scars of battle. Every wall was peppered with bullet holes, and frozen blood—thick and dark—had splattered and streaked its surfaces like grotesque paintings. Rowan's eyes followed mutilated and eerie footprints in the ice, a trail suggesting that the fallen had been dragged away into the endless gloom.

The haunting scene from the previous night played over Rowan's mind as he paused beneath a shattered skylight. Snowflakes drifted down from the broken skylight, cascading like frozen confetti amid the wreckage—a strangely beautiful anomaly in this ravaged world.

Moving with meticulous caution, Buirke kept a wary eye on Jasper, who, despite his earlier misstep, now trailed quietly. "Next time, let your father do all the talking and thinking. You'd save yourself a lot of trouble," Haider whispered with a blend of humor and admonition as he passed Jasper to assume the lead.

Jasper bit his tongue and fell silent, the lesson duly noted. After an exhaustive initial scan of the area, the group reassembled under the broken skylight. Rowan then began to recount their eerie history. "Not long after we arrived in old London, our clan leader, Larissa, sent us on a ridiculous scouting mission. We took shelter in the Gherkin building. Later that night, we heard the sound of gunfire coming from the warehouse. We immediately assumed it was another raiding party."

Rowan's voice grew somber as he detailed how, upon their return to the clan, they discovered that everyone had been wiped out, finding, to their horror, one of the abominations feasting on Larissa's corpse.

"It was like nothing any of us had ever seen, creatures poured in from every direction. We were lucky you all found us then," he explained.

"It wasn't luck, Rowan," Buirke interjected, nodding toward Val with a respectful smile. "Luck has nothing to do with escaping a swarm of stalkers. It all comes down to training—a lesson Haven clearly could use. I'm grateful for every extra able hand."

Rowan offered a grudging smile as he nodded. "I appreciate that. Perhaps we'll all learn something today."

"In this life," Buirke replied with quiet gravity, "survival is key."

Rowan's gaze drifted toward a narrow hallway leading to the scene where Larissa had met her grim fate. "Without my team, I wouldn't be here," he murmured. "Hold on for a sec, I need to check something out."

"Make it quick. We'll scout the vicinity while you're gone," Buirke instructed.

With deliberate care, Rowan advanced along the creaking wooden floor. Each step produced a groan from the ancient boards, echoing in the stark silence of the warehouse. With his back pressed against the wall and his favorite HVT rifle cradled at his shoulder, Rowan slid along the corridor. His senses were hyper-attuned; every small sound and flicker of movement mattered. His uncanny battlefield awareness had been his lifeline for years, allowing him to perceive what others missed.

Everything was as it had been during their last visit. The door at the end of the hall, where Larissa had met her untimely end, was left ajar. Slowing his pace, Rowan edged closer. Peering inside, he found the room disturbingly empty. Lowering his rifle to his side, he unfastened his radio, "Spence, come in."

"Go ahead, Spence," came the crackly response.

Rowan crouched near the blood-stained floor where his former leader had lain motionless while the beast feasted upon her remains.

"I don't like what I see," he murmured, almost to himself. "There are no survivors here—not even Larissa's body. And we all know she went down. Perhaps some cannibals swept through and took the remains; this weather is like a giant, frigid vault for those freaks." His eyes then narrowed as he considered another possibility. "Yet, that wouldn't explain the weapons left behind. No bandit or scavenger would be foolish enough to leave them. What's our situation out there?"

"That's what I was getting at," Spence agreed.

"How's it looking out there?" Rowan asked, kneeling, he carefully shifted debris aside and uncovered Larissa's prized 1873 Winchester. Holding the rifle, he felt as though he was touching a piece of history. For years, he had yearned to handle this very rifle, now smudged with the weight of lost time and duty. Larissa had safeguarded it, mounting it on a wall in the Mammoth with pride. He marveled at its simplicity—the devastating power of its 357 Magnum rounds at close range. With methodical precision, he inspected the chamber, relieved to find it loaded, a small testament to her vigilance. Bringing the rifle's finely crafted wooden stock to his shoulder, he admired its balance and construction one last time.

"Larissa really knew how to maintain quality—it looks damn new," Rowan thought, before carefully stowing it in his second rifle holster attached to his backpack.

Over the radio, Spence's voice came through again, "Despite the bone-chilling cold, the Mammoth is intact—just as Larissa left it. All the fuel's here, and our armory hasn't been tampered with. Rook and Mia have loaded every weapon they could locate."

"Good work," Rowan replied. "When you finish out there, I spotted a few inside to grab. Then, prep for our next destination."

"Copy that. Spence out," came the measured confirmation as he reattached his radio.

Nearby, Rook chuckled lowly, leaning close enough for his voice to barely be heard. "You're lucky Rowan told you to stay back with us. Because that little blond kid was about to rip you a new one."

"What's that supposed to mean?" Spence asked.

"You know exactly what I mean, that kid was about to beat your ass," Rook continued to tease.

"You wish. That little shit wouldn't know a pot to piss in if he saw it. Let alone take me on. Fact is the Irish don't go down easily," Spence said with a hint of mischief.

"You're one to talk. Remember Dublin? You got shot in the ass back then!" Rook retorted with a smile of his own.

"That I did, no denying that," Spence laughed heartily,

lightening the atmosphere as they moved back inside.

Within the warehouse, Val lingered against a dilapidated wall, keeping watch, while the rest—Buirke, Rowan, Jasper, Haider, and Al—scoured the vast space for anything useful. Al ambled through the aisles, his curiosity piqued by remnants of shoeboxes and forgotten crates. Halfway down one aisle, he discovered a lone, weathered brown box on the lowest shelf. Its lid clung precariously, half-removed as if in surrender to time.

"Ahh, what do we have here?" Al whispered to himself, tilting his head in intrigue. He carefully lifted the lid, revealing a pristine pair of beige leather dress shoes. They still carried that unmistakable new-leather aroma and even boasted an absurd price tag of $699. With a quiet chuckle, he muttered, "I think I can afford this," before tucking the shoes away in his backpack. Satisfaction lit his face—but the moment was abruptly shattered when he stopped dead in his tracks. "Rowan!" he bellowed, his voice echoing through the cavernous space, ensuring everyone heard his urgent call.

Chapter 17

Ending his transmission with Spence, Rowan's eyes remained fixed on the gruesome aftermath of Larissa's death—a scene he could scarcely believe. The creak of the floor behind him made him whirl around, sidearm swiftly drawn to confront an unseen threat. Instead, he found Val leaning casually against a half-collapsed wall.

"Didn't think you cared enough for her to pay respects?" Val said, her tone teasing yet edged with concern as she glanced at the blood-soaked rubble beneath his boots.

Rowan replied curtly, "Just here to pick something up," holstering his weapon with deliberate ease.

Val's eyes sparkled wryly as she smirked, "Ah, that thing. You always claimed you'd get it eventually—guess that time has finally arrived, albeit in a very unexpected fashion." Then, lowering her voice, she added, "There's something you need to see downstairs."

"Right behind you," he said, before shifting his gaze back to the spot dappled with red, *"Larissa, you're lucky it wasn't me that put you down."* Facing Val once more, "Lead the way."

Minutes later, Rowan and Val descended the stairs, where they met Buirke, Al, Jasper, and Haider gathered in a tense huddle. The room felt choked with anticipation.

"What's the story here?" Rowan demanded as he stepped up beside Al, whose silence was as pointed as his raised weapon aimed ahead without a word.

"Spence, you guys, come on inside. You might want to check this out," Rowan's voice erupted over the radio, carrying a mix of urgency and dread.

Streaked in dark, desperate blood, the wall bore the chilling message: *They're here, the creatures are changing, nowhere is safe now.*

Val's whisper barely broke the heavy silence, "What in the world?"

Rowan's eyes narrowed as he faced Buirke. "Explain: What do you suppose they mean by 'changing'?"

Buirke's response was as calm as a storm's eye. "I wish I knew, Rowan. It could mean anything. More savage, adapting to the light. I could be any number of things."

Rowan's frustration built. "That's not good enough. I get it, we're the new kids on the block. But how are we to cover each other's backs out here, when no one has a straight answer for us? Clearly, Haven knows more than what it's putting on. You guys have been fighting them for some time."

As if cued by Rowan's loud voice, Mia, Spence, and Rook joined the group.

"Rook, over here," Rowan commanded, his voice firm, catching sight of their entry into the structure from his peripheral vision.

"What's the situation?" Rook asked, as the group reassembled.

Rowan continued, "Buirke was about to fill us in on the city's chaos." His eyes stayed locked on Buirke while Val gestured subtly toward the blood-written warning.

"What's with all this cryptic crap?" Spence snapped.

"I see you have all eyes on me now, Rowan. So I'll say this once: I don't have an issue with either of you, as long as you do your part. With that, everything I said earlier still holds. You're soldiers—you took orders before, and I took mine. I'm just the messenger, so suit up and take your questions back to Haven. I brought you here, secured your gear, and now it's time we nab a generator. Once that's done, we can head back and you can get the answers from those who sent you," Buirke declared evenly, his eyes locked with Rowan's.

Silence fell for several long seconds until Rowan finally broke it. "Fine. We wrap up here, grab the generator, and head back to Haven. My team needs clarity." Stepping across Buirke's path, his team fanned out behind him. "Team, get back to the Mammoth and Scorpion. I want them prepped to leave proto. Val, you're on Mammoth with Al and Mia. Rook, Spence, and I take the Scorpion."

Once outside the battered shoe warehouse storefront, the group paused to take in the life that was theirs now to live.

"Give me a few minutes—I need to refuel the Mammoth. Looks like Larissa's goons forgot to top her off when we arrived. There's no telling how far the generator is from here," Val said, watching the constant snowfall.

"Mia, help Val with the refuel and have Al stand guard. We can't afford any surprises," Rowan ordered.

Mia gave him a brisk nod, and together, she and Val headed for the Mammoth. Rowan watched them trudge through the biting snow toward the vehicles, while Haider approached silently.

"Mr. Rowan, the generator site is roughly twenty minutes from here—could be less if visibility holds. We're waiting in the vehicle," Haider reported.

Rowan's focus locked on the Mammoth ahead. "Understood. Tell Buirke we'll be ready in fifteen."

Haider paused as if to add more, then continued, "One more thing, Mr. Rowan." He stopped in his tracks, his voice softening as he recounted, "I've been at Haven for eight years now, and I used to wonder these same things. But my family wasn't as lucky. We were brutally attacked by these creatures. I had to drag my daughter's body through the forest, and every step reminded me of my lost wife, my parents, my children—everything stolen by those beasts. This scar on my face? It's my mark from Allah, a constant reminder of my failure as a husband and father, and of how these creatures ended my happiness. I joined the Devils to seek vengeance, but even after countless take downs, I never found satisfaction. Now, I only see peace and mercy left in the hands of the Creator. I pray you get your answers soon, and don't spend your life chasing ghosts." With that, Haider turned and walked away, leaving a heavy silence in his wake.

Rowan stood alone for a moment, his thoughts coiling like the biting wind at his back. Everything he believed was now shrouded in a fog of secrecy. His team was his family, and he would do whatever it took to keep them alive—even if that meant venturing further into the white. The mission was clear: one objective completed today, another to go—and eventually, he'll demand answers from those who held them.

Ω∎Ω∎Ω∎Ω

Their intel pinpointed the generator at Hephaestus—a home improvement store nearly two kilometers south of their last position. However, debris blocked their vehicles from navigating the narrow street leading to the store, forcing the teams to abandon the vehicles and proceed on foot.

They moved silently down a narrow street off Garratt Lane, organized in two single-file lines flanking either side of the pavement. Rowan led one side and Haider led the other with his Tec-comm maps up, their guns locked forward, those in the middle vigilantly scanning the rooftops, while the rearguard watched for any signs of an ambush.

Shuttered shops lined the street—electronics, tattoo and piercing parlors, antique and comic book stores—now mere husks, looted long ago and left in eerie abandonment.

"Stay alert, everyone," Rowan said with a whispered holler, his uneasiness growing with every step along the bottle-necked street. The threat of ambush lurks in every shadow. "How much further?" he hissed, his whisper tense enough to slice the cold air.

Haider consulted his Tec-comm and replied softly, "The entrance to Hephaestus should be coming up in the next thirty feet or so, on our left." Suddenly, his body tensed, and he dropped to one knee, an alert in his eyes as he thought he spied movement.

"What did you see?" Buirke queried, his tone laced with cautious concern.

"Could be nothing—probably just a trick of the light," Haider muttered.

Rowan leaned in, voice hushed yet firm, "We can't afford to stop. Let's keep moving."

"Understood," Haider responded, and the group resumed their careful advance.

After twenty-five tense yards, they reached a corner. With

his back pressed against a cold wall, Haider peered around the corner. "We've got a situation—a makeshift wall's blocking the entrance."

Mia's face tightened with worry as she exchanged a questioning glance with Rook, who silently traced the outline of the wall with his eyes.

The wall rose from the frozen ground, a patchwork of weathered wooden boards, rusted sheet metal, and an assortment of scavenged remnants. Amongst the jumble, you could spot pieces of abandoned vehicles, twisted pipes, and even a shattered neon sign half-buried in

the icy soil. Each material bore the scars of time and wear, telling silent tales of past lives and desperate ingenuity that had gone into fortifying this barrier against the relentless cold winds that swept through the desolate landscape.

"There's no movement, no alternative route," Haider continued grimly.

Hurrying forward, Buirke inspected the obstacle. "That wall's at least twelve feet high. Climbing it? Not an option."

Rowan strode to his side, scanning the impassable barrier. "If we can't go around, maybe we can go over."

"Scaling it isn't feasible," Buirke countered sharply.

Rowan's eyes lit up as he pointed across the street. "But who said we need to climb? The guitar shop—from the third-story window. I bet we could clear this gap and land on the roof to get around the wall."

Buirke squinted at the gap. "That's at least five meters. It's a long shot."

"Do we have any other options?" Rowan pressed, his tone resolute. "At this point, not really."

Rowan's calloused fingers danced in a series of precise

gestures, communicating the revised strategy to his team without a word as they cautiously made their way towards the abandoned storefront.

Spence murmured under his breath, "Who built this god-damn wall in the first place?"

Rock's low response echoed his sentiment, "I'm with you, Spence. Whoever did, they were trying to keep something out."

Buirke was the first to make his way through the broken storefront, cautious in every step. "Keep your eyes peeled. If they built that wall, they intended to keep something or someone secure."

Rowan moved with precision, his team in a calculated formation. As they infiltrated the building, their synchronized steps echoed softly in the silence. The narrow staircase loomed ahead, its ancient wood groaning under their weight. Val signaled silently, and they ascended, each member covering a different angle. Reaching the third level, Val advanced cautiously to a window, her keen eyes scanning the neighboring roof for any signs of movement or danger.

"That jump's no walk in the park," Val remarked, half in awe, half with pragmatic caution, as Rowan joined her side.

"You can say that again. Who's brave enough to go first?" Rowan asked, gently prying the window from its frame to inspect the snowy drop spanning two stories down.

Without hesitation, Mia pushed to the front. Ignoring soft objections from both Val and Rowan, she focused her gaze on the daunting gap. She nodded at the two of them as if to say, "*I got this*," despite the peril.

Rowan stepped aside with a nod. Mia took a few deep, steadying steps back, then launched herself toward the window. At the critical last moment, she planted her foot on the frame and propelled herself into a daring leap. For several heart-stopping seconds, she flew through the icy air above a white, snow-laden expanse. Finally, she landed atop the opposite roof with a soft thud, executing a smooth tuck-and-roll to absorb the impact. Before springing to her feet and shooting a triumphant thumbs-up to her team.

"She got guts," Jasper commented from near the window, his tone a mixture of incredulity and admiration.

One by one, nine more figures followed Mia's lead, each employing a careful tuck-and-roll as they landed on the adjoining roof.

"Man, my old bones nearly gave out on that jump," Rook groaned.

Al chimed in with playful banter, "Stop complaining, Rook. You've still got at least another year or two in you."

Rook grinned despite himself, "Thanks for the pep talk, buddy."

"Anytime," Al replied lightly.

"For real thought, sometimes I wonder if I'll see those extra years," Rook added somberly. "Ever since leaving Haven, shit just haven't felt right."

Rowan clapped him on the shoulder, "We have no time for regrets. Let's complete the mission. When it comes down to it, we know what we're capable of." Passing by the others, he reached Buirke at the front. "Your move," he said quietly, eyes locked on Buirke.

Buirke stood silent as the rest of the group gathered around him. "Haider said the depot is just ahead. I located a fire escape we can use to descend to ground level," he stated coolly, weapon at the ready."

"Then why are we sightseeing?" Rowan asked.

Buirke gave a slight smile before striding away for the fire escape.

Chapter 18

A forlorn wind howled relentlessly across the desolate expanse, its icy gusts whipping up drifting snow into a blinding, near-whiteout that obscured everything in its path. In the midst of this frozen chaos, a ten-man unit trudged forward, their silhouettes evoking the image of old-time Arctic explorers. Yet, rather than crude tools like hooks and pickaxes, each man carried modern, high-powered weaponry and bundles of volatile explosives glinting under the bleak light.

Buirke led the charge toward the looming structure known as Hephaestus Home and Gardening Depot. Unlike the crumbling, huddled buildings of Old London, Hephaestus loomed in solitary isolation, encircled by an expansive three-acre parking lot that stretched out like a barren wasteland. At first glance, the sight was both eerie and compelling: someone had clearly attempted to transform this once-bustling department store into a makeshift settlement. Haphazard barricades made of chained shopping carts and a chaotic scatter of wrecked vehicles and salvaged building materials formed a crude wall around the store's entrance, though a large section of it was violently torn away as if wrenched out by desperate hands.

As the group cautiously closed in on the breach, every detail betrayed the failed security of the settlement. Bullet-pocked surfaces and scorched, twisted metal testified to a ferocious battle fought just within that ragged, makeshift barrier. It was a familiar sight to Rowan, who had witnessed the rise and crushing collapse of many such communities in the years following the catastrophe. In the face of dwindling resources and mounting desperation, even once-hoped-for unifications ended in violent raids and the disintegration of fragile alliances.

The team moved carefully across the abandoned lot until they reached the shattered glass doors of the store, whose windows were splintered into jagged shards that glittered under the cloud-covered gray sky. With a mutual, wordless agreement to proceed with caution, they stepped into the store's cavernous interior. From the very first impression—the disarray, the fallen merchandise, the scattering of debris—Rowan doubted they would even find any operational generator within these walls.

"Rook, Al—stay sharp and watch our entrance. We're going to canvas this area," Rowan ordered, his voice low but resolute in the eerie quiet.

"Jasper, hang back with them and be ready to assist if any locals tail us. I suggest the rest of us split up to cover more ground," Buirke added, his tone both commanding and cautious.

Rowan's eyes swept the shadowed interior as he continued, "I agree—no one goes anywhere alone. Spence, head left with Haidar; Val, Mia, take the right side; and Buirke and I will check the central aisles. Watch your corners."

After a final check of their gear, ensuring weapons were at the ready, flashlights mounted and ammo secure, the group set off as one cohesive unit. "Keep your eyes peeled and never lose sight of your partner. Meet back here in twenty minutes—no exceptions," Rowan instructed, his voice echoing slightly in the vast, somber space.

"We gotcha, Rowan," came Spence's muffled affirmation, while Mia offered a determined nod.

In an instant, the darkness was punctured by the harsh beams of their mounted flashlights. With arms wrapped around cold, battle-worn weapons, the team dispersed into the store's labyrinthine aisles, fully aware that the deeper they ventured, the more they depended solely upon their artificial light.

Although Hephaestus Home and Gardening retained the imposing presence of a home improvement warehouse—complete with towering orange storage racks—it now resembled a post-apocalyptic relic. Items that once belonged neatly on shelves now lay scattered across aisles like forgotten confetti, and their beams cast elongated, monstrous shadows upon the worn concrete floor and cold steel structures.

After turning down several aisles, Rowan and Buirke found themselves in a section dedicated to lumber supplies. Stacks of variously cut pieces of wood formed uneven barricades along both sides of the aisle.

"I'm surprised there's still this much lumber left," Rowan remarked, sweeping his flashlight's beam over the weathered planks, each scarred by time. "Maybe the Stalkers have something to do with that?"

Buirke's measured reply came as he slowed, "Most people hid indoors once the snow began to fall, and they stayed safe until food shortages forced them out. In those days, building a shelter was the last thing on their minds." Then, lowering his voice slightly, he added, "Since we're alone right now, there's something more urgent I need to discuss. I apologize if I've seemed secretive, but believe me when I say Haven is a sanctuary—a place that, with people like Dr. Orion, will spur remarkable advancements."

Rowan halted abruptly, turning to face him with intensity. "I'm not one to mince words, Buirke. I deal with things as they are, not as you're eager to present them. First, you requested our help, not the reverse. And secondly, I can't accept that everyone in Haven is an angel cloaked in secrecy. In our world, secrets are as filthy as the dirt beneath our boots. You never know what might be festering in there. Third, frankly, I don't care so long as my team and I aren't targeted. Yes, I'm a bandit—used to be a bandit, but I'm here now. As you said, the past doesn't matter, right? And don't get me started on the Stalkers you seemed not to want to talk about. If no one likes my team or me, then so be it. Once we secure this generator, we can part ways," Rowan declared, locking eyes with Buirke in a silent, seething challenge.

"Anyone can talk a good game, but true character reveals itself in a crisis. We aren't in need of any more loose cannons, though I acknowledge you've already proven your worth," Buirke conceded.

"Best we keep moving," Rowan replied curtly as he turned away, leaving Buirke lingering in the dim gloom.

"I guess that means we're in agreement then," came the steady retort as Buirke readied his weapon and followed suit.

Ahead, Rowan lifted his flashlight to reveal a sign hanging above an aisle reading *Outdoor Equipment.* Quickening his pace, he scanned each shelf meticulously, the beam of his light dancing across scattered merchandise in search of the prized generator—a ticket back to Haven and a way to escape the relentless encroachment of the White. It wasn't long before his persistence was rewarded.

"I found it," he called out sharply, alerting Buirke, who trailed just a few feet behind. Inspecting the generator with careful scrutiny, he mused, "This beast weighs no less than three hundred pounds. Hauling it back to the Mammoth will be no small feat."

"Good work," Buirke said approvingly as he joined him. "For once, Intel was right about something. I'll radio in—get our guys to assist." He pulled back his sleeve to speak into his Tec-Com. "Jasper, you there?"

"I'm here," came the immediate reply on the channel.

"Locate Spence and Haidar. Head to aisle twenty-four. We've discovered the generator and will need extra hands to drag it out. Keep your eyes open for anything we can use— there was some lumber on the way here, maybe grab a few pieces of timber."

A few minutes later, Haidar, Jasper, and Spence emerged down the aisle. Jasper balanced a heavy section of plywood, while Haidar clutched a length of sturdy rope.

"What's this?" Rowan asked, eyeing the trio. "I expected you'd haul something to move the generator."

Jasper explained, "The snow is deep enough that using wheels alone would just have us sinking. I scavenged some tools from the carpenter section and punctured several holes in this plywood. With the rope, I figured we could create a makeshift sleigh and haul the dam thing."

"Initially, I had the same thought, but the kid's idea is far more ingenious," Spence added enthusiastically.

"Alright then—get it rigged up and ready to haul," Rowan commanded.

"Nice work," Buirke complimented, patting his son on the shoulder just as a distant, pitiful canine howl drifted through the corridors.

"What was that?" Rowan queried, tightening his grip on his weapon.

"Sounded like a howl," Spence replied, confusion clear in his tone.

"Can't be... It's been years since we last saw wolves," Rowan murmured.

"I hear you, but I'm telling that was a wolf," Spence said, causing Buirke, Jasper, and Haidar to share a glance.

Rowan's gaze flicked to them, each appearing unnervingly calm despite the unsettling sound. For Rowan and Spence, even a distant animal cry was significant; so many of the world's creatures had vanished under drastic climate shifts that the presence of any was a portent of deeper trouble. Their expressions confirmed his silent fears.

"See what I mean, Buirke, secrets," Rowan said, naturally readying his weapon.

"Aye yo, Boss, I think you should get up front ASAP," Rook's voice crackled over the radio.

"Roger that, Rook. In route," Rowan turned to Jasper and Haidar. "Secure that generator and meet us at the front. Buirke, Spence—stick with me."

Jasper and Haidar exchanged a brief glance with Buirke before he barked, "Do it," and then bolted toward the entrance with Rowan and Spence close behind.

The three of them quickly navigated their way back through the depot, and upon reaching the building's front, Rowan found Al, Mia, Rook, and Val hunkered behind a half-wall constructed from repurposed shopping carts. Their entrenched positions allowed them to peer out into the windswept, desolate parking lot beyond the shattered barricade.

"What's the situation?" Rowan asked, dropping beside Rook as he crouched low.

"Take a look for yourself," Rook grunted, motioning toward the small roof they had scaled to reach Hephaestus. "Val and Mia just returned when they showed up."

Pulling a miniature binoculars from within his vest, Rowan slowly scanned the bleak, snow-dusted parking lot. Perched upon the roof was a solitary figure—not the mysterious specter he'd seen before their camp's attack, but someone much shorter. The person's face was concealed behind reflective goggles and a tattered scarf, and their leather stitch clothing.

Clutched in one hand was a rugged leather leash, its other end linked to a hideous beast that, though canine in outline, was anything but familiar. The creature crouched on all fours, nearly four feet tall, its hairless, purple-tinted skin stretched over bulging muscles. Elongated limbs elevated its body from the snow as it growled lowly, saliva visible on its fanged snarl, all while fixated on its next gruesome meal.

"Skin-walkers, scouts—and they have Wulvers with them!" Buirke murmured, his voice heavy with dread.

"I'm beginning to sound like a broken record here. But Skin-walkers? What are you saying?" Rowan asked incredulously, lowering the binoculars. "You know these creatures?"

"Let me see that," Spence demanded, reaching for the optics.

"Rowan, there's much you need to learn about. But now isn't the time," Buirke interjected firmly.

"Damn right, this isn't the time. Five more just arrived, and with them, another pack of those Rottweiler look-alikes,"

Spence added.

"They are both right, Rowan. And I doubt whoever they are, they're not here to talk it out," Val stated gravely.

Rowan's attention veered away from Buirke's cautious whispers, drawn instead to the edge of the half-wall. In the distance, silhouetted against the icy horizon, six ominous figures stood in a grim formation. Their commanding presence was matched by the Wulvers at their side, sinewy creatures with elongated limbs and a menacing aura. As Rowan watched, a primal urge seemed to ignite within the beasts; they strained against their restraints with an unsettling eagerness, emitting guttural howls that echoed through the desolate landscape like a chilling harbinger of death.

"Weapons ready, but hold fire. Buirke, check on your team and see what the holdup on the generator is," Rowan ordered.

In unison, everyone aimed their weapons toward the emerging threat. One final glance at the Skin-walkers and their snarling Wulvers confirmed the grim reality. With a sudden, sharp nod, Buirke pivoted and began making his way back toward Jasper and Haidar. Seeing him break from the group, the Skin-walkers gave a unified war cry that traveled on the wind as they released the deadly beast.

Chapter 19

With the agility and raw ferocity of a prowling predator, the Wulvers easily vaulted down from the rooftop high above onto the snow-laden parking lot, each leap stirring plumes of powdery white with every bound as they closed in on their targets.

"Time to let these mutts have it. Open up," Rowan ordered with a steely calm.

Bullets erupted in a synchronized frenzy, a storm of metal hurtling towards the approaching Wulvers. The lead creature crumpled instantly, its body careening down in a gruesome slide that painted the icy ground with splatters of blood and debris. The rest of the pack dispersed swiftly under the unyielding barrage, each volley tearing through snow and shattered concrete, forcing them to zigzag frantically to evade the onslaught from all directions. Their strength, speed, and tireless energy far surpassed that of any common canine.

"Damn, they're nimble—can't seem to land a solid hit on these fuckers," Spence bellowed, his weapon swaying amidst the chaos.

"Fall back into the store now!" Rowan shouted as he squeezed off additional rounds and seeing the gap between them and their attackers closing. "Val, you lead."

Following his order, Val unleashed controlled bursts to cover their retreat, moving with the precision of a seasoned soldier. In swift succession, the team leapfrogged further inside, making it to cover before protecting the retreat of the others into the store. Rowan was the last to break cover from the half-wall, his retreat timed mere seconds before the remaining Wulvers vaulted over, as if it were a bump on the road.

Upon entering, a pair of the creatures swiftly climbed towering shelves to hunt their victims from elevated vantage points, while the remaining trio stealthily maneuvered into the shadowy depths of the aisles.

Silence reclaimed the space as all gunfire ceased, leaving behind an eerie symphony of heavy breathing, the steady thud of boots, and the occasional clatter of a stray object falling somewhere in the darkness.

"You know the drill—stay alert," Rowan whispered urgently, his voice a razor edge in the quiet as they circled, backs to one another, advancing cautiously through the aisles in search of Buirke and his men. Each measured step was underscored by the knowledge that an attack was imminent.

Val swiftly signaled, raising a clenched fist in the air as a shiver ran down her spine. Taking a deep breath to steady herself, she swept the beam of her flashlight through the ominous darkness around them. Slowly, a soft, incessant tapping began all around them—a rhythmic, unnerving sound like long nails lightly drumming against cold metal.

Low snarls echoed from above, alerting her. Swiftly lifting her flashlight, she illuminated the rafters to reveal a crouched Wulver, poised to strike. Reacting instantly, she squeezed the trigger, sending a barrage of shots that tore through the creature's chest with deadly accuracy. Stepping aside deftly, she watched as the lifeless body of the Wulver crashed to the ground with a heavy thud. Immediately unleashing a swift kick to the fallen beast's carcass—a brutal blow that snapped its jaw noisily.

All eyes were fixed on the grim trophy, and Rook couldn't help but lean over. "Geez, that thing's hideous," he commented softly, his flashlight illuminating the creature's horrifying details.

"Not now, Rook. There's no time for a post-mortem walk-through; there are still four more out there," Rowan snapped, urgently rallying the team. "Keep moving back to the others!"

Before anyone could respond, sporadic bursts of gunfire erupted again, echoing off the store's battered walls.

"Buirke!" Rowan shouted as he pivoted on his heel. "Double time!"

"Man, this is some twisted shit—each moment gets weirder," Al murmured under his breath, anxiety mingling with dark humor.

Winding their way through the maze of aisles, the group eventually reached an atrium crowned with a large skylight. In the center of this open space, two towering shadows burst forth from the darkness like nightmare incarnate. In a heartbeat, one enormous beast charged directly toward Rook. Its sheer mass slammed into him, sending him hurtling sideways into a precariously piled stockpile of shelves. His limp form was forcefully swept out the opposite side, buried under a cascade of fallen DIY merchandise.

In that chaotic moment, the team instinctively scrambled for their weapons. While their attention was focused on rescuing Rook, the second beast exploited their distraction. It lunged from an unseen side, pouncing onto Al's back and viciously raking through his backpack. The beast's grip dragged him across the cold floor like a rag doll, its monstrous claws leaving brutal marks in its wake. As weight and fear bore down upon him, Al's struggles echoed the terror of being singled out by a creature fueled solely by blood lust.

With the beast lost in its own thirst for flesh, Rowan seized his own moment of opportunity. He advanced with lethal precision, drawing his handgun in one fluid motion, aiming squarely at the beast's head. The shot was deafening in its finality; the creature's brain seemed to erupt in a grisly spectacle before its lifeless body crumpled to the floor. A purposeful shove from his boot sent the carcass tumbling off Al, who lay gasping for every stolen breath.

Mia, Val, and Spence stood firm as another monstrous beast thundered towards them from the dark aisle's end. Its jaws, a menacing row of jagged teeth, gleamed in the dim light. Without hesitation, the trio synchronized their movements with practiced precision. They released a combination of semi and automatic fire.

The creature spasmed violently as the onslaught of projectiles tore through its twisted form. Blood sprayed in gruesome patterns as it struggled against the barrage of firepower. With a final shudder, the beast succumbed to its wounds, crashing heavily to the icy ground in a grotesque display of defeat. The metallic tang of spent ammunition hung thick in the frigid air of the depot.

"Anyone got a count on that train of nightmares?" Rook groaned as he clawed himself from the debris.

Spence was quick to respond, "I got you, bro," pulling him up.

"That thing just came out of nowhere," Rook continued, dusting himself off, staggering amidst the chaos.

"Rook, you alright?" Rowan asked, holstering his handgun in a moment of brief concern.

"I'm fine… just a bit of air knocked out of me. Just need a few, that's all. That fucker hit like a truck," Rook replied with a rueful chuckle.

Not willing to waste more time.

"Val, Spence, you two come with me. The rest, stay back with Rook until he recovers," Rowan commanded.

Before Mia and Al could silently nod, they were already in motion for Buirke.

Rowan pushed himself with every ounce of strength as he sprinted toward Devil Squad's last known position, knowing that, while the immediate rescue of them wasn't his highest priority. However, Buirke's insights might provide crucial answers about Old London's calamities, making it a necessity.

Not far off, the aisles crackled with gunfire, casting fleeting light on the scene where Jasper and Haidar had readied the generator. The flashes sliced through the darkness like shards of ice, revealing tense shadows and sharp movements in the frigid air. Rowan, Val, and Spence hurried through the maze of shelves, their breath visible in the cold as they closed in on Jasper. He stood there, panting heavily, wrestling a lifeless Wulver off Haidar while gripping his blood-smeared knife. Meanwhile, Buirke was spotted in the distance, his rifle blazing towards a retreating Wulver as it vanished into the darkness.

"What took you so long?" Buirke bellowed, pausing briefly to scan the area, ever alert for another ambush.

Rowan's voice was both sarcastic and weary, "You know as well as I do that these things are harder to kill than cockroaches.

Besides, we weren't exactly briefed on what we're facing out here, were we?"

After a momentary silence, Buirke replied, his tone grim, "Don't get too comfortable. One of them is still out there."

"Nice way to react, Jasper. If you hadn't, I'd have been its meal—my gun jammed and that thing was on me before I could reach for my sidearm," Haidar recounted, wiping the crimson smear from his knife before returning it to its sheath.

Rowan then addressed Jasper, "Were you able to prep the generator to move?"

"We just finished constructing a litter when the Wulvers burst in," Jasper answered succinctly.

"Good work. Spence, Jasper, Haidar, and I will haul it out. Buirke and Val, cover our retreat," Rowan ordered calmly, before taking hold of his walkie. "Al, meet us at the entrance."

"Sure thing," Al's voice responded to him.

Seconds later, the four men hoisted the cumbersome litter and raised the three-hundred–pound generator with gritted will.

Minutes passed in strained silence, punctuated only by the laboring grunts of the men and the steady rhythm of combat boots on concrete.

"Keep your eyes open, Buirke—I know it's nearby. I can feel its presence," Val murmured, her flashlight beam dancing across the darkened outlines of shelving.

"Yeah, eyes peeled. I don't fancy a bite to the arse," Spence grumbled, readjusting his grip.

"Focus, everyone," Rowan interjected. "Val's right. It's out there, stalking us. It's alone, and we need to be ready for its next move."

Though he continued to lend his strength to the heaving

generator, Rowan's eyes darted around every dark crevice and shifting shadow. With Val covering the team's left flank and Buirke guarding the right, they pressed onward toward their rendezvous.

A thunderous snarl shattered the eerie quiet as they navigated past a looming storage shelf. Without warning, a Wulver burst forth from the shadows beneath the lower rack, its movements swift and savage like a primal force unleashed. In a blur of motion, its razor-sharp jaws clamped down on Buirke's right leg with brutal force, teeth sinking deep into his flesh with a sickening crack that echoed through the icy air. A cry of anguish tore from Buirke's lips, the intense pain cutting through the frozen stillness as he fought to stay upright against the relentless assault of the beast.

In a heartbeat, their eyes met—Rowan's grim gaze locking with Buirke's pained, steadfast look—just before the creature yanked Buirke violently beneath the lower shelf, dragging him out of sight.

"Dad!" Jasper screamed, dropping the litter in a panic.

"Jasper, I got him," Rowan replied sharply, seizing the boy's arm and halting any impulsive chase. "Val, take my position and get to the others."

With that, Rowan bolted off in a desperate sprint into the swirling darkness.

Buirke plunged into darkness as the creature dragged him beneath the shelving, his rifle slipping from his grip. Struggling against its relentless hold, he reached for his sidearm, firing off shots in rapid succession. The Wulver's sharp teeth sank into his leg, but he refused to yield, each bullet missing as the beast thrashed him around sharp corners. Its menacing growls echoed through the air, sending a wave of fear down his spine. Isolated and defenseless, Buirke fought against the odds with every ounce of strength he had left, his survival hanging by a thread.

Released abruptly, the Wulver let go of Buirke, who tumbled into a cluster of shattered windows nearby. Sunlight pierced through the thick clouds, casting an eerie glow on the retreating creature. Its snarl echoed faintly as it prowled away, its powerful chest rising and falling with each step. Circling Buirke like a predator sizing up its prey, the Wulver drew closer, anticipation curling its lips. With unwavering resolve amidst fear, Buirke raised his weapon, aiming with precision at the monster's forehead. In a swift motion, he pulled the trigger as tension filled the air.

Click...Click...

Lowering his weapon, Buirke's gaze locked onto the towering Wulver. The creature's claws tapped ominously on the cold concrete floor with each deliberate step. Suddenly, it lunged forward in a blur of motion. Time stretched as fear gripped him, but Buirke stood firm, refusing to avert his eyes even in the face of impending danger.

In a breathless whisper, he muttered, "As I walk through the valley of death," steeling himself for the imminent clash.

As the creature lunged, its fangs gleaming menacingly, a thunderous barrage of gunfire shattered the air. The Wulver was sent hurtling through the air, crashing violently into a barricade of overturned shelves. Rowan burst into view at the aisle's end, his HVT-Viper gripped firmly across his chest in a stance of lethal readiness. Surveying the scene swiftly, he recounted the fallen beast, *one dropped in the parking lot, Val's takedown, the ones that had ambushed Al and Rook, Jasper's swift kill,* and now this final foe—Rowan mentally tallied up the casualties. Six beasts down. A solitary sigh escaped him as he grappled with the gravity of their ordeal.

"What a shit show, I've got us into?" he muttered under his breath, bitterness lacing his words.

With the danger subdued, Rowan rushed to Buirke's side, his footsteps quick in the icy silence. Kneeling beside him, "The valley of death, huh?" A faint grin tugged at the corner of his lips as he added hoarsely, "I've faced worse." Slipping his weapon across his back, Rowan retrieved his worn scarf from his coat pocket and bound it tightly around Buirke's wounded leg.

"Ow—" Buirke winced, yet added with forced humor, "Other than my pride and my leg, I'm still kicking."

Observing Buirke's struggle to stand, Rowan helped him up, he said, "I got you. By the way, I found this along the way," offering his lost rifle with a gesture that spoke of gratitude and urgency.

"Much appreciated," Buirke replied, gingerly shifting his weight onto his uninjured leg and reloading his sidearm with precision.

"Ready to regroup with the others?" Rowan asked softly.

"As ready as I can be," came the resolute reply.

Rowan draped Buirke's arm over his shoulder. As each man re-armed their sidearm, an unspoken understanding passed between them.

"Buirke, since we're here so close—let me ask you something," Rowan began, tone tempered by the intimacy of shared peril.

"You saved my hide, so I owe you a few answers," Buirke replied wryly.

"Why don't the Wulvers turn on their masters?" Rowan

inquired, his voice low and intense.

Buirke paused, contemplating the question with a heavy sigh. "From the sparse intel we've gathered, it's likely linked to pheromones. The Skin-walkers themselves wear the skins of their trophies, be they human or otherwise, and my guess is that by donning the skins of Stalkers, the Wulvers mistake them for one of their own."

A beat of silence passed before Rowan countered, "And you guys never thought of doing the same?"

"Rowan, my friend, even if the world's gone to hell, we at Haven still cling to the vestiges of civilization if we hope to rebuild the Earth," Buirke grunted through his pain.

Rowan shook his head, a wild glimmer in his tired eyes. "Allow me to enlighten you, old friend: sometimes, to survive in this savage world, you have no choice but to be savage with it."

Burke's voice was grim as he replied, "The moment you turn savagely, you forfeit your humanity—and in doing so, you become something far worse than any beast. But I agree, maybe there's a way to replicate the pheromones."

Amid the crumbling ruins of a grand department store, its glass facade shattered and debris strewn across the icy floor, two weary survivors trudged forward. The air was thick with the acrid scent of gun smoke, punctuated by the sharp cracks of gunfire reverberating through the desolate space. Each footstep they took echoed like a haunting drumbeat in the silence, a stark reminder of their relentless fight for existence.

Their faces, etched with exhaustion, betrayed the harsh reality they faced - a world where every decision could mean life or death. With wary eyes scanning their surroundings, they moved cautiously, knowing that in this unforgiving landscape, the line between humanity and savagery was blurred beyond recognition. Every corner could hold unseen dangers, every darkened alcove whispered of impending peril yet to reveal itself.

Chapter 20

Making their way cautiously through Hephaestus' isles, Rowan and Buirke joined the others at the weathered storefront's entrance. As they neared the group, Jasper's eyes widened when he caught sight of his wounded father being carefully assisted out; without hesitation, Jasper ran toward them, his determined stride mirrored by Haider trailing closely behind.

As Jasper helped hold his father, no words were necessary—as he grateful nod toward Rowan, who firmly supported his father on the opposite side, spoke volumes.

"Al, Buirke needs patching up," Rowan said with an edge of concern.

"On it," Al replied briskly, unzipping his backpack to reveal neatly organized medical supplies.

Rowan then stepped closer to the group as Haider seamlessly took over supporting the injured Buirke. "How's it looking out there, Val?" he queried, his voice low. "Haider, get your people on comms and have them ready to receive Buirke immediately."

Haider acknowledged with a firm nod, replying, "Absolutely."

Now kneeling beside Val, Rowan listened as she shifted her

focus back to the rifle scope that scanned the snow-dusted parking lot outside. "It's been as quiet—at least ten minutes since we last saw a Skin-walker," she reported, her eyes never leaving the crisp, shifting view through her scope.

Rowan took a slow sip from his canteen, the cool liquid briefly easing the tension in his throat. "That's what I like to hear," he whispered, his voice barely audible over the distant howls of the wind. Then, with a sense of urgency that matched the fading twilight, he called out, "Spence, get the generator ready to move. Make sure everyone is loaded with fresh mags, and let Haider know he's responsible for making sure Buirke doesn't slow the group down."

"On it," Spence spoke out. "And what's the plan after that?"

"Nothing elaborate. We'll haul ourselves and the generator back to the vehicles. The men will carry the generator, and Val and Mia will cover. But once we're back at Haven, I plan on having a long, uninterrupted chat with Mitch," Rowan explained, his gaze briefly drifting to watch Buirke as Al bandaged his injury. With Spence departing to execute his task, Rowan took another measured drink from his canteen before tucking it away. He glanced over to Val, whose silence seemed to carry the weight of her thoughts. "What's wrong?" he asked softly as he peered over the half wall, his eyes straining to catch any disturbance in the store's snow-swept parking lot.

Val's voice, calm yet edged with worry, broke through the quiet. "This entire ordeal has me thinking—those scouts, why come after us? Something tells me they didn't act on a whim. It almost seems like they were testing us, gauging our reaction to a perfectly orchestrated ambush. I can't shake the feeling we're being swept up into something far bigger and more insidious than we can comprehend."

Rowan's eyes narrowed in agreement as several tense seconds passed with the two of them scanning the silent, snowy expanse. "I agree," he admitted, the layers of their shared unease palpable. "They had us on our heels. If the scouts had attacked at the same time, they could have easily finished us off," he paused as if thinking on his words. "But one thing's for sure—let's not stick around long enough to find out if they decide to come back."

Almost as if on cue, Al returned, his voice carrying a mix of relief and urgency. "Rowan, Buirke's all patched up and ready to roll."

"How's he holding up?" Rowan inquired, his concern evident.

"Other than a broken leg, he's stable. I managed to secure a splint, though we should get him back to safe ground to be sure. I'm more worried about the threat of infection—the skin around the wound is already showing signs of discoloration. Who knows what bacteria Wulvers carry? And we don't have anything to ward off a fever if it kicks in."

Rowan's tone softened as he replied, "Okay, good work. See that Haider has him ready to move at a moment's notice."

With a clear directive, Al announced, "Time to move. It's getting late, and I don't need to remind anyone how critical it is to be back before darkness sets in." His words cut through the lingering silence as he strode toward the generator, stationed just outside the store's entrance.

Haider's arm provided a sturdy crutch for Buirke as he pressed forward, his gait unsteady from the injury. The team had gathered by the generator, their faces etched with purpose rather than fear. Each member moved with a sense of purpose as they followed silent cues, swiftly securing the generator. Val and Mia positioned themselves strategically in the front in back. Their eyes scanned the desolate expanse of Hephaestus' parking lot, alert to any potential threats.

Taking command of the moment, Rowan inhaled deeply, drawing strength from the cold air before he brusquely ordered, "Let's go."

They hustled across the parking lot, their hurried steps echoing on the hard, cracked pavement as they reached a wall that had earlier thwarted their progress. Without hesitation, Mia retrieved explosives from her backpack, planting them deftly along the wall. With practiced precision, she and the team cleared the area before she detonated the charges, and seconds a breach was formed—a door to the narrow street beyond.

As the team made their swift descent down the narrow street of Garratt Lane, they arrived at their vehicles only to be pleasantly surprised by their intact condition. After a quick but thorough scan for any unusual disturbances, the all-clear was given; the generator was then placed on Mammoth for transport.

Rowan ensured that Buirke was carefully placed into the Mammoth so that Al could keep a vigilant watch over him. Meanwhile, Rowan took his seat in the passenger compartment of the rugged Scorpion, with Val in the driver's seat dutifully following behind Haider and Jasper, who led the determined convoy back to Haven.

Clutching his radio, "Haider, what's our ETA?"

After a brief pause, Haider responded, "Maybe thirty-five minutes, if the weather holds up."

"Copy that," Rowan replied, setting the radio atop the

dashboard and leaning back, his head briefly resting against the worn seat. Almost rhetorically, he then asked, "Val, I'm not sure this is or us after all?" His voice was soft, touched with a hint of wry humor as he gazed out the windshield into the icy twilight.

Val offered him a steady, reassuring look. "You're doing what you think is best, and that's all we need from you," she answered, her eyes returning to the road as if the tracks of fate lay ahead.

Suppressing the tempest of his emotions, Rowan fell silent. With the hum of the vehicle as his only lullaby, he closed his eyes for a brief respite, finding solace in the calm before the inevitable storm.

Chapter 21

After what felt like endless hours of sleep, Val gently shook Rowan awake from his heavy slumber.

"Check this out," she said.

Outside, the storm had momentarily relented, and the once-ferocious snow drifts were now settling into quiet dignity. With the snowy haze gone, Rowan's eyes feasted upon Haven, where the once-familiar London Mall unfurled its long stretch toward Buckingham Palace. The majestic trees that once heralded the palace's approach had now given way to tall, imposing fences, a testament to the heightened security precautions Mitch had meticulously installed.

Drifting past these sights, Rowan's gaze swept over a labyrinth of defenses—notably, a tremendous minefield extending outward more than a hundred yards from Haven's outer wall. This lethal barrier could only be safely traversed by following the illuminated, carefully marked pathway when provided or by relying on the sophisticated navigation systems embedded within the specialized Tec-Comms.

Past the treacherous minefield, a daunting obstacle loomed ahead: a ramshackle fifteen-foot barrier fashioned from salvaged remnants of the old world. At its pinnacle, jagged razor wire caught the feeble sunlight, casting ominous glints across the desolate landscape. Originally a makeshift defense, plans for a sturdier replacement were underway.

Along the makeshift barricade, Haven's resilient denizens toiled ceaselessly to raise a new structure - a solid ten-foot brick wall positioned strategically behind the razor wire fence. This intermediary zone provided ample space for vigilant sentries to maintain constant vigilance, an essential measure in a territory plagued by relentless and savage storms.

At the fence's entrance, two sturdy, roofed watchtowers flanked the retractable gate. Perched atop these watchtowers, two guards clad in heavy snow fatigue parkas maintained swift vigilance over the area, their eyes scanning the surroundings with disciplined alertness. Below them, two immaculate white snowmobiles promised rapid intervention should the need arise.

As Haider's vehicle approached, one of the guards swiftly waved him through while the retractable gates parted with a smooth mechanical elegance. Haider carefully maneuvered his vehicle into the secure compound, coming to a stop just inside the main gate before engaging in quiet conversation with the watchtower guards. After a few tense seconds during which the guard's wary glance lingered on the rugged exterior of the Scorpion vehicle, Haider was given the silent clearance to proceed.

Inside the fortified gates, the caravan pivoted left at a meticulously maintained quad that sat proudly at the heart of Haven, guiding them southwestward. Dominating the center of this open space was the magnificent eighty-two-foot-high Victor Memorial. On its apex stood a radiant golden statue of Queen Victoria, encrusted with icicles that never melted— a detail that had earned her the affectionate nickname "the

Ice Queen" from the local children. Carved from gleaming white marble, the memorial boasted ornate figures, angelic and heroic, etched along its base. The sight was nothing short of breathtaking, serving as a poignant reminder of a glorious past that had once shone with promise.

As Rowan's journey continued outside Haven's southern wing, he observed an eclectic mix of people diligently toiling within expansive greenhouses, nearly as large as professional basketball courts. Adjacent structures buzzed with the activity of farm animals, their quiet companionship contrasting with the severe chill of the outside world, temperatures that dropped well below 25°. Strikingly, the workers inside donned attire more suited to balmy days. It was increasingly clear that the resilient people of Haven were here to stay, willing to rebuild their lives and their community.

By day, Haven thrummed with life. People moved purposefully in all directions, each fulfilling their daily duties, while vigilant soldiers patrolled the vicinity on ATVs and snowmobiles. Children could be seen playing soccer on a freshly plowed patch of ground—a heartening reminder to Rowan that a good life was still possible. In every joyous detail, from the camaraderie that filled the air to the quiet hum of hard work, Haven exuded a genuine sense of community—something Rowan had not witnessed since the collapse of the NWF.

It was not long before their vehicles were pulling up in front of the sprawling garage, the team collectively watched three caution lights begin flashing on the control panel. With a resonating creak, two enormous hydraulic doors slowly split aside, unleashing a cascade of swirling snow that fell like a delicate curtain from above. As the doors parted fully, what lay beyond was a vibrant hive of activity: men and women burst about in organized chaos, each engrossed in their tasks, while vehicle parts swung overhead suspended from mechanized rafters and lifts. Two men stationed on either side of the door waved them toward a neatly designated parking spot, orchestrating the arrival with brisk efficiency. It all reminded Rowan of his early years of wandering numerous military bases.

Once all three vehicles were parked in their assigned places, three steadfast members of Haven's crew promptly approached the Mammoth. Within seconds, the doors were open, and Buirke was being whisked away to the infirmary while Al accompanied them, offering what aid he could.

"I haven't said this in a long time, but I'm glad to be back," Spence remarked warmly as he approached Rowan, his weapon slung casually across his shoulder.

"At the moment, I wish I felt the same," Rowan replied somberly, his eyes following Buirke's hurried departure.

Before Rowan could dwell further on these thoughts, he found himself surrounded by Mitch and two of his armed officers—one of them being the ever-reliable Trevor.

"I thought I'd never see the day when bandits—excuse me, former bandits—kept their word. I guess humanity isn't as doomed as we once feared," Mitch said with a satisfied smile playing on his lips. "I want to thank you all for your aid in this matter." As his remaining squad members joined Rowan, the tension was palpable.

"Success? We damn near died out there," Rook blurted out, his tone edged with urgency, while Mia nodded in earnest agreement at his side.

"Hold off, Rook," Rowan interjected, raising his hand to

pacify the outburst. "But he does have a point, Mitch. The mission was a narrow escape, and we nearly lost Buirke. I wouldn't call this a triumph. True success is built on trust, and frankly, you essentially sent us on a suicide mission. At the very least, you could have briefed us about the Skin-walkers or their pets. My team risked everything for a generator—the least you could have done was provide proper intel."

Mitch's expression softened as he replied, "You're right on several counts, Rowan. But remember, I just met you only hours ago. I'm not one to extend my trust to outsiders without caution. This mission wasn't just about reclaiming a generator; it was a test to gauge how you and your team handled extreme circumstances. And I must say, everyone performed admirably. In my view, the mission was a success. You recovered the generator, protected my men, and earned your place among us. If that isn't success, then I challenge your very definition of the term. Dr. Orion questioned your viability to complete the mission, but Buirke swore to her that your team could be a valuable asset for our community—and so far, I believe he's right."

"*Orion,*" Rowan's mind drifted for a moment to Dr. Orion—the enigmatic doctor who had sent them on this convoluted quest for the generator. "*Why would she be concerned about us?*"

"We appreciate the gratitude," Rowan finally said, his voice both measured and firm. "But if mishaps like this occur again, more than just words will need to be exchanged." Taking a deliberate step closer to Mitch, his tone grew resolute.

"Your point is taken, Rowan. I'll ensure that doesn't happen again. Now, where is the generator?" Mitch inquired, shifting the conversation without missing a beat.

"It's in the Mammoth. Rook, can you show them?" Rowan instructed without hesitation.

"Gotcha," Rook replied instantly as Mitch directed his team to follow.

"Rowan, while the generator is being taken care of, can we have a private word?" Mitch asked, his tone low and conspiratorial.

Rowan glanced at his team, each member wearing expressions ranging from apprehensive to skeptical, then met Mitch's eyes. "Sure. Guys, restock the vehicles and get them cleaned up—it's been a while," he ordered before stepping away with Mitch.

Exiting the bustling garage into the cool embrace of the South Wing, with his hands clasped behind his back, Mitch broke the silence. "Rowan, I know you might think I'm secretive. But in order to keep a place like Haven operational, some things must remain under wraps. You were once a military man, after all." He paused, his voice dropping to a reflective murmur. "You're a strong leader, and I wager what little I own that it's due to genuine prowess. Not everyone who calls themselves a leader can bear the weight of that title. Leadership is forged in blood and honed in fire."

Silent steps echoed as Rowan strode next to him through the extended, lavishly adorned hallway. As he had not seen much of Haven, his gaze swept across the fusion of old-world charm and futuristic elements: windows gleaming with golden gilding, columns bearing intricate carvings, paintings immortalizing England's historical legends, and transparent screens displaying live updates on routes, drills, and the day's culinary offerings.

"Now that we've got the generator secured, there's something I need to know. What exactly are these Stalkers, and what's their origin?" Rowan inquired, his tone grave as he halted abruptly in the hall.

Mitch sighed, pausing in his tracks, "Look, I promised to let you into Haven, not to become your personal informant. You can't expect me to hand over the keys to this city in a single day. Building trust takes time and demonstrated dedication. That said, Mr. Rowan, with you here, we could achieve great things. With that, I also appreciate your saving Buirke; his loss would have been irreparable. I'll share something with you: nearly a decade ago, the Consul stationed me here to manage security at the fort. In those days, much of the NWF administration had immense faith in my abilities—and looking around at what Fort Haven has become, I'd say their faith was well-placed. Most of the soldiers here were once part of my personal security detail. The others either came from the outside or were born here. When state officials abandoned their posts in the name of survival, we stayed behind and made a promise— to take in outcasts and salvage what was left of humanity. True sacrifice paved the way for our new beginning."

"What does this have to do with Stalkers?" Rowan said.

"Have patience, Rowan. I'm getting to that. Before anyone is allowed to settle in Haven's community, they must be tested for harmful pathogens. With that, I had my doctor sample your blood for such dangers."

Rowan's eyes widened in disbelief. "You took our blood without permission? I thought this place was civilized."

Mitch's tone softened but remained strong, "To administer proper treatment for any potential injuries as you came in, it had to be done immediately. Everyone was unconscious, so I made the call. I do apologize, but it was a necessary measure."

Rowan pressed further, "And what did the tests show?"

"Continue with me," Mitch directed with a firm tone, motioning for Rowan to follow. Guiding them towards a massive steel door that stood sentinel, flanked by a lone guard, Mitch elaborated, "The medical team confirmed that all is in excellent order with you and your people." He pivoted to address the soldier standing watch, who briefly appraised Rowan before receiving assurance from Mitch. "Stand down, soldier. He's with me, of course."

"But sir, regulation says—"

"And who wrote those regulations, soldier?" Mitch asked with authority.

"That would be you, sir," the soldier said.

"Then he's with me," Mitch added.

"Of course, sir," the guard said, with a nod of acknowledgment, smoothly swiping his magnetic key card over the reader. As the door parted with a soft hiss, it unveiled a realm that beckoned Rowan into its heart—a sprawling expanse alive with the hum of machinery and the focused energy of scientists engrossed in their work. The air thrummed with an undercurrent of innovation, each corner adorned with intricate devices and holographic displays that painted a scene of advanced technology unlike anything Rowan had laid eyes on since before the world fell apart.

"So here we are, standing at the threshold of a partnership which can potentially help not only us but also those less fortunate. You've shown your capabilities, and so, I stand by my word: you help me, and I help you. What do you say?" Mitch said, extending his hand in a gesture both sincere and binding.

Rowan's mind raced as memories of years spent with Larissa

intermingled with visions of Haven—the smiling faces, the resilient spirit of its people. He needed this new life as much as his team did. Finally, meeting Mitch's expectant gaze, he extended his own hand. Locking eyes with Mitch, he declared, "If you ever go back on your word, or sabotage my team. I'll be sure to turn all my capabilities on you and anyone else who attempts to stand in my way. What do you say?"

Mitch smiled broadly and nodded in agreement. "I think we are in agreement, Mr. Rowan." Releasing his grip.

"What's in there?" Rowan asked, gesturing to the secured room where scientists worked diligently in their white coats.

"Well, that's why you are here," Mitch added as he turned and strode through the guarded door marked *Authorized Personnel Only.*

Rowan gave the soldier one more glance before following suit, as the heavy steel doors closed behind them. The weight of new alliances and hard-won truths is settling within.

Chapter 22

While Rowan strode away with Mitch, the rest of the squad lingered behind, sticking to orders despite the grim task ahead. No one particularly relished the chore of scrubbing down the battered vehicles, their surfaces uncleaned for years since the last proper maintenance.

Val and Rook shouldered the responsibility of managing the battered Scorpion, while Mia meticulously unloaded an arsenal from the Mammoth. Meanwhile, Trevor, deep in his own anxious thoughts, nervously crept up behind the group.

"Merry Christmas," said Trevor, walking up to the group, finding Mia preoccupied with her task. His unexpected greeting caused everyone to cease their rut task and turn their attention toward him.

"Thank you, Pal. It's been ages since I heard those kind words," Spence replied with a warm, wry smile. "Hell, I didn't even realize it was that time of year; it's looked the same outside for nearly a decade."

Before anyone could protest, Trevor raised a hand toward Mia. "Sorry, but I was talking to the lady," he said with a roll of his eyes, nodding in her direction.

Spence scoffed, "What... Mia, she's no lady—she's one of us." No sooner had the words left his mouth than Mia used one of the rifles she was carrying to give a sharp retort in the form of a strike to his side.

"Owch!" Spence squealed, clutching his wound.

"Don't pay that fool no mind," Al said, stepping forward with a cocky grin. "He's bitter that nobody's paying him any attention."

"Can I speak with you privately?" Trevor said, stepping closer to Mia. "I was wondering if you're planning to hit up the feast tonight. Would you mind joining me?"

Mia raised an eyebrow before glancing at Al. After doing her own form of hand language with Al, she looks back at Trevor.

Spence blinked incredulously before saying, "Really? This is something you have to do right now?" He shrugged and then returned to unloading, dismissing their conversation.

Al then interprets Mia's message for Trevor, "She says, I didn't already know there was a feast tonight."

Trevor his eyes darted between Mia and Val, confused as to why Al was speaking for her.

"Yeah, kid, she doesn't speak," Al said matter-of-factly.

"Uh, sorry, I didn't know, didn't realize," Trevor said, trying to correct his mistake, causing Mia to laugh. Facing Mia once more, "Yeah, there's one every year," Trevor said, trying to mask the excitement in his voice with a deep, measured breath. Seeing her hesitation, he motioned her to step aside into a slightly quieter corner near the Mammoth. "Since I'm part of the guard unit – we split into two teams, rotating duties between festivities and keeping watch – I figured it wouldn't hurt if you joined me."

Mia glanced over at the ammo crates. She couldn't help but smile, feeling butterflies in her stomach, but doing her best not to show it before sign language once more.

"Sure," Al interpreted for Mia.

"Great..." Trevor stammered, fighting back genuine enthusiasm. "I'll see you tonight then." He adjusted the rifle slung over his shoulder, his eyes locked on her as she resumed her task.

Trevor lingered for a long moment, watching Mia go back to work. She walked away with a graceful stride that made him forget the perilous world around him. Ever since the day he'd first seen her, something deep had drawn him in. With a newfound sense of purpose, he trudged back to his bunk, feeling reborn in a way he had never experienced before.

Val emerged from the Scorpion as Mia and Trevor parted ways. With a mix of concern and curiosity, she eyed Mia's subtle smile—a message that said, without words, *I'm interested.* Trevor, meanwhile, kept a careful eye on Mia before heading off on his own.

Val put the items in her hand down and walked to Spence, "What was that all about?" Her eyes were fixed on Mia, a mixture of protectiveness and suspicion in her gaze.

"The guy asked Mia to some Christmas dinner tonight," Spence shrugged with a lazy smile. "And if I had to guess, the boy just managed to snag the lady's number."

Val shot him a stern, deadpan look. "Hey, you asked," Spence teased, sauntering up the ramp.

Walking with a purposeful stride, Val approached Mia, who was busy kneeling and organizing ammunition crates. "Mia, can I have a word?"

Mia looked up and wiped grease from her hands as if to say *Sure.*

Val's voice was low and steady. "What did Trevor want with you?"

Mia's cheek twitched as she quickly signed the words *boy, asked, eat, dance, tonight.*

"And how did you answer?" Val pressed, her tone soft but insistent.

Mia frowned, *Why?* she signed.

"Well, I guess your smile said enough," Val said, her eyes scanning the room warily before lowering her voice further. "I get that Trevor seems like a charming guy, but we barely know him or anyone around here. We need to stick together, watch our backs. We can't afford to trust too freely."

Mia's eyes flickered with inner conflict before signing her own version of saying, *I understand, but how can we ever learn to trust if we don't give them a chance? Val, honestly, you only trust Rowan. Out there in the whiteout, it's easy to forget what normal feels like. Even simple acts of trust seem like luxuries after all that we've been through; we all deserve a break.* She paused, gathering her thoughts. *Besides, getting to know him could at least let me see what's really going on here.*

Val sighed, struggling between caution and understanding. "I'm not trying to meddle in your life, Mia. I just worry—we can't allow ourselves to be blindsided by strangers, however appealing they might be."

Mia closed the crate and started to walk away before facing her once more, *I am not the one you should be talking to. He's the only one taking tours. Maybe he agrees with me,* she ended her sign language.

Left standing alone, Val couldn't help but acknowledge the harsh truth in Mia's words. Yes, Mia's natural reserve meant that she trusted no one easily, but that very wariness had also kept her alive. Even as Haven offered a final respite from the bitter cold and relentless violence, Val's senses did not allow her to open herself up so freely. All she could do was remain vigilant and protect the team at all costs.

Chapter 23

As they walk deeper into Haven's lab, Mitch guides Rowan through a labyrinth of state-of-the-art labs. The air hummed with the electricity of innovation, and Rowan couldn't help but marvel at the technological prowess displayed around him.

He watched as scientists, their faces intense with concentration, worked in separate glass-walled cubicles. Each lab was a self-contained world of advanced tech, where researchers hunched over complex machinery and manipulated holographic displays that shimmered like ghostly apparitions in the dim light.

Rowan's eyes were drawn to one particular display - a three-dimensional projection of what appeared to be a Stalker. It rotated slowly in mid-air, its grotesque form captured in chilling detail. He could see every twisted sinew, every mutated bone structure. A scientist stood before it, her fingers dancing across an invisible keyboard as she tweaked parameters on the creature's digital doppelganger.

"Quite something, isn't it?" Mitch broke the silence between them. His voice echoed slightly off the sterile white walls and glass partitions.

Rowan grunted in response, his gaze still transfixed on the holographic beast. "Never seen anything like this," he admitted gruffly.

Mitch chuckled lightly at that. "Welcome to Haven's heart," he said grandly with an expansive gesture towards their surroundings.

As they walked further into the maze-like complex, Mitch raised his hand and called out to someone ahead of them. "Dr. Orion!" His voice cut sharply through the low hum of activity around them.

After a brief moment, Dr. Orion turned from where she had been delivering instructions to an assistant. Her eyes were sharp and intelligent behind her protective goggles; her stance exuded authority even from a distance.

Her gaze shifted from Mitch to Rowan as they approached, assessing him with clinical precision that made him feel somewhat like another specimen under her microscope.

"Mitch," giving him a nod. "It's good to see you again to Mr. Rowan," Dr. Orion greeted as they stopped in front of her.

"Nice to see you as well," Rowan greeted in return, looking into her deep eyes. He was baffled at how he failed to notice the hint of green in her light brown eyes. It was something about them that made him feel as though she could look into his very being. A feeling that made him slightly uncomfortable. Straightening up his posture, "And it's just Rowan by the way."

"Alright, Rowan. Also, before it slips my mind, I would like to apologize for the manner I displayed myself earlier today in the garage. With so much going on and personal deadlines, I don't know what came over me, that's not my usual persona," she said.

"It's not a problem, as much as it pains me to say, but I'm used to it," Rowan said.

'Anyways, what brings you to my laboratories?" she placed

her hand into her lab coat pockets.

"I brought him here to check out the labs. I figured if he and his squad are going to be staying here and working on the expedition crews, he should at least know of Project Eve like everyone else," taking a cigar from his shirt pocket and lighting it. Taking a good pull and exhaled, "No more secrets."

"Okay, I see where this is going," clasping her hands together. "Shall we proceed with this tour?"

"I think we should," Mitch agreed with a smile.

"Follow me," Orion said and turned on her heels.

Shortly after, they arrived at a set of imposing double sliding doors flanked by more vigilant guards. With a subtle gesture, the guards yielded, and the sleek automatic doors parted smoothly with a hydraulic hiss. The laboratory wing mirrored Haven's grandeur, boasting a lofty vaulted ceiling and windows adorned with intricate golden frames. Gone were the elegant chandeliers of old; in their place stood precise rows of humming fluorescent tubes that bathed the space in clinical brightness, illuminating every detail for the diligent scientists within.

Workstations with sleek glass countertops gleamed under the bright overhead lights, showcasing an array of specialized tools and devices neatly organized in each cabinet. The scientists, clad in pristine white lab coats, moved with practiced efficiency within the grid-like layout of the room. Rowan continued to marvel at their meticulous work as they manipulated intricate instruments with unwavering concentration, each motion deliberate and purposeful.

It struck Rowan how every individual seamlessly integrated into this complex choreography of scientific exploration, akin to a finely tuned mechanism where every cog had its place and function. The scene before him was not just a workspace; it was a living testament to expertise and dedication, a harmonious ballet of intellect and technology, something he could appreciate.

"Like I said, Rowan, initially we were running this place as the NWF left it. But once Dr. Orion came on board, it wasn't long before it started to come into its current state. And did not take long before we started gathering resources at the nearby colleges and hospitals, which provided critical technology to run this place," Mitch informed.

"Don't forget that once governments collapsed, people were looking frantically to find a place to belong. And lucky for us, many of them found their way here," Orion added as she walked and observed the happenings of the lab. "Jerry, don't forget to bring me those calculations I asked for," spotting one of her scientists sitting at their desk.

"I should have them too soon," they responded, never taking their eyes from the holographic display in front of them.

"Look, all this is nice and all. But I'm not going to beat around the giant bush here. So, what is this lab really about? And I'm smart enough to know that you guys are not growing cabbages. How does this fit in with the stalkers and needing our blood?" Rowan asked, trading looks with the two of them.

"Well, I see that Mitch has shared some information with you," she added, tucking loose hair that fell to her face behind her ear.

"The way I see it, Dr. Orion, I promised him there would be no more secrets as long as he and his team are putting their lives on the line," Mitch chimed in.

"Such a noble endeavor," she murmured, proceeding towards a staircase crafted from stone and glass positioned at the heart of the lab. "Honestly, I think the work happening in this facility could spark a resurgence of life on this icy world, benefiting not just humans but all creatures, whether living or extinct," she expressed as she ascended the steps, with Rowan walking beside her and Mitch trailing close behind.

"I'm not sure I follow," Rowan responded.

"When those meteoroids began to strike the planet, everyone had guaranteed that millions upon millions of species would die. Either from the initial impacts increasing global temperatures that caused many unseen processes, the de-salination of the oceans, or this wintry climate. What I'm attempting to do...excuse me. What we're trying to do is rekindle life all over the planet, or at least allow what's left to flourish," she finished, reaching the top stairs.

Ascending the final flight of stairs, Dr. Orion pulled her magnetic card from her lab coat and waved it in front of the reader. The door to the third-floor laboratories yielded to her touch, granting access to a realm that seemed plucked from the vivid pages of a futuristic novel rather than reality. Unlike the clinical efficiency of the second floor, this section exuded an otherworldly aura.

Within this enclave of scientific marvels, intricate glass cylinders stood sentinel in varying sizes and shapes, each housing a unique tableau. Some enclosures cradled verdant flora in delicate bloom, their leaves unfurling like emerald whispers against the transparent walls. Others held suspended figures - not mere specimens but Stalkers themselves - ensconced in an enigmatic liquid medium that refracted light in mesmerizing patterns.

The scene was a symphony of contrasts: life flourishing amidst containment, beauty entwined with danger in these glass-bound worlds that hinted at both the fragility and resilience of existence.

"What's this? You're keeping Stalkers here, too?" Rowan inquired, studying the creatures intently.

"The teams occasionally bring in specimens for them to study," Mitch replied, taking a step up to the container.

"What better way to understand them if not by examining their physical structure under the microscope," Dr. Orion said, placing her badge back in her coat.

"So, what did you learn about them?" Rowan asked.

"A lot, actually. In most cases, each one possessed human genes and other genes from the local wildlife," Orion said, circling the container with the Stalker."

"Human genes....that's impossible. That's impossible, right? That would only mean they're—," Rowan responded, trying to read what she was leading to.

"Human," Mitch continued, cutting Rowan off. "You'll be absolutely correct, Mr. Rowan. And to be more precise, they are family and friends of ours, and once lived here," he said, placing his hands in his pocket, and giving Orion a quick glance.

Rowan stood in stunned silence, grappling with the overwhelming question that echoed through his mind, leaving him at a loss for words. "How is that?" he finally muttered.

"Remember the alien that we mentioned earlier? Well, it's not what you may think. It's a microbe-organism, the same organism that allows us to grow vegetation and livestock faster. Exactly five times faster," she continued as she made her way to a nearby board containing written formulas and pictures of wildlife in various stages of growth and transformation. We call this organism EVE, for Evolutionary Enhancements."

"EVE, the mother of us all. And that which will bring life back to this white planet," Mitch commented.

Unlike the first Eve who failed mankind, this one will benefit in unimaginable ways. You see, this organism is nothing like anything on earth. In fact, classifying it as a bacteria is wrong; it just happens to fit in that category better than a virus, as viruses usually destroy cells. This species takes resources, energy from its host without the host dying. In fact, it helps the host produce more energy effectively by making it stronger and more durable. Thus, by multiplying itself and merging with every cell in the host's body, the host benefits, and the bacteria have an endless supply of energy provided by the host," Orion continued.

"A partnership," Rowan added, as Mitch began to walk the lab, allowing them to talk.

"Symbioses to be exact....Once this partnership, as you call it, has been established, the host can grow stronger, healthier, and invulnerable to other diseases. Drastically increasing its life span. A few years back, Haven was on the verge of critically low resources, and we had no choice but to inject the EVE into our animals, making them fit and increase offspring output. As for vegetation, we splice the seeds with EVE before germination. This allowed our plants to grow in unforgiving environments, even with minimal light," Dr. Orion explained.

"EVE searches for the perfect host, increasing the host's natural attributes. There are literally unimaginable possibilities, including longevity of life. As it constantly repairs degenerated and damaged cells," Orion continued.

"Seems like you're hinting at eternal life, Doc?" Rowan remarked, his gaze shifting from the tanks to Dr. Orion.

"Not eternal life but longevity. I've theorized that if EVE can constantly repair degenerated cells, its host can possibly live past its normal expectancy."

"And, somehow, you don't see this as playing God," Rowan commented.

"God left this planet a long time ago," Dr. Orion declared with unwavering certainty. "If anything, this is literally a gift from the heavens. But if you still see this as playing God, then mankind has been playing God for thousands of years. Did you know that when the bulb of an onion is cut and it is planted, the onion that grows is just cloned from the onion it was cut from? As the germinated bulb grows, it will have the same DNA structure as the first," she smiled, "Think of what we are doing here as preserving what has already been created. EVE came from the heavens as a gift to mankind. We simply need to take it by the horns, as you Americans like to say. And sometimes that even requires sacrifices."

"What kind of sacrifices are you talking about. I know this has to have an effect on people when they eat what's cooked up in this lab," Rowan said, looking for an answer from either of them.

"You're right again. EVE does have both positive and negative attributes to those who consume foods treated with the bacteria. As I stated earlier, the benefit of EVE is that it makes everything affected by it less vulnerable to illnesses. In some rare cases, it can even improve muscle structure, giving an increase in speed and strength. Which, for us, means more meat and labor from our livestock," she continued, sliding him pictures of healthy cattle.

"Now what about the negatives?" Rowan asked.

"The negatives are even rarer but are more drastic. The only negative that we can currently explain is that of the B+ blood type," taking a deep breath, she continued, "Any individual with B+ blood type who is treated with EVE, they begin to change.

"You mean, infected," Rowan said firmly.

Ignoring his comment, "Losing all knowledge of who they are. With no sense of family or community. They become...."

"Whoa....Whoa...Whoa! So the Stalkers are really your people?" Rowan asked, taking a step back from the table. "So that's what you meant about family. How in the hell do they become blood thirsty that way?"

"Like we said, it has to do with the B+ blood type. EVE somehow and ways taps into that genetic makeup and evolves it beyond what others experience. Stalkers have increases in all senses, along with an increase in strength and speed. But like every step in evolution, there is a trade off. With their increase, there is a decrease in their intellectual level."

"Rowan, you have to understand," Mitch interjected, coming back to rejoin them. "As the good doctor has shared, it was only a few years ago that Haven was running extremely low on resources, making it mandatory that all began to ration. At this point, we no longer had the benefit of testing the negative effects of EVE. So, on the verge of extinction, I ordered that EVE be put into effect. That call not only saved Haven by increasing our food output, but it also bought us more time to study its effects on the human body. Which Dr. Orion has been working towards since."

"What became of those who were first affected?" Rowan inquired of Dr. Orion, noticing her gaze shift downward.

A tense hush fell over the room before Mitch spoke on behalf of Dr. Orion, "The original residents present during the initial outbreak refer to it as the Exodus. When we realized who was at risk we couldn't bear to harm our loved ones. Therefore, before their transformation into those creatures was complete, we offered them the choice to depart Haven and face the unknown outside our walls."

"And if they stayed, that only meant their end anyway," Rowan said, finishing Mitch's sentence, glancing at Dr. Orion again, who had finally raised her head.

"That's correct. Their presence here as infected would only have increased the amount of bloodshed as they turned. Their natural instinct of violence always overrides their rational thinking. At the time, the Exodus was our and remains our only option until we find the reasons behind the AB+ marker mutation."

Taking a moment to gather his thoughts, "This is not the type of information you hide from people. You invited us in and fed us contaminated food, infected with alien bacteria. That means anyone from my team could be infected without them knowing," locking eyes with them.

"Don't worry. You remember the blood test that everyone was given the day you arrived. Well, it was not a prevention to keep us from getting infected. It was a precaution to make sure you were not B+. Keeping us from infecting you," Mitch answered.

"What if we were AB+?"

"Simple. We would have sent you on your way, with no food and basic medical treatment," Mitch answered.

"I can't believe this. You should have allowed us to at least consent to being treated with this EVE," Rowan continued.

"We did, when I gave you the option to leave or help us and stay," Mitch added.

"Don't worry, Rowan, all measures have been taken. As

everyone living here is aware of EVE and is happy to be a part of such history-making. No one is left in the dark," Orion started to reassure him. "The test we have is simply a way to ensure that another Exodus does not take place. Which ultimately means that we can take in more outsiders like yourself."

"That brings to mind," Mitch said as he reached into his back pocket and removed a mag-card. "Here you go," extending it to Rowan.

"What's this for?" He asked.

"As you may have noticed, many of the doors around Haven have a magnetic card reader and locks. This card will give you access to areas that you would need to reach, such as the garage, living quarters, and the weapons depot. Your team can pick theirs up from the security office. The card contains information about you, your name, and blood type. They also track the movement of each individual who wears them, allowing security to keep an eye on everyone from a single place. Even children are issued cards at the age of six. Each card can be deactivated in the event that the cardholder needs to be quarantined."

"Why is my blood type provided here?" glancing down at the tan and white card with the letter B written in bold on it.

"Blood types are presented to decrease the likelihood that the forbidden blood type would be born. Having both men and women enclosed from the outside forces, they are bound to have offspring, so there is no need to try to keep it from happening. However, we can make everyone aware of what blood types are more likely to create B+. We hope that by doing this, individuals take the correct measures to prevent it from happening," Orion added.

"Because of this openness, the number of babies born with

AB+ blood type has decreased to zero since introducing this protocol," Mitch chimed in.

Rowan's grip tightened around the magnetic card, his gaze fixed on its surface. The information bombarding him was overwhelming, leaving him unsure of how to process it logically. While he recognized the necessity of the safety protocols in Haven to contain Stalker threats, a surge of anger made him want to unload his weapons on both individuals responsible for their current bizarre situation. The sudden shift from battling bloodthirsty creatures one night to waking up among those who birthed them, only to discover an alien parasite within himself, was beyond surreal. This week was spiraling into the most chaotic period he had ever experienced.

"Mr. Rowan, I know this is a lot to take in, but we do mean well by you, your people, and everyone else here at Haven," Mitch said. "Anyways, let me take you back to your people. I just wanted to hold up my promises. There are no secrets at Haven. My job is to maintain that and to keep this place safe. And now with you and your team, I hope you will help remain with us to keep that mission a priority."

Despite glimpsing Haven's concealed truths, an unshakable sense of underlying mystery lingered in his mind, hinting at a veiled secret beyond his reach. "You're correct. I must return to my comrades. Appreciate the card and your kindness," he murmured, tapping the card gently. Casting a final glance at the pair, "Mitch... Dr. Orion," he acknowledged with a nod before pivoting away. "I'll navigate my way back."

"Hold on. No need for that. I'll see you out," Dr. Orion said, stepping up beside him.

"I'll stay here in the lab to check on a few things. Oh, another thing, Rowan," Mitch said, getting him to turn and face him.

"I would prefer if training started tomorrow. I will have all attendees report to the Training Hall at 0600 hours." Mitch commented while clasping his hands behind his back. "Also, don't forget about the holiday dinner tonight in the Grand Ballroom. It would be an honor if you and your team joined us."

Silently, Rowan gave a nod, and Orion left through the exit on the laboratory's third level. As he departed, Rowan's gaze lingered on a glass enclosure containing a specimen of a Stalker.

"Progress," he muttered to himself.

Once out of earshot, "So how does EVE affect animals, and how do you deal with it? As I don't see any Stalker dogs running around here," Rowan asked Dr. Orion.

"Yes, I assume you're referring to the Wulvers. They're a nasty beast. Pretty much means Werewolf to the Scotts. Someone said the name, and it stuck. Did you encounter them out there?

"I practically kept one from kissing Buirke," he answered.

"Truth be told, we are not exactly sure how EVE affects animals on a genetic level as of yet. That is one of my primary goals to figure out. To answer your question of how we deal with it, easily, we isolate the suspected host, observe them after exposure, document and study any changes, then we exterminate the carrier," Dr. Orion responded with unwavering certainty.

Chapter 24

Wandering alone through the corridors of Haven after leaving Buirke in the medical bay, Al's mind buzzed with uneasy thoughts. The medical staff had confidently assured him that Buirke's injuries were nothing more than superficial scrapes—nothing life-threatening. Yet, as Al mulled it over, he recalled that Buirke had sustained a bite to his shin that completely fractured it. For a man of his age, even a well-treated shin break would demand no less than several weeks of recovery, if not more. And if he did recover, his walk would not be the same.

What unsettled him further was that when Buirke arrived at the med bay, the only things the staff had prepared were simple gauze pads; there were no sutures, no medications, nothing that suggested a meticulous plan to mend or place bone.

Though he barely knew the man, Al couldn't help but feel a pang of sympathy. As a soldier himself, the idea of being forced to leave the only life he'd ever known was unthinkable. Every day, he risked his life, yet since meeting Rowan at that rundown bar in Brazil and joining the ragtag crew, no other pursuit had managed to fill the void with a hint of purpose. Rowan used to say, with a glint in his eye before the world turned upside down, "Being a soldier isn't just a job—it's an all-consuming lifestyle."

That fateful night at the bar, where the neon lights battled the creeping darkness outside, had been a turning point. After being booted from the Boxing Federation amid whispers of alleged steroid use, he had drowned his sorrows in bitter alcohol and reckless pub brawls, desperate not to be left with an empty shell. He still chuckled wryly, remembering how he once thought it brilliant to flirt outrageously with a local thug's girlfriend before staggering into the proprietor's own bar. Typically, five-on-one odds were a challenge he relished, but after a few too many drinks, even a single adversary could spell disaster.

From the far corner of that smoky bar, Rowan and Spence had watched the melee unfold with unique calm. Amid the chaos of fists and shattered faces—one thug getting knocked senseless, another's nose brutally broken until he scrambled off—the duo had finally stepped in, their movements as precise as a well-rehearsed dance. In mere moments, they had dispatched the remaining three thugs, effectively ending the brawl Al had unwittingly ignited. Helping him up from the blood-spattered floor, Rowan had guided him to a table where an unexpected invitation awaited: an offer to join the ranks as a mercenary. In that gritty moment, a bond was forged that would eventually see Al become the medic for Rowan's newly assembled squad—a family he'd come to treasure.

Emerging from his reverie, Al's boots halted when his eyes caught a familiar sign posted on a nearby wall. It matched the one he had seen near the medical bay—a pristine white board edged in red, emblazoned with a magnetic card and the edict: All persons must carry their reader at all times. No exceptions.

"What's this all about?" he murmured softly, his voice barely audible as he scanned down the deserted, echoing corridor where identical signs punctuated every fifty yards like silent sentinels. With a slow, measured pace, he retraced his steps back to their quarters over the next fifteen minutes, hoping to catch a glimpse of his comrades.

$$\Omega \blacksquare \Omega \blacksquare \Omega \blacksquare \Omega$$

Meanwhile, the team had been shifted from the isolated quarters outside to squad communal quarters on the second floor of the West Wing. This area, redesigned for the recovery expedition teams, had shed its antique trappings to make way for functional bedding—walls freshly painted, its erstwhile classic look replaced by a modern air that better suited its hardened inhabitants. A small exhibit in the South Wing now housed the treasured paintings, left behind for those with a taste for nostalgia, while expedition teams kept their surroundings stark and unembellished, much like the harsh world awaiting them beyond Haven's gates.

Inside this refurbished space, Rowan found the room sprawling and identical in size to their old communal quarters, complete with long rows of military bunk beds. Those with families were granted separate chambers whenever possible, a luxury amid these pragmatic arrangements. His team, already settled in a clearly marked section of the room, was busily unpacking personal effects into foot lockers or huddled in animated clusters discussing their day.

"As if the spotlight hadn't found its way to you already," Spence grinned as Rowan made his entrance, clapping him on the back. "I took the honor of lugging your heavy gear up while you got your VIP pampering. So, tell me—where's my tip?" he teased, extending a calloused hand.

"You'll get it as soon as I track it down," Rowan replied with a mischievous half-smile.

"Ah, isn't that always my luck—always taking the short end of the stick," Spence quipped, his tone light but edged with genuine ribbing.

Rowan's smile softened as he glanced around at his five-man team. "Listen up," he began, his voice firm yet warm, "I know it feels almost surreal being here among all these people, but there's something important you need to know." For the next several minutes, he recounted the unsettling details relayed by Mitch and Dr. Orion—from the EVE infection sweeping through them to the need for magnetic cards, and even Haven's dark ties to the creation of the notorious Stalkers.

"I knew this was too good to be true," Rook interrupted with a skeptical scoff. "Look, as much as I love the free food and the steady heat, I'd gladly trade it all just to keep alien filth out of my system."

"I'm with you on that, Mia, it is something out of a night-mare," Al said, observing Mia's hands in constant motion, her gestures vividly expressing her exasperation.

Rowan raised his hands in a calming gesture. "The fact is, every single one of us here is infected. Dr. Orion explained that the bacteria lurk in everything—meats, fruits, you name it—and only the B+ blood types are negatively affected. The Positive is that luckily enough, none of us fall into that category."

"Positive? Seriously, what could ever possibly be a positive of harboring an alien organism inside you?" Al interjected sharply, his tone laced with incredulity.

"Ease up, Al," Val ordered, her voice cool and measured.

"Ease up? Are you for real? How can I possibly relax when we've been marked by aliens? Fighting little green men is one thing, but this is—" Al retorted, his frustration bubbling over.

"It's not like we had a say in this," Val's calm demeanor breaking as she cut him off. "You heard Rowan, the minute we arrived here, they took our blood to ensure we couldn't morph into Stalkers. Once we took that initial bite or drink, our bodies were claimed by EVE. We just have to accept it."

A heavy silence fell over the group as each member absorbed the weight of their new reality, faces etched with anger and uncertainty. Spence's low mutter cut through the quiet: "This is unreal. I used to fight beasts, but now we have one inside us."

Rowan's gaze swept over the team as he continued, "Beast or bacteria, if anything, we should be happy just to have that collar gone. You all agreed to follow me, and so we've been here for days without any of us falling ill. We've overcome worse than this before, so now is not the time for panic." He paused, scrutinizing Al in particular. "Last thing, Mitch invited us to tonight's Christmas dinner, so that the population can see and greet us. Make sure you report to security to get your ID card; without it, you won't gain access. Remember, these cards log your blood type and track your movements, so keep them on you at all times."

Before he could finish, the door to their chambers opened up, "Good day to you all. I see you've finally heard the word on EVE," came a clear, assertive female voice.

Turning around, Rowan found himself facing a tall brunette in her late thirties, standing at 5'9" with a lithe, well-defined build and nearly flawless skin that belied the harsh world outside. Dressed in rugged brown cargo pants and a dated NWF tactical vest emblazoned with a diamond Raven on the left shoulder.

"Hey there," Rook managed with a faint smile as she approached.

"The name's Lilian, but around here, everyone just calls me Lili. I lead the Raven expedition team," she announced, extending a strong, confident hand.

"Nice to meet you, Lili," Rowan replied warmly, shaking her hand. "I'm Rowan. This is Val, my second in command, along with Spence, Mia, Rook, and Al."

"Pleased to meet you all," she said, stepping back with her hands resting confidently on her hips. "I heard Mitch added you to the Devils, correct?"

"That's right," Rowan confirmed.

"Great to have you with us. You'll see we're short on manpower around here these days - our ranks have thinned out a lot. Oh, and just so you know, Buirke's one reliable fella," Lili said.

"Yeah, he's a good man," Rowan agreed, careful not to reveal that Buirke wouldn't be back anytime soon, and would possibly mean he'll have temporary command of the Devils.

"I apologize for not coming earlier. I try to know the other teams, which helps to maintain relationships between squads. But Mitch has put us on a last-minute expedition outside the walls. We'll be back long before tonight's dinner. And speaking of dinner, are you coming? Trust me, you don't want to miss it. The food here is, well, out of this world," she added with a twinkle in her eye.

"Please, spare us any talk of alien meat," Spence whispered under his breath.

"We'll definitely be there," Rowan replied, his tone light yet sincere.

"Alright, I've got a few more things to handle before the evening. It was a pleasure meeting you all," Lili said as she began to walk away, then paused at the door. "And don't worry about Buirke—he's in good hands. EVE will have him up and about before you know it," she finished, her words lingering as she disappeared down the corridor.

For a few charged seconds, everyone stared after her. Finally, Spence broke the silence with a wry comment, "Is it just me, or is everyone in this place annoyingly friendly?"

"I'd rather have friendly than them turning into flesh-eating beasts," Val shot back, a sardonic smile playing on her lips.

"She can be nice to me any day," Rook chimed in, earning a few knowing glances from his comrades. "I mean, who'd have thought someone could be both kind and, dare I say, attractive nowadays?"

"Come on, man—we didn't think you could find anything outside of nuts, bolts, and engines attractive," Spence teased, drawing a round of laughter.

Mia teased Rook further, forming a heart shape with her thumbs and pointer fingers.

"It's been a while," Rook remarked, his shoulders lifting in a nonchalant gesture.

"Honestly, Rook, you spend more time with the Scorpion than with any of us. I'm surprised you haven't asked Rowan for permission to marry it yet," Spence added, and the banter carried on until even the tight atmosphere began to lighten.

Rowan watched his team—his makeshift family—laugh and bond, a warmth stirring in him despite the looming uncertainties. After so long in the suffocating isolation of The White, where survival often meant losing one's humanity, these moments of camaraderie were as precious as they were rare.

"Alright, everyone," Rowan finally commanded, his tone firm as he scanned the room. "Don't dawdle—get your ID cards made before tonight. We want to at least try to fit in."

"No worries, Rowan," Val replied crisply. "I'll see to it that everyone's sorted."

Stepping away from the group, Al lingered behind and approached Rowan. "Hey, can I have a word?" he said, his tone tentative yet earnest as he glanced at Val, who excused herself.

"What's up, Al?" Rowan asked, genuine concern lacing his voice.

"I wanted to say I'm sorry," Al began quietly. "I didn't mean to question your decisions earlier. I was just...reacting to all this news. I can't shake the feeling that we really don't know what this infection will do in the long haul. I'm not sure if you caught what Lili said at the end. There's no way Buirke is coming back anytime soon. With a fractured shin, recovery in a few days is impossible." He glanced around furtively, as though sharing a secret. "What exactly does EVE do to our bodies?"

Rowan's gaze softened as he glanced at the others nearby. "Well, Dr. Orion mentioned something about EVE existing with its host. To make it stronger, maybe this includes healing as well. But I'm no scientist, this is speculation about all of this."

"What if they are not the ones affected and we are? What if they infected us, just to observe how we react," Al asked.

"Al, I get all that. And just because we are here, doesn't

mean we are putting all our trust in them. But I agree with you, we've got to keep our eyes open and watch out for any signs they might be hiding something. And like every other day, we pull together and get through it."

With that, Al nodded and rejoined the others. Rowan then trudged over to his bed and collapsed onto it, seeking refuge in a moment of quiet solitude. As he stared upward at the soaring, vaulted ceiling, his body sank into the comfort of the bed. Breathing in deeply, he allowed a sense of peace to wash over him, transporting his thoughts back to a time before the Impact—a fleeting reprieve in a turbulent world.

He had long since accepted that he was an old soldier in a rapidly changing new world—a world that demanded he live with the scars of his past and perhaps, someday, find redemption. With his final thoughts lingering on the comrades, he let himself drift into a somber, reflective sleep.

Chapter 25

Ever since Mitch assumed management of Haven, the winter feast had evolved into a celebrated tradition. Originally established as an Old World diversion meant to distract everyone from daily survival struggles, the discovery of EVE had transformed the occasion into a grander annual tribute—a celebration of Haven's newfound ability to host a thriving community.

A few hours preceding the event, Mitch's aides had delivered meticulously tailored penguin tuxedos for the men and flowing dresses paired with elegant makeup kits for the women. Although a few grumbled at the notion of donning such attire, Rowan's silver-tongued persuasion ultimately won them over for one unforgettable night.

Stepping as one cohesive group into the Grand Ballroom felt like being transported back in time. The spacious room glistened as if it had been freshly constructed, its immaculate white walls serving as a canvas for ornate paintings that seemed to shimmer beneath the soft, golden glow of antique chandeliers. Grand tables draped in crisp white and bold red tablecloths lined the perimeter, framing an expansive central floor where a band clad entirely in white played gentle, lilting tunes, summoning the brave souls willing to lose themselves in dance.

Just a few feet inside, amidst clusters of animated conversation and graceful sways, the feast unfolded like a scene plucked from a classic film. A cheerful voice broke through the hum of festivities from their right. "I'm glad everyone made it tonight," said Trevor, his tone warm yet professional. "Mitch asked me to escort you to your seats if you choose to join." His eyes landed on Mia, who dazzled in a backless red silk dress that cinched tightly at her waist before cascading loosely to her feet, revealing her almond-toned skin. "Mia, you look stunning tonight," he added with a playful smile.

Mia's lips trembled into a mischievous, almost childlike grin before signing *Thank You*, which caused a fleeting moment where Trevor's boyish charm and effortless grace had her heart fluttering with unspoken yearning.

However, a subtle tension glowed in the air when Trevor caught sight of Val glaring at him. Quickly, he spun around, lowering his voice in an apologetic murmur, "I'm sorry, Val—you look exquisite as ever." She offered a half-smile in return, the warmth in her eyes softening her quiet reserve.

"Where's Mitch?" Rowan queried, his gaze scanning the room with a practiced leader's precision.

"He's still finalizing a few details. He'll be with us shortly. In the meantime, allow me to guide you to your table," Trevor explained, adding with a conspiratorial wink that Mitch had arranged for their team to be seated closer to the front—a subtle honor weighed with camaraderie and respect.

As they moved steadily toward their designated seats, Spence found himself unable to take his eyes off Val. For the first time, he truly admired her in the gentle luminescence of the ballroom; her pristine white cashmere dress appeared custom-tailored to accentuate every graceful curve of her toned figure. Years of unspoken admiration had built an unyielding familiarity between them, and tonight, Spence entertained hopes of voicing feelings he'd long harbored.

Leaning in from behind, he murmured, "You look amazing, Val," his voice barely above a whisper, not giving her a moment to respond, he continued past her to join Rowan at the forefront.

Val's lips curved into a knowing smile as she continued forward, her quiet confidence commanding respect.

"Did I hear you say what I think you said?" Rowan teased, glancing sideways at Al.

"Yes, you did," Spence replied with a crooked grin, eyes fixed ahead.

"How'd it go?" Rowan added with a soft chuckle

"I suppose you'll know if I ever disappear," Spence laughed.

At the front of the room, Trevor ushered the group to their seats situated just left of the stage, where the band's soft music intertwined with the murmur of delighted conversation and clinking champagne glasses.

Seated comfortably, Rowan savored the sight—the opulent surroundings, the gentle effervescence of celebration—and allowed himself a rare, heartfelt smile.

"So, what's on tonight's menu, Trevor?" Rook asked, clasping his hands together in anticipation.

Trevor replied in his measured, enthusiastic tone, "Expect a lavish spread: a spectrum of meats—beef, lamb, pork, and chicken—accompanied by fresh, vibrant vegetables. Mitch spares no expense during the winter feast; it's the one time of year he really boasts about Haven's abundant surplus. Trust me, our chef conjures up some of the best cuisines this side of the old world." As he settled next to Mia, his eyes twinkled with mischief.

Amid the murmurs of approval, a softly dignified voice greeted from across the table. "Good evening," Dr. Orion announced. The group turned, and Rowan's heart skipped a beat—this was the first time he saw Dr. Orion out of her customary lab coat. Her long hair was artfully swept into a neat bun, framing delicate pearl earrings and a matching necklace that caught the light with every subtle movement.

Trevor quickly looked up and said, "Dr. Orion, it's wonderful to see you! If you haven't found a seat yet, please join us."

"I do hope I'm not intruding," Dr. Orion replied, her tone measured as she surveyed the table for any hint of objection.

"No intrusion at all," Trevor assured cheerfully. "In fact, there's an open seat next to Rowan."

With a subtle, conspiratorial glance between Rowan and Trevor, and noticing Mia's gentle smile, Rowan slid his chair aside to create more space for Orion, who accepted with a warm, grateful nod.

"Doctor," Rowan greeted with respectful formality.

And as she took her seat, it allowed him to get a smell of her perfume, which had a delicate, soft fragrance of wildflowers, reminiscent of spring meadows.

"Call me Orion tonight," she replied.

Not far away, Spence leaned towards the table and marveled aloud, "Nice to see you again, Orion," his tone light yet sincere—a comment that earned Rook a playful, exasperated look.

"Before I forget," Orion continued, drawing the group's attention, "I must thank everyone for assisting in retrieving that generator. It's going to be a tremendous boost for our research. I'm also saddened by the news of Buirke's injury—truly, the man is a walking encyclopedia of these lands. Without him, we'd lose one of our bravest guides on the expeditions." A heavy pause followed before the conversation resumed.

"My apologies for cutting through this moment," Al interjected, "but what exactly is the generator being used for? Hopefully something worth risking our lives for?" His inquiry hung in the air, bordering on impatience.

Spence promptly added, "Al, just enjoy the evening."

"We've been over this already. Let it go for now," Val said, with a gentle firmness.

Yet Al persisted, "I'm merely curious—a pretty face might distract a man, but it won't leave him in the dark."

Before more could be said, Orion interjected softly, "Enough. For clarity's sake, the generators you recovered are going to be converted into bio-generators, using plant oils produced on-site. These bio-generators would power everything—from vehicles and generators to the hot showers we all enjoy. With Haven's rising population, these resources, alongside EVE's contributions, are absolutely crucial. Without them, we'd have no power or food," she ended, allowing the table to fall into a reflective hush as her words sank in.

"Alright, that's enough talk for now—I'm off to grab some grub!" Spence declared, breaking the somber mood. Rising with determined cheer, he headed toward the buffet tables.

His quick movement drew a hearty, "On your six!" from Rook.

Soon enough, the entire table was up, Al momentarily behind.

An astonishing array of culinary delights awaited them at

the buffet. Three enormous roasted pigs were presented on gleaming silver platters, each one invitingly ready to be carved. It was a bounty unlike any feast they'd known in the harsh wilderness—a veritable banquet set in fine China and polished silverware, where each guest eagerly piled their plate high. Even Al, ever the skeptic of Haven's promises, could not resist slicing generous portions of succulent pork.

Contentment radiated from every face as the clatter of plates harmonized with murmurs of satisfaction—a marked contrast from the lean, meager meals of their past. Over the next several minutes, the room filled with laughter, appreciative grunts from the men, and soft smiles from the women observing the communal pleasure.

"Mia, what do you think of this feast?" Trevor asked, sampling a bite of the tender pork.

With playful candor, Mia replied with a nod and smile, as she happily chewed on a mouthful.

Trevor leaned in conspiratorially, "One of our chefs is an old friend of mine—I could arrange a tour of the kitchen after dinner if you're interested."

Immediately getting a thumbs up from her.

"Come on, give us a moment," Spence, his eyes never leaving his heaping plate. "We all know a proper meal is hard to come by these days."

Mia rolled her eyes and waved them off.

"This is the best food we've had in years," Rook, with a gentle smile, added. "I'm not going to lie—if the food is always this good, then at least Haven is working in our favor, even if those labs are brewing up some strange experiments. What do you say, Val? You've been quiet tonight."

After a pause, with every eye on her, Val met their gaze and murmured, "As Rowan said, we're here to support each other. That's what matters."

In response, Spence pulled out his flask and offered, "Anyone care for a taste?" Passing it around gently, he received only modest headshakes.

"No one wants paint thinner with their meal," Rowan laughed loudly.

Al quickly snatched the flask, grumbling good-naturedly, "Hand that over—I could certainly use a bit of that right now!"

"You see, everyone, take note. This man here knows a good thing when he sees it," Spence quipped, observing Al's hearty gulp from the flask.

At that moment, the applause in the ballroom crescendoed as Mitch entered in his distinctive Penguin tuxedo. But the real thrill was reserved for Buirke. Encircled by exuberant cheers, Buirke made his grand entrance in a mechanized wheelchair, his wife Maggie and Jasper standing on either side. The crowd parted gracefully, forming a respectful aisle as the quartet ambled confidently toward the front, exchanging firm handshakes and warm greetings with every step.

Mia's hands moved in silent gestures, *Why all the cheering*, she asked, her eyes reflecting genuine curiosity. Rook took on the task of interpreting her signs for Trevor.

"Listen, you're new to our ways. Every expedition team— and especially the notorious Devils—is revered as heroes here. Their daring encounters, like Buirke's near-death escape, fill the bedtime stories of our children. He's a renowned figure among our teams, vital for recovering the supplies and people that keep Haven running," Trevor explained.

It pleases Rowan to see people being honored for their worth once again. Having fought shoulder-to-shoulder with

Buirke, he understood the unspoken bond of combat—a bond that spoke of sacrifice, bravery, and hope for mankind's redemption.

Guided to a table under a raised podium, Buirke and his family settled amidst the continuing applause. Mitch took center stage and, with a raised hand, silenced the crowd.

"It is a privilege to stand before you, my sisters and brothers. Tonight's feast isn't merely about food—it commemorates our survival, our unity. Someone once remarked that life is granted only to the fittest. And here you are, exemplifying that fitness: our chefs, our engineers, the greenhouses and animal caretakers, and our soldiers stationed throughout Haven, even those who couldn't join us tonight. But there's one group that truly stands out—the courageous hunters among us." At his cue, the room erupted with whistles, shouts, and heartfelt applause.

Mitch continued, his voice resonating with both pride and urgency, "Without these brave souls, Haven would not have the power or the sustenance we rely on. Tonight, I honor every man and woman who has risked everything for the promise of a new beginning—for our future and the world's rebirth." Accepting a glass of champagne brought quietly from the side, he raised it high. "To Haven's Expedition Forces!" he proclaimed, taking a deliberate sip as the room echoed his toast. "Enough of my rambling, band, please, carry us away with your music. Enjoy yourselves, dance, and eat to your heart's content."

With that, Trevor leapt to his feet, turning to Mia with an almost reverent excitement. "Those were the words I was waiting for. May I have this dance?"

A hush fell over the team as all eyes fell on Mia, waiting for her response. After several long seconds, Mia gracefully stood and accepted his invitation. Gently taking her hand, Trevor led her to the center of the dance floor where, under the soft cadence of the band's notes, they began to sway in a slow, intimate dance.

"Hey, look at that. Who thinks the girl could dance?" Rook said, surprisingly.

"Can you believe this? The world's become a snowball, and they're all acting as if this is the Titanic."

Spence chuckled, adding, "Yeah, perhaps it's not the best time to invest too much emotion." He exchanged a knowing glance with Val, who watched the proceedings with quiet amusement.

Not to be left out, Rook called out, "I don't care about any spooky experiments brewing in those labs. Tonight, any moment is a good moment to experience a little normalcy. Val, how about joining me for a dance?"

After a small pause and a brief glance at Spence, Val smiled and softly replied, "Sure, why not?" The pair steadily made their way to the dance floor, their quiet steps drawing appreciative glances from nearby tablemates.

"What's happening here?" Al mused with a wry smile, observing Val head over to share this moment.

Meanwhile, Rowan's attention was drawn as Mitch made his way toward Buirke's table. Before Mitch could engage in conversation, a solemn guard approached him. Mitch's surprise was evident as he exchanged a brief, meaningful look with Rowan. After listening intently to the guard's report, Mitch excused himself, weaving through the throng to reach Rowan.

"Good evening, everyone," Mitch greeted everyone calmly

upon reaching their table. After receiving nods and quiet waves, he continued, "I trust you're enjoying this splendid evening. Dr. Orion, it's wonderful to see you—your radiance always brightens the room."

"Thank you, Mitch," she replied softly.

"Is everything okay. I saw the soldier debriefing you—did something occur?" Rowan asked.

"As straightforward and observant as in day one," Mitch said, he paused, gathering his thoughts before replying in a steady, measured tone, "At 1400 hours, Raven Squad departed on a routine supply expedition just beyond District-A, a few kilometers north of Haven, and they've yet to return. With only a few hours of daylight left, this is unprecedented for the squad."

"I'm sure Lily is fine," Orion reassured him. "She's well trained and knows what to do if the sun falls."

Mitch's expression remained etched with concern, "I'd like to believe so, but it's unusual for her to delay return this close to sunset. Moreover, communication with them went silent nearly an hour ago. There was one final transmission..." He turned his gaze toward Rowan. "I need you and your team to accompany me."

Rowan studied those at the table and was already aware of where Mitch was taking the situation.

"This is bullshit," Spence blurted out, and saying what Rowan was thinking.

Rowan turned his attention back to Mitch, "At the moment, my team is enjoying the dinner, you asked them to attend. I would prefer them to wind down after what happened this morning."

"First, I'm asking as an associate. And I hope that I don't

have to ask as the director of Haven," Mitch insisted calmly.

"What's going on here?" Rook asked, returning to the table with Val at his side.

"It appears that our festivities are being cut short," Rowan said, his glare sharp and piercing.

Chapter 26

It was a brief, brisk walk through the cool, echoing corridors to the communication room perched on the third floor of the west wing. Dr. Orion walked alongside them, her eyes soft with concern for Lily, whom she regarded not only as a trusted friend but also as an extra set of attentive ears for her sometimes tumultuous thoughts. In her mind, offering emotional support was the very least she could do.

Nestled in the heart of the West Wing, the communication room was the beating nerve center of every expedition. Its staffed consoles provided each team with precise objective locations and essential weather pattern reports. On the roof, large radio towers, expansive radar dishes, and a tangled array of antennas reached skyward, eagerly grasping any signal that might guide them through the endless winter white.

In stark contrast to the rest of the building, with its sleek glass control panels and shimmering holographic terminals, the Comms Room was a unique blend of antiquity and modernity. Many of its systems were relics fashioned before the advent of satellite technology. Years of patient gathering had produced this eclectic collection, salvaged from local museums and painstakingly refitted for present use. Since the catastrophic Fire Storm Impact, the international communication network had fallen silent, leaving this room as their sole tether to distant echoes.

No sooner had Mitch stepped in than he barked an order, his voice cutting through the low hum of machinery, "I need a Situation Report on Raven Squad now." His eyes swept the room for anyone who could provide details. "Any word from my daughter?"

"Daughter? That explains his heightened attachment," Rowan mused.

Within moments, a timid yet clear voice responded from behind a communication panel, "Sir, Raven Squad has been dark for well over an hour now." A lean, somewhat wiry man rose and adjusted his threadbare uniform before continuing, "Our last transmission came not too long after they entered District A."

"Mr. Edler, I thought you were taking the evening off to rest," Mitch inquired, a mix of mild reproach and genuine concern in his tone.

"I did—until word came in that we were missing a team. And more alarmingly, that it was Raven Squad," Edler replied, his pale German features set in a somber expression.

Known for his deep expertise in communications technology, Edler had been among the first at Fort Buckingham when the Fire Storm struck. With no ties to family or life beyond work, his solitary nature had made remaining at what was now known as Haven an uncomplicated choice.

Mitch then extended introductions. "Your concern and efforts are much appreciated. Mr. Edler, this is Rowan. He and his people have joined forces with the remnants of the Devil Squad. However, further formalities will have to wait."

"It's a pleasure to meet you, Mr. Adler. Do you have any

further information that can shed light on what happened to the squad and their mission? Perhaps you can locate them using the surveillance cameras that tracked us," Rowan interjected, his tone brisk and insistent.

A brief pause followed before Edler sighed, "Unfortunately, District A is not equipped with surveillance at this time. With supplies scarce, only about six percent of the city has such coverage. Come to think of it, we did record a short video transmission from Squad leader Lily." He shot a quick glance at Mitch. "Over here," he said, beckoning the group to follow him. "Bring up the video on The Eye," he commanded one of the other workers in the room.

The Eye stood as an intricate hub of command and control, integrated into a sturdy platform the size of a table. It boasted numerous projection arrays that could conjure intricate three-dimensional holograms. As they assembled around it, Edler calmly tapped a green button on the console. After a brief, suspenseful pause filled with static, a recognizable figure materialized—Lily appeared suspended in the middle of the table, wrapped in a thick white parka that obscured much of her visage, her features gently softened by the unyielding winds swirling around her.

"Tower, this is Raven Squad leader," her voice crackled through her coms bracelet.

"Go ahead, Squad leader, this is Tower," came a clear female response.

"Tower, we're pressing into District A," she declared before static surged once again. "All is going as schedu..." followed by a burst of interference.

"Squad leader, you're breaking up—can you repeat?" the female voice prompted.

"We should be reaching our destination soon…" Lily began, but then, amidst more static and overlapping sounds, she called anxiously, "Hold on, Tower… What do you mean you saw something? In what direction?" A tense pause ensued, and then the sound of rapid gunfire erupted over the recording. "Tower, they have us surrou—" she yelled, just as the transmission was abruptly cut off by interference.

"That's all we have," Edler reported, his voice laden with a mix of regret and urgency. "My team exhausted every effort to reestablish contact with Raven Squad. Even with the video, the whiteout conditions left us struggling to pinpoint any nearby landmarks."

Edler's slender fingers danced over the controls, coaxing the icy projection of Lili to fade away. In its wake, a vivid depiction of the city's decay emerged, each detail etched in frozen ruin. "However," he spoke with precision, his gestures illustrating his point, "By tracking their vehicles' path, we suspect they have ventured into this sector of District A. We trust that you might uncover remnants of their presence there," Edler concluded, withdrawing his hand from the holographic display.

Rowan, his tone fierce yet measured, added, "Well, Mitch, I know why you brought us here. And now that we know they did not simply vanish into the night, the next move is squarely in your hands." His words carried the weight of experience, and though he despised being a mere pawn in someone else's control, he knew any defiance against Mitch would endanger their fragile arrangement, especially when emotions are involved.

A heavy silence fell over the room as every eye fixed upon Mitch. He understood intimately that his coming decision could determine lives—decisions he made all too frequently. Yet this time, the stakes were heartbreakingly personal, for it involved his only daughter, Lily. Their relationship had grown bitter over recent months, yet his paternal heart still beat with the same fierce love as the day she was born.

Mitch had always opposed her joining the scavenging teams, but fate and his own training in military tactics and close combat had led her into that dangerous path. She had become everything he had ever wanted in a soldier—a living legacy of his own tradition. Now, he faced two grim choices: either wait until dawn to send a search party in hopes of picking up her trail, or deploy Rowan's team immediately, risking further exposure in the hostile White after dusk. Both decisions weighed heavily upon him.

"Rowan, you and your team have proven your mettle as true soldiers of Haven. And now I am asking you to once again step beyond our safe walls to conduct a search and rescue," Mitch declared, his voice steady despite the emotional tremor underlying his words.

Glancing at his assembled team, Rowan replied, "I'm just hoping that the general is making a well-thought-out decision in sending people out to search for those who may already be dead. It might not end as neatly as during the Congo Rebellion." His gaze locked on Mitch, punctuating the tension.

Mitch paused before picking his words carefully. "How long have you known?" he asked inquisitively.

"From the moment you told me your name. With a reputation as renowned as yours, even the harsh White Out cannot hide the truth," Rowan responded sharply.

"Not many around here are aware of the Rebellion, and much has changed since those days. You will never fully know,"

Mitch mused, a gnawing regret mingling with determination. "I was once part of NWF, supposed to be a civilized force. Yes, I once made decisions that cost lives in pursuit of our mission's success. Much like the rebellion, I continue to make calls that can cause others to buckle under the weight of consequence. Some might see it as the wrong call—as if I'm like the Consul—but what they fail to realize is that although I am not out there fighting those creatures directly, I'm always in the trenches. I make these decisions not to condemn but to save, to keep hope alive for humanity. It was the public's hope in me that kept the Consul from banishing me, and it is that same hope which drives me now to bring everyone home safely."

The weight of his words bore into each member of his team as they waited silently for his command. Rowan asked, "When should we suit up?"

"Immediately. We must capitalize on the dwindling daylight. I'll personally contact the garage to ensure your vehicles are primed and ready," Mitch replied, his tone decisive.

"How do we locate their last known position?" Val asked.

"With satellite tracking now extinct, every vehicle in Haven—including the Scorpion—has been fitted with tracking devices. With the Comms-Tec system, you can narrow down their direction and distance within mere feet," Mitch explained.

A voice from the doorway interrupted, "I hope you're not tracking without my men." Heads turned to see Buirke wheeling into the communication room, Jasper and Haider closely following.

"Going out at this hour is risky, so you're going to need every bit of firepower. Jasper and Haider know these districts intimately; they'll help navigate the terrain. We heard about

Raven Squad's disappearance, so we're here to support you. If anyone can complete this mission, I believe you, Rowan," Buirke continued, his eyes serious. "Although I don't know you on a personal level, I know you as a soldier. Because of you and your team, I'm still alive. And in my eyes, you are as much a member of Haven as anyone else."

Rowan nodded appreciatively. "The additional manpower is a welcome reinforcement. We're grateful for your help."

Buirke smiled slightly as Jasper produced a small duffle bag slung across his shoulder. "Jasper has a little something for you all," he said. Opening the bag, Rowan discovered six state-of-the-art Tec-Comm devices. "Don't worry about the thanks—we're a team now. That's how Devil Squad gets the job done," Buirke added, handing Rowan his meticulously cleaned purple scarf from the suit's inner pocket. "Take this too. It might one day save another life."

Rowan took the scarf, his gaze sweeping across the room, then declared, "With our numbers squared away and if no one has anything further to add, we shouldn't waste another second. Let's change, gear up, and be ready to depart from the garage in thirty minutes."

After a final look at The Eye, with Old London and its towering relics, Rowan pivots away and exits the communication chamber.

Ω▪Ω▪Ω▪Ω

Thirty minutes later, the eight-man team was split between two vehicles at Haven's main gate. Haider drove the first vehicle flanked by Al, Jasper, and Mia, while the Scorpion trailed closely behind with Rook at the helm, Rowan in the passenger seat, and Val and Spence crammed in the back.

In the quiet cabin of the Scorpion, Rowan sat silently, his gaze drifting out the window to the bleak, gray expanse. Rare shafts of sunlight pierced through the dense, turbulent clouds, casting shimmering reflections off the dilapidated skyscrapers of Old London. It was barely an hour or two before twilight, he mused. Countless cycles had slipped away into the unforgiving expanse of snow, but the fleeting sanctuary found at Haven appeared to have justified every moment sacrificed to the icy wasteland. Now, as they set out to search for Mitch's missing squad—possibly lost for good—the shadows of doubt crept in. His thoughts turned grimly to the nocturnal beasts that would soon be prowling in the dark.

"Heads up, Rowan. Raven's last known location is one kilometer out," Jasper announced over the Tec-comm, his voice carrying through the quiet tension.

"I copy. Al, take your team and secure Raven's vehicles. The rest of us will secure the surrounding area," Rowan ordered crisply.

With that, the crew began donning their weather gear with hurried precision. The elements, like any other foe, was a force to reckon with in their own right.

Haven was more than just a shelter—it was a lasting settlement clinging to the remnants of civilized ideals in a world seemingly spiraling into barbarism. Mitch had meticulously divided prominent areas in London into districts, allowing for the easy marking of which sections had been scavenged for resources.

The northern section of Marylebone had been the first to be resourced and was now known as District A. Before the collapse, Marylebone had thrived as a bustling, extravagant neighborhood, its elegant brick buildings converted into chic storefronts. Even when cloaked under a heavy gray sky and blanketed with snow, the area retained an air of dignified elegance.

As the vehicles crept along at a measured pace, the tracking device began to beep and flicker steadily, heralding the imminent appearance of Raven's vehicles.

"Rowan, we have eyes on the package," Jasper announced as the vehicles slowed, their tires crunching over fresh snow.

"Alright, team, we've touched down. Grab your gear," Rowan declared, rising from the front seat and moving purposefully toward the rear compartment to retrieve his equipment.

With his backpack secured, sidearm holstered, and both his HVT assault rifle and the 1873 Winchester strapped to his back. Satisfied with the silent nods and thumbs up from his comrades, he pressed the button to release the rear ramp. Adjusting his snow goggles snugly over his eyes and pulling up his scarf, he observed in silence as the hydraulically operated ramp lowered with a metallic exhale. A blast of arctic wind swept into the vehicle—a stark reminder of the wild, unforgiving world they now inhabited. One by one, every member of the team stepped out, weapons slung tightly over their shoulders, eyes scanning every conceivable angle for possible ambushes.

Rowan was the first to exit the Scorpion. He paused, dropping to kneel several feet behind the vehicle while the rest took up positions at the front and sides, forming an impromptu semicircle around him. As his vigilant eyes roved over the barren scene, it became unsettlingly clear: this area had been turned into a kill zone.

Evidently, Raven Squad had been ambushed in a place that

unsuspectingly provided a perfect trap for intruders—a grim irony born from the misplaced assumption that District A was safe. Once again, Rowan was forced to shoulder the burden of cleaning up a catastrophic mess.

The tracking device attached to Raven Squad's vehicle led them to Gloucester Place—a lengthy stretch of road running northward from Haven, bordered by stately five-story homes on each side. As the team moved deliberately toward the designated mark, Rowan maintained a watchful eye on the upper windows of the surrounding buildings, the most likely vantage points for an unseen foe. Finding only the haunting sound of wind and no immediate threats, he halted his group near a cluster of abandoned vehicles.

The scene that unfolded before them was nothing short of a warzone. Crimson stains collected in small, sinister pools of blood on the pristine white snow. Half of the team began sifting through the wreckage of the vehicles while the others scanned rooftops and windows for any sign of movement.

Approaching the dirge-like scene with grim caution, Jasper murmured, "This is definitely Raven Squad," his voice trembling as he checked his Comm-Tec device, which beeped frantically until he managed to silence it with a tap.

"Is anyone seeing the snow speeders?" Haider asked as he cautiously opened the door of Raven's truck, only to find it abandoned. "No one inside."

Mia and Al were walking the perimeter several feet away when she tapped Al's arm, swiftly communicating through her unique sign language, then motioned towards a path diverging from Raven Squad's parked vehicles.

"I hear you, Mia," Al said before initiating his Tec-comm. "Rowan, if you're looking for the speeders, our best bet is to search in that direction," he ended.

"Be right there," Rowan responded over the coms.

With the other, Rowan stepped up to Al and Mia.

"That way," Al suggested, "Mia found them while surveying the area," pointing at a series of imprints in the snow. "It appears that whoever attacked them seized the speeders and headed northwest."

"Good job, Mia," Rowan said while studying the tracks.

"Whoever took them wasn't alone—these tracks indicate heavy machinery was involved. Perhaps some kind of transport vehicle," Rook added, bending down to examine the deep tire impressions. And I'd wager it was something vintage, judging by the tread patterns. Rowan, Haider—what do you think?"

After a moment of inspection, Rowan said, "They definitely had a heavy vehicle—one capable of hauling prisoners. How many were in Raven Squad?"

"Raven is an eight-team unit. If they were taken, that leaves Skin-walkers behind this. Which means that Raven Squad is in a truly dire situation. They didn't earn that name simply by skinning stalkers and wearing their flesh, but rather from devouring anything they capture—man or beast alike," Haider explained.

"Give it to me straight, Haider. What are their chances of making it?" Rowan inquired with his usual directness.

Pausing as if thinking about how to respond, "I say, fifty-fifty. All depends on if Raven Squad is already dead or if the Skin-walkers are keeping them around as cattle," Haider grimly elaborated.

"Then our mission is clear—we must rescue them," Jasper commanded with renewed urgency.

"Hold on, Greeny," Spence interjected firmly. "We need to think this through first. The best course of action is to plan our approach meticulously."

"I hear you, Spence, but the harsh truth remains—the longer we wait, the graver the situation becomes," Jasper retorted.

Rowan finally interjected, slinging his rifle over his shoulder. "Both of you have valid points. Charging in unprepared might get us all skinned, yet we cannot afford inaction." He gestured towards the direction of the heavy tracks. "Haider, are there any major structures along that route?"

"There are a few," Haider replied, fingers dancing over his Tec-Comm as he pulled up a luminescent projection of the city's map. "There's The Landmark London Hotel here, and the London Business School directly ahead on Gloucester Place."

Rowan's finger hovered over another point on the map. "What about this location here? There's a vast, empty expanse surrounding this building. What sits here?"

"That's Marylebone Station," Haider identified.

"If I had to guess a likely hideout—a place that could be defended by a small, agile team, with tunnels offering cover from the elements and muffling desperate cries—this would be it," Rowan murmured thoughtfully, then met Haider's doubtful look.

"It's impossible that the Skin-walkers would have a hideout so close to Haven. And Tower would have advised us otherwise," Haider countered.

"You may have your concerns, and I understand them, but know that I do not make decisions that recklessly endanger my team. I am here to complete a mission. If they're not there, we can easily sling shot back around to search the other locations.

I was bought on for a reason, trust in my decisions—and that trust must start now."

Haider fell silent, exchanging uncertain glances with Jasper. Finally, he conceded, "Alright then, we head to Marylebone Station. But if we find nothing, we'll push further into the city."

"Excellent," Rowan remarked. "Time to head back to the vehicles. Daylight is waning," he directed, urging the squad to swiftly make their way back to their transport.

Every second now felt laden with tension as the team steeled itself for what lay ahead.

Chapter 27

Devil Squad had battled through the relentless, bone-chilling blizzard as they neared Marylebone Station, strategically parking their vehicles at a safe distance and advancing silently on foot. They gathered inside a shuttered building adjacent to the station—a crumbling relic with frost-encrusted windows—to scout the area and prepare for their entry.

True to Rowan's suspicions, Marylebone's train and subway station lay in a state of desolation. The once-grand entrance now appeared as a ghostly remnant, ravaged by a decade of winter storms. Massive icicles clung to its regal red-brick chimneys and slate roof, appearing dull under the disappearing light. A formidable nine-foot gate of metal and brick guarded the main entrance, evoking eerie memories for Rowan. It was hard to fathom that this threshold had once seen thousands of commuters daily—now, only the relentless, icy winds stirred the silence.

"Seems like you nailed it, Rowan," said Haider with a nod, his voice low and measured as he eyed Rowan intently. "The tracks lead straight into the station."

Rowan's reply was grim. "Right or wrong doesn't matter now—we just need to make sure we all get out of here in one piece and with the rest of the team."

"You're right," Haider said, checking the increasing gusts of wind. Another operative remarked, "We should move soon. The whiteout is coming; we can use it to slip by undetected. Remember, stealth is our ally. Now's the time—any objections?"

Jasper's tone was resolute as he added, "Time to bring our people back."

"No kidding," Spence shot back, placing a reassuring hand on Jasper's shoulder. "And then we hightail it out of this icebox."

Rowan's authoritative voice cut through the murmurs. "Val, take Jasper, Rook, and Al. Approach the gates from the east. I'll lead the team from the west. And remember—radio silence as much as possible." With that, Rowan gave the signal to move.

Once again, in unison, the teams split up and began a cautious dash toward the station's entrance. Snow-laden winds howled like spectral forces wrapping the area in an icy shroud. Visibility was reduced to a mere twenty meters, obscuring their every move from patrolling sentries.

Both teams reached the opposite sides of the grand, decaying station simultaneously and advanced toward the center gate, only to find it secured with a heavy lock and chain. With a series of subtle hand signals, Rook was summoned to move forward. He swiftly removed his backpack upon reaching the gate, setting it carefully in the snow as he knelt down. After rummaging through the contents with practiced speed, he extracted his salvage torch—one of his many indispensable tools deployed in emergencies.

Rook's calloused hand gripped the trigger of the salvage torch, unleashing a searing blue-white blaze that danced against the icy metal surface. His goggles automatically adjusted to the intense light, casting sharp shadows, revealing every imperfection as the flame sliced effortlessly through the frozen barrier. As he silenced the torch, its hiss fading into the frigid air, Rook deftly stowed away the cutter into his pack and resumed his position.

Rowan himself carefully unhooked the chain with stealthy precision, ensuring not even a whisper of noise. Once the chain was off, the heavy barred gate creaked open. Both teams surged in simultaneously—Val's group first, with weapons raised and eyes scanning for any lurking threat, and Rowan's team following suit from the opposite side.

Inside the sprawling main gate, Rowan's thoughts drifted back to the digital map Haider had provided. Marylebone Station was divided into two distinct sections: the open, frost-covered train platforms at ground level and the subterranean subway system below, accessed by two grand staircases flanking the entrance. Even now, evidence of pre-Impact construction lay scattered—massive tunneling machines, dragging equipment, and other industrial paraphernalia that spoke of a time when the station thrummed with life.

Silence fell over the group as the howling winds subsided and the snow began to fall in a steady, almost hypnotic rhythm. Yet Rowan couldn't shake the unsettling feeling that they were being watched. The abandoned appearance of the station contrasted sharply with the tracks that boldly cut through the main gate, hinting at hidden secrets.

"Val, do you feel it? Something's off," Rowan's voice crackled through the Tec-Comms, his tone laced with apprehension.

"I know what you mean..." came her measured reply. "It's too quiet."

Rowan continued, "As much as my gut is warning us to leave, we are here and need to find Mitch's people. Take your team, scout around, and keep your eyes open."

"Copy that," Val acknowledged.

Before they could respond further, a piercing, eerie squeal erupted over the station's intercom. Instantly, Devil Squad's instincts snapped to combat readiness; hands moved to grips of rifles, fingers caressed the triggers as every soldier's eyes flitted across the shadowed corridors.

"Everyone inside—move, now!" ordered Rowan, rallying his squad into decisive motion as they stormed deeper into the station.

A booming female voice cascaded over the loudspeakers: "Greetings, neighbors of Fort Buckingham! You might not have been on the guest list, but consider yourselves most welcome. Sit back, relax, and enjoy our hospitality!" Her sinister tone was followed by one last high-pitched squeal as the transmission ended.

With a single hand, Mia signed, *This is not good.*

Rowan's tone was resolute. "Don't worry—we're not planning on waiting around for that twisted hospitality. Val, continue your sweep of the ground level. Keep in constant communication and, if you locate the package, extract immediately with no delays," he ended, then gestured for his team to head down the left staircase into the subway, while Val and her group veered away to the right.

Inside the subway, the once-pristine, white-tiled corridors were dimly lit, the only illumination provided by sporadically burning steel barrels placed every few yards. Flickering flames cast enormous, shifting shadows against the tiles, transforming the corridor into a nightmarish passageway where every step seemed to echo the saints' laments of lost souls. He could not help but think of the Skin-Walkers victims, likely guided here like helpless sheep to their slaughter—a true descent through the gates of Hell on earth, where the last kiss of natural daylight was violently stripped away.

Regardless, for Rowan, this was another mission—another chance to dispatch bad guys with precise shots from his rifle. With unwavering nerves, he and his team advanced further into the subterranean maze.

They descended a decrepit, rusting escalator and emerged onto a dark, partially constructed, three-tiered subway platform. The aftermath of hasty construction was evident: abandoned dredgers, tunneling equipment, and miscellaneous items—frozen in time—littered the scene. As they penetrated deeper, the flashlights revealed a horrifying tableau: a grim tapestry of human and inhuman remains carpeting the floor, a visceral reminder of the carnage inflicted here.

On the second level, Spence broke the silence, his voice echoing off the cold walls. "There's no doubt we're in the right spot now."

Rowan's keen eyes scrutinized every inch of the floor. "Looks that way," he agreed, vigilant for traps. But instead of devious contraptions, his beam caught sight of something decidedly more macabre—a foot, partly obscured behind a rusted cage. Slowly, the light traced upward along a body until it revealed a metal collar around its victim's neck and chained to the subway wall like a mark of ownership.

"That's Joseph, one of Lily's men," whispered Haider as he knelt near the cage, his hand gently tapping on the soldier's shoulder. "Joseph, come on, buddy."

"I don't think that's necessary, buddy," Spence added, his

voice held a mix of disbelief and sorrow as his flashlight revealed the mutilated left arm of the man, from just below the elbow down, a pool of frozen blood spreading beneath.

"He... he must have just died. His body's still warm," Haider said.

A heavy silence followed before Spence muttered, "Man, that's a horrible way for any soldier to go."

Without saying another word, Haider placed his hands reverently on the soldier's head and began a low, guttural chant in Arabic.

"No time for this!" Spence interjected briskly.

"Let him be, Spence," Rowan ordered shortly, trying to restore order. Rising slowly, Haider softly countered, "There's always time to guide a soul to Heaven—especially after surviving this Hell." His eyes locked onto Spence's, patience mingled with grief.

Spence murmured his apology, "You're right... I'm sorry. But we've got to keep moving if we're going to—"

Rowan raised a hand, cutting him off. "Quiet," he hissed, his light scanning deeper into the chilling darkness. "There's something ahead." The entire team followed his gaze, tense as their eyes adjusted to the dark and moving with the beam of light

Soon, the sound of clattering chains and distant, anguished moans filled the air. Five captives, like helpless sheep, their hands bound behind their back, gagged, their necks chained to the wall, their fate nearly sealed.

Muffled moans cried from their gagged mouths, eyes imploring for help upon seeing Haider approach.

"Shh, we got you, we're here," Haider pleaded with them.

"Cut them loose—now!" Rowan ordered, his eyes narrowing at the way the chains were digging into their flesh.

Mia advanced with a practiced calm, taking out her own salvage torch and began cutting at the chains.

"Cover her!" Rowan commanded as she went to work, the flame sending sparks dancing along the frozen ground.

Rowan, Haider, and Spence dropped to a knee crouch around Mia, as their flashlight scanned the darkness.

"Rowan, I didn't see Lily with them," Haider noted, tension in his whispers.

"Noted. Maybe they're holding her somewhere else," Rowan said, clearly frustrated.

"What's the move? We can't haul everyone back if things go sideways," Spence said.

Rowan's mind raced. "For now, get these folks closer to the stairs as fast as possible."

"They took Lili, they took Lili somewhere else," someone from Raven Squad said aloud behind them.

Glancing at what remained of Raven Squad, Haider interjected, "Give them a few minutes; EVE will patch them up in no time. Any weakness or drugs they were given should wear off soon."

A heavy silence fell over the team as Rowan weighed their options. "Alright, but do anything to help speed up the process," Rowan ordered.

"On it," Haider said, turning to help Mia.

"Rowan, you copy?" Val's whispered voice came crackling over the Tec-Comms.

"Rowan here," he responded, his eyes never leaving the shadowy corridor.

Suddenly, Val's voice returned, tinged with urgency: "We located the package in an abandoned train car. We're en route back to you. Also, we spotted a group of Skin-Walkers entering the station shortly after our split—I counted eleven. Hold on... I have tangos moving in—"

As soon as the transmission had ended, pandemonium erupted. Automatic gunfire blared in the distance.

"We've got contact," Val reported over the comm, her voice tight with adrenaline.

"How many?" Rowan demanded.

"At present, I can only pick out a handful," she replied as she unleashed a rapid burst of gunfire, each shot echoing ominously through the crypt-like corridors.

"Copy that, keep me posted. Rowan out." His voice was curt and commanding as he rallied the team. "Tighten up, everyone! We're about to have unwanted guests. Haider, status on our packages?" His eyes now locked on the broken escalators, they came down.

"They're up and moving. I expect a few minutes. The severely injured will still need a hand." Haider responded with pragmatic efficiency.

"Do what you can. Mia, continue lending a hand. Spence, stick with me." Rowan said, moving low behind a marble square column near the escalator. Spence took cover behind a barricade of large, strapped pipes, his eyes vigilantly scanning every shadow.

Listening intently, Rowan's grip tightened on his weapon. Footsteps echoed steadily down the corridor. "Go dark," he instructed calmly, turning off his mounted flashlight. Adjusting his scope, the world transformed into a ghostly green hue as his goggles instantly transitioned to night vision, with the others following suit. "Let the first few come down before going live," he said in a whispered shout, prompting a nod from Spence.

As they waited, the sounds of rapidly approaching footsteps swelled, until the first silhouette of a Skin-Walker broke through the green-tinged gloom above. The approaching pack slowed as they descended the stairs, their forms ghostlike and menacing against the darkness. Rowan firmed his grip, steeling himself for the onslaught.

When the first three Skin-Walkers reached halfway down the stairs, Rowan opened fire with his HVT-Viper rifle. At the same moment, Spence let loose with his AK-47, depositing several foes in a tangle of lifeless bodies. The combined barrage of gunshots was deafening—a violent symphony that sent the remaining Skin-Walkers into a panic as they ducked behind whatever scant cover they could find.

Recognizing the platform now under Rowan's team control, a second wave of Skin-Walkers poured onto the escalator, their movements. Like shadows come to life, they swiftly split into two groups, taking up positions on both sides of the exit. With superior numbers, the Skin-walkers began laying down suppressive fire on both Rowan and Spence, pinning them behind their cover.

"Raven Squad—get up and fall back!" Rowan barked, peering out briefly to unleash a well-calibrated stream of suppressive fire, then rushing out to reposition himself at the far end of the platform. He managed to find cover behind a massive marble pillar that shielded him from enemy fire.

He was happy to see that Spence had done the same, taking up position at a twin pillar. Bullets whizzed past, striking the elegant marble that once adorned the grand station, fracturing it into debris.

"Rowan, it appears they have the tunnels walled off, for

some reason," Haider chimed in over the coms.

"Hell," Rowan said to himself. "I hear you, Haider. You and Mia stay with Raven Squad, Spence and I will hold them off."

"I copy Rowan," Haider ended.

The first wave of Skin-Walkers surged ahead from the escalator, closing in on Rowan's team, who stood pinned down with no escape route in sight. Caught between advancing foes and a dead-end, tension mounted as they faced imminent danger.

"Rowan, we can't hold out much longer!" Spence shouted over the cacophony of the firefight, his voice strained as he fired a controlled burst at a cluster of advancing enemies. A precise shot hit its mark, propelling the figure backward off the edge of the platform, disappearing into the shadows of the train's rails.

Tell me something I don't know, Spence," Rowan replied, eyes locked onto his handheld Tec-Comms as he swiftly pulled up his sleeve to access a secure channel for Val.

"Rocket incoming," Spence yelled, before Rowan could relay further instructions.

A figure clad in a tattered skin cloak, the wind billowing its ragged edges, stood tall. On their shoulders, a launcher perched confidently before it unleashed its payload with a swift pull of the trigger. In an instant, a rocket roared towards their position. With no time to spare, he sought refuge behind protective cover as the explosive projectile collided with a sturdy column. The impact sent marble and concrete shrapnel scattering in all directions.

The earth ruptured beneath Rowan in an instant, swallowing him into the twisting underground passage. In the tumultuous descent, he tumbled through what seemed like multiple levels before finally crashing onto the elevated platform of the third railway station. A shower of debris struck his head, casting his sight into obscurity as swirling dust and crumbling fragments enveloped the collapsing tunnel.

Chapter 28

Coming to, Rowan found himself buried alone in the subway tunnel. His first act was to dig himself from beneath the rubble. His head throbbed as he stood. Rubbing his head, he found no injuries, yet his head was caked with dried blood. He had managed to hold onto most of his gear, though there were no signs of the Winchester anywhere.

"How long was I out?" hearing the silence of battle. With winds blowing through the tunnel, he turned on his mounted flashlight. "This can't be good," seeing that he had been out for over an hour and was now in the dark hours. "Val, you copy?" *Silence.* "Haider, you there?"

He gave his Tec-comm a quick glance, which revealed its cracked interface. As he examined the device, his gaze caught the attention of something on the ground. Directing his light toward the floor, he uncovered a grim sight: he was standing on a small pile of the skeletal remains of humans and those of something else.

"How can this day get any worse?" he muttered to himself, adjusting the rifle strap. "Those psychos are sacrificing people," sliding down from the pile

Then came a familiar sound from deep within the tunnel, the growing sound of scraping claws brought him back to reality, more importantly, that he needed to get moving now.

"That explains why the Skin-walkers blocked off the tunnel," he said.

He quickly turned off his light, thankful that his goggles were still intact. He quickly took off, finding an alcove twenty-five yards away. As his eyes promptly adjusted to the night vision, he peeked from behind cover and realized the creatures were further back than he thought. His past training and experience had taught him how to best gauge time and distance, most people tend to think they have more time than they do, not the other way around.

Before he could think more about it, three shadows darted past. He waited to ensure no others lagged behind. As the others scrambled over the debris, their bat-like nostrils flared, sniffing the air as if attempting to grasp the source of the disturbance. Rowan took a long look down the tunnel, seeing that the cost was clear of others. Confident he had the drop on the Stalkers, he shouldered his weapon and stepped out for the kill.

Rowan switched his weapon to semi-auto, conserving precious ammo as he unleashed a shot at one of the beasts. The creature, however, caught the sound of stones crunching underfoot and dodged just in time. The round struck its leg, splintering the femur with a sickening crack. Without hesitation, Rowan shifted his focus to the two remaining stalkers. One lunged forward, jaws agape and ready to tear into him. Meanwhile, the third defied gravity, its claws gripping the concrete as it scaled the subway wall for a deadly aerial assault.

With the wounded one holding back, Rowan dropped to one knee and took aim at the creature charging directly at him.

Taking calm breaths, he released two quick shots, hitting the creature square in the face. As its face shattered, the sudden impact caused the beast to face plant into the tracks, its momentum flipping it over onto its back.

As the second beast crumpled to the ground, Rowan whipped his gaze upward, but his initial shots at the third Stalker went wide. The creature darted through the tunnel, weaving erratically as Rowan fired round after round, each bullet ricocheting off the concrete walls with sharp cracks. Just as his rifle clicked empty, the Stalker pivoted in an instant—its instincts honed to recognize the sound of a spent magazine—and lunged forward, closing the gap between them in mere strides.

With a sudden surge, the creature lunged at him. Rowan hit the ground hard, landing on his back as he instinctively drew his pistol. In one fluid motion, he fired several rounds into the beast's midsection just as it barreled overhead, crashing against the wall with a deafening thud. He rolled away just in time to avoid its razor-sharp claws slicing through the ground his head had just been on. Coming to rest on his stomach, Rowan steadied his aim at the monster's head. Four shots rang out in the confined tunnel; two struck its hand as it tried to shield its face, while the other two pierced through flesh, halting the Stalker in its tracks.

Aware that the fight was far from finished, Rowan pivoted sharply to confront the last Stalker. But it had vanished from his memory's grasp. He spun around in a frantic search until he finally spotted it, crouched in the center of the track, eyes fixated on something lurking behind him. Heart pounding, he turned slowly and froze at the sight—two more Stalkers flanked a much larger one at their center. The monstrous figure scrutinized him with an unsettling intensity, its outline hauntingly familiar. The smaller Stalkers flickered glances at their colossal companion, as if awaiting a silent command to strike.

"Not good," he said with a whisper, taking the moment to reload his pistol, yet they remained in position. Not passing up another opportunity, he promptly reloaded his HVT-Viper. As his magazine locked into place, the monster gave a blood-curdling roar that sent the other three charging toward him.

"So, it begins?"

The wounded Stalker surged forward, its injured leg seemingly forgotten as it charged at him with a primal fury. Rowan's strategy was straightforward: eliminate it like the others. He squeezed the trigger three times, but the creature twisted mid-air, narrowly evading his shots and landing just a few feet away. Out of the corner of his eye, he spotted another Stalker launching itself from the wall. With lightning-fast reflexes, as though the world had slowed, he executed a dodge roll just as its claws slashed through the air where he had stood moments before. Now, behind the first Stalker, Rowan sprang to his feet and seized the thick fur on its head, yanking it back with all his strength.

"Gotcha," he thought.

With a swift motion, Rowan pressed the barrel of his pistol against the base of the creature's skull and pulled the trigger, shattering its head in a gruesome spray. The sight sent one of the last two monsters stumbling backward in panic. Without missing a beat, Rowan holstered his sidearm and swung his rifle onto his shoulder, flipping it to full auto as he did. The fleeing beast barely managed ten paces before a hail of bullets tore through its chest, splattering blood across the frozen ground. It crumpled to the earth just moments after its faceless companion.

Rowan swiftly tallies the shots he's fired against the rounds still in his magazine—fifteen left. Just as he raises his rifle to fire, the creature lunges, scooping up gravel from the ground and hurling it at him like a barrage of bullets. Reacting on instinct, he jerks his head aside and raises his forearm to shield himself from the flying debris, but still fires blindly at the spot where the Stalker had been lurking moments before.

The creature howled in agony as a bullet tore into its gut. Lowering his arm, he found the beast lunging toward him with its claws. With no time to think, he swung his rifle up like a staff, deflecting the strike just in time. The impact shattered the high-impact plastic of his weapon, sending splinters flying. The monster's momentum caused it to barrel past him, and as it did, he drew his pistol and zeroed in on its back and fired.

As the final shell casing clinked against the frozen ground, the creature lay face down, its lower body twitching helplessly. Rowan gazed at the mangled remnants of its spine, a testament to his lethal accuracy. Despite being immobilized, the beast thrashed on its belly, clawing at him with wild desperation as its useless legs tangled in the rusted rail tracks. By the time it managed to extricate itself, Rowan had swiftly reloaded his pistol and leveled it at the creature's head.

"This time, stay down," pulling the trigger, ending the Stalker's movement.

Facing the final and largest Stalker, Rowan activated the LED light mounted on his rifle. The creature stood still, having observed its minions being slaughtered with a chilling patience. He could sense its eagerness for confrontation as its massive shoulders heaved rhythmically. Then, an unsettling sound reached his ears—what seemed like a chuckle.

It was hard to believe; a beast that should have been devoid of intelligence, driven only by instinct, was mocking him. If he had been one of Haven's scientists, he might have found this phenomenon intriguing. But he wasn't one of them. Instead, he lifted his handgun, steadied his aim at the creature's heart, and pulled the trigger.

The beast surged forward with a speed that defied its massive frame, veering to its right and slipping into the shadows, evading the hail of gunfire. Anticipating its move, he rolled onto his shoulder and pivoted, his instincts honed to perfection. As he regained his footing, the creature landed mere feet away, towering over him with a grotesque face marred by countless imperfections. In one fluid motion, he raised his weapon, finger poised on the trigger. But the monster was quicker; it lashed out with a powerful backhand, sending the gun flying from his grasp and into the abyss of the dark tunnel.

Before he could even catch a glimpse of where it had crashed, a crushing grip clamped around his throat, yanking him off the ground. Panic surged as he struggled for breath; the pressure was relentless, squeezing his throat shut. He pounded at its wrist with desperate fists, each strike futile against the monstrous strength. After what felt like an eternity suspended in midair, the creature hoisted him to its eye level, mere inches from its grotesque face. In that harrowing moment, Rowan froze—his breath stolen not just by the grip but by the recognition of who stood before him.

Before him loomed not merely a product of scientific experimentation or an extraterrestrial parasite. It was a beast spawned from brutality, anguish, animosity, and an insatiable thirst for dominance. The parasite had merely revealed her true nature, amplifying what she had always been. The last time he beheld her, she appeared as a motionless cadaver, sprawled on her back.

"Rowan," she spluttered, her voice a distorted rasp as her feline-like eyes locked onto him.

Despite her transformation, Rowan recognized that the thrill of the hunt still coursed through her veins. He struggled to discern whether it was a raw survival instinct driving her to kill for sustenance or a darker enjoyment in the act itself. Her nose twitched as if catching an unseen scent, and her skin glowed with an eerie purple hue from the harsh elements, yet he could not deny who she had once been.

Thick drool dripped from her lips as she bared her sharpened fangs in a menacing snarl.

"Loose...collar," she said, tightening her grip around his neck.

"The collar!" he recalled, a flash of memory surfacing as he remembered that Buirke had returned them to him.

He instinctively reached for the collar at the back of his belt. Interpreting his gesture as a threat, Larissa hurled him down the tunnel with terrifying ease. He landed twenty feet away, hitting the ground with a thud that knocked the breath from his lungs. As he gasped for air, a groan escaped him; he belatedly registered that he had skidded face-first across the rough terrain.

As his eyesight slowly came into focus, he discarded his shattered goggles, letting them slip from his grasp. Shaking off the lingering haze, he noticed a door slightly open to his left. He redirected his focus to her; she was watching him with an impatient intensity.

"Of course, she wants to hunt her prey," he thought aloud,

rising to his feet and brushing away the blood that dripped into his vision.

He cracked his neck from side to side. Larissa let out a low snort, dropping onto all fours, readying herself to spring.

"I stand no chance against her in the open. I need to restrict her movements," he thought, eying the door.

"Come get me, you fat, ugly, bi—"

His voice faltered as Larissa's primal scream erupted, a sound that sliced through the air like a jagged blade.

Without hesitating, he dashed toward the door, covering the distance in five swift strides. As he pushed it open, a narrow concrete maintenance corridor unfolded before him. The atmosphere was unsettling, filled with decaying rusted pipes, tangled cables, and scattered bones. He eased his speed as the beam from his rifle-mounted light gradually brightened the shadowy hall.

A thunderous crash echoed behind him as Larissa battered her way through the narrow door, casting a shadow that swallowed the light from behind her. Even in the dark, Rowan realized his sight was somewhat sharper than usual, at least compared to what he recalled. But with a three-hundred-pound beast on his tail, he had little time to ponder how that was possible.

Chapter 29

Large, rusted pipes with square brackets clamped to the wall stretched along nearly every inch of the dim, claustrophobic maintenance corridor. Their cold, industrial presence complicated every step Rowan took, forcing him to contort his body around them—a minor nuisance compared to the relentless hound-like predator chasing him. If these obstructions slowed him down, he reasoned grimly, they'd only serve to hinder Larissa even more.

Despite the cramped space and the occasional stumble over debris and exposed wiring, Rowan maintained a steady, desperate pace. He wasn't keeping track of time playing this twisted game of hide and seek, but the stakes were crystal clear: if he didn't flip the roles soon, he might very well become dinner for his former bosses.

Larissa, by now, was little more than a feral force of nature—an almost perfect predator with supercharged vision, smell, hearing, and raw strength. All Rowan had to fight back were rounds for the Winchester, a combat knife, a handful of survival gadgets, and one precious item: a collar rigged with explosives.

His plan was audacious—a booby-trapped leash, if you will, to deliver a spark of explosive retribution. Yet he doubted it would encircle her thick, powerful neck. Still, if it landed, the small explosion might be enough to finish her off. The only catch was he'd have to close the gap—a risky proposition, even when she was human.

The corridor was a morass of old pipes and machinery, and as Larissa thundered forward, smashing through sections of piping, Rowan was forced to pick up the pace. He kept his lean form pressed close against the wall to avoid the deadly protrusions on the opposite side. Every crunch of metal and concrete echoed ominously as if the structure itself was protesting the chaos. Occasionally, a guttural sound—something akin to an animal's curse—broke through the cacophony. Rowan, half-amused despite himself, could swear she managed a "Fuck" amidst the grunts, though the sound was nearly swallowed by her snarls.

Then, as he rounded yet another battered corner, something caught his attention—a sudden eerie silence. Everything ceased: the muffled sound of footfalls, even his own ragged breathing, filled the void. Rowan halted mid-stride. His senses went on high alert: sight yielded nothing but oppressive darkness, the smell was a sickly blend of abandoned subway dampness and decay, the taste in his mouth was bitter with fear, and underfoot, he felt nothing but the coarse texture of concrete and dust. But most telling was the silence where Larissa's rampage had once indicated her presence.

"Did she give up? No way—" he mused bitterly, "I'm not that lucky. She's too damn stubborn!"

Before he could reassemble his hurried thoughts, a sound assaulted him like knives digging into concrete. As he realizes, like the other Stalkers, she had climbed the wall, his nerve momentarily fracturing into panic. But his internal battle was cut short as another guttural roar filled the corridor.

Larissa's ungainly, monstrous movements betrayed her feral nature, yet somehow they translated to an accelerating pace. Now, she was merely twenty feet away, her presence a looming specter of terrible inevitability.

"How in hell did she even fit in this tunnel?" Rowan wondered aloud, the question muffled by his racing heartbeat, as he dodged another ferocious swipe—the scrape of her claws embedding into concrete sent a shudder down his spine.

Her panting escalated into raw, animalistic exertions. In that frantic moment, he could picture her twisted visage clearly: a sinister, knowing smile stretching across a mouth filled with yellow, deformed fangs, all glistening with saliva.

"Oh, fuck!" Rowan shouted, cursing the collapsing wall that knocked him sideways, bouncing him off another metal bracket like a rag doll.

Larissa, ever relentless, vaulted from the ceiling with ter-rifying unpredictability—as if gravity betrayed her form— and Rowan found himself dodging her actual trajectory by ricocheting off a corner. Metal brackets and pipes crumbled under her weight as she turned the pursuit into a chaotic ballet of destruction.

Stumbling back to his feet, dazed but undeterred, Rowan sprinted down the hall. Though it was pitch black, he was able to see through the gloom, revealing a path cluttered with industrial detritus that barely slowed his desperate flight. All the while, Larissa was in hot pursuit, lunging on all fours, her heightened senses homing in on his every scent and sound. His hope rested on somehow neutralizing her keen sense of smell, knowing that as long as she could track him by scent, silence—or stealth—would be wasted.

Navigating the corridor like a pinball bouncing off every obstacle, Rowan suddenly reached a T-intersection. With Larissa nearly upon him, he smirked bitterly, "Come get me, you ugly bitch," his voice a gritty blend of defiance and exhaustion as he fixed his gaze toward the darkened tunnel beyond. He shut out all other distractions in his mind and concentrated tallying the measured steps of her approaches—

"One... Two... Three... Four..."—each crunch of claws growing louder until a full-throated roar signaled his moment.

In a blur of movement, Rowan dove aside as Larissa barreled by, her momentum throwing him off balance as she collided with a wall, the impact accompanied by a high-pitched yelp that hinted at excruciating pain. In that split second, he had two choices: risk a close-quarter confrontation by lunging with his combat knife to drive it deep into her skull, or wrestle with fate by aiming for a less risky target.

Choosing the latter, he drove his knife deep into her calf muscle. With every ounce of strength he could muster, he twisted the handle, slicing through sinews, tendons, and ligaments, down to her heel.

The beast's howl of agony was immediate. In retaliation, Larissa swiped with her claws, her strike missing violently as Rowan dropped flat onto the gritty floor. Regaining his footing, he twisted and pulled her arm, attempting to reposition his blade underhanded, aiming a slicing blow at her wrist. A spray of blood decorated the concrete—a grim tapestry marking the collision of human ingenuity and monstrous fury. Yet, her instincts to survive kicked in: she pulled her arm free, knocking the blade from his grasp.

Though Rowan mourned the loss of his weapon, the damage had been done; Larissa was crippled, her ferocity momentarily dampened. He rolled backward as her good hand smashed the ground in front of him. Seizing the opening, he dashed down the corridor, bolstered by the conviction that a wounded predator was more dangerous and unpredictable than one already dead.

He eased into a jog to save his strength, realizing for the first time that his breath came easily. After everything he had endured, he felt far less fatigued than he ought to be.

"No time to dwell on that now. Let's just get out of here first, Rowan," he thought.

His pulse surged with adrenaline and grim purpose as he planned his next move. Minutes later, Rowan discovered a heavy, creaking door in a narrow alcove. He turned the knob gingerly and, glancing back, could hear Larissa's ragged recovery behind him—her pace slower now but no less threatening. Steeling himself, he stepped inside, every instinct warning him that if the room had no other exit, he'd find himself cornered.

Cursing under his breath, he realized this was a calculated risk he had to take. The door groaned in protest as its rusted hinges creaked for the first time in ages. Even in the darkness, his eyes darted over the room: a subterranean maintenance bay beneath a ruined Earth, replete with ancient tools and hulking machines.

A quick scan revealed two sets of tracks and rickety scaffolding reaching toward the ceiling; temporary walls, stacks of rebar, a small drum of gasoline beside a silent generator, and an assortment of tools—nail guns, wrenches, screwdrivers—lay scattered about. There was plenty to work with, but time was quickly slipping away.

No sooner had he settled on a plan than the door shuddered under Larissa's onslaught.

"Come and get it, Larissa," he taunted, turning his back on the approaching threat as if daring her to make a move.

His attempt at verbal jabs, however, barely registered with the beast. With each brutal battering, the door creaked closer to collapse. Then a sudden realization struck him: Larissa wasn't mindlessly bashing the door; she was deliberately targeting its weak points—a chilling testament to the residual cunning of a creature that was once human.

Frantic, Rowan scrambled for a length of rebar and a heavy chain, improvising a platform of sorts. His eyes locked onto a half-full drum of gasoline. With trembling urgency, he dragged it towards the door, pried its lid off, and tipped it on its side. The fuel spilled in a serpentine trail across the floor. He snatched up the welding torch's flint, his fingers numb and tense, and awaited the critical moment.

He counted in his head, knowing he might only have one or two more bashes before the door was wrenched from its frame. With deep, calibrated breaths, he slowed his breathing even more to meld into the darkness. This was it—his final gambit. As the door finally crashed in, landing with a heavy thud onto the gasoline-soaked floor, a malevolent calm descended over him. Larissa's ragged, heaving silhouette emerged in the doorway, her nose twitching as the acrid scent of gasoline mingled with her own musky odor. A low, evil laugh—harsh and demonic—bubbled up from her throat as the smell took over her senses.

"Hear something to laugh about?" he snarled, striking the flint and igniting the spilled fuel.

A flickering red inferno erupted, casting grotesque shadows on Larissa's form. With a predatory tenacity, she used the door as a makeshift bridge to cross the flames, her wounded leg making every step a battle. Rowan tensed, aware that when she emerged from the fire, all hell would break loose.

Larissa's recovery came in a flash. Despite her injuries, she lunged at him with a swiftness that belied her battered state. Rowan barely dodged her wild strike, rolling aside in a desperate bid to avoid being hit. As he peered around, he saw Larissa crouched low, one knee planted on the scorched floor and her entire body poised to pounce, only to suddenly shift left.

Thinking quickly, Rowan reasoned, *"Of course, the other way you could have landed in the fire."*

He charged with newfound resolve. Gripping a length of chain in one hand and a fallen rebar in the other, he aimed to outmaneuver her.

Their chaotic dance escalated—a blend of primitive instinct and desperate strategy. As Larissa's claws lashed out, throwing a cloud of dirty grit into his face, Rowan dove aside. He landed near her injured flank, which afforded him a brief window to recalibrate his attack. Yet she wasn't done; she anticipated his moves. Ducking a savage slash aimed high, Rowan countered with a powerful swing of the rebar aimed at her good knee. The solid impact felt like clashing against a brick wall—his rebar clattered from his hand, but not without drawing an agonized howl from her.

Enraged beyond measure, Larissa's response was immediate and brutal. Roaring with animalistic fury, she struck back, her claws tearing through the back of his gear and biting into his shoulder with unforgiving precision. Pain exploded through Rowan's body as both combatants collapsed to their knees in a frozen tableau of mutual defiance. As Larissa slowly pushed herself up, Rowan lunged, attempting a swing with the chain. Instead, he grimaced at the fresh, searing wound on his shoulder.

Without missing a beat, he sprinted toward the flickering flame to grasp another rebar. In a twist of fate, Larissa moved with a similar purpose, snatching up the very piece he had dropped. Limping forward, she resembled a monstrous troll wielding a crude branch, her clawed grip uncertain yet with lethal potential. Scanning his surroundings desperately, Rowan's gaze fell upon one of the pouches secured to his vest—a full magazine, his last token of chance.

A new idea blossomed in his mind. Slowly, deliberately, he removed his tactical vest, all the while clinging tightly to the rebar. With calculated caution, he detached the explosive collar from his body. As Larissa advanced with a look of morbid confidence twisted on her savage features, she did something unexpected—a voice, deep and otherworldly, emerged.

"Little roach still clings to his collar," she growled, her words rough around the edges yet laced with a dark intelligence. "You won't need it much longer." The blend of bestial ferocity and lingering human cunning was unsettlingly clear.

Rowan smirked despite the pain, replying through gritted teeth, "I'm the handsome one, girl. Sorry, can't say the same about you." His quip was met only with a vicious snarl. "Your delusions of grandeur will make your end all the more fitting. Your crimes against humanity will not go unpunished," he spat, voice dripping with contempt.

Using her vanity against her, Rowan tried to bait her further. Slowly, he edged clockwise toward the growing inferno of the spilled gasoline. Larissa's laugh—a grim, mocking sound—followed him as she paralleled his movement. His mind raced: arrogance aside, he was no mere hunter of animals. Larissa was a deadly convergence of beast and man, and he now understood her tactics all too well.

With a swift, almost ritualistic toss, he heaved his vest into the fire, shedding his extra weight.

"Rowaaan..." she mocked, drawing out his name as if relishing every second. "You know nothing."

They circled each other, taking measured steps. Finally, when Larissa positioned herself directly between him and the vest, Rowan said, "Maybe, but at least I'll be around to find out. You controlled for far too long. Time to return the gift of servitude."

In a horrifying moment, the heat ignited the gunpowder in the spent rounds, discharging a chaotic spray of rounds in every direction. One stray bullet found its mark in the back of Larissa's shoulder, causing her to stumble like a wounded animal. Seizing the chance, Rowan sprinted forward; in two rapid steps, he trampled the distance between them. With a swift, crushing swing of the rebar, he slammed into her uninjured hand, the impact cracking bone and forcing her to relinquish her weapon. Without pausing, he struck her face with a brutal blow, feeling her jawbone shatter under the onslaught.

Larissa toppled onto her back, instinctively using her claws to shield her bruised face as crimson blood and saliva mixed grotesquely from a gash in her mouth. Momentum carried her to a rolling, desperate scramble back onto all fours. She waited for him to overcommit, and at the very last fraction of a second, tried a backhand slashing strike. Anticipating her attack, Rowan slammed the rebar into her forearm. The sickening snap of bone echoed in the confined space as her tough skin gave way.

Roaring in pain and fury, Rowan maneuvered behind her and snatched the nail gun. In a flurry of calculated strikes, he drove two nails into her opposite shoulder blade to cripple her arm and another into her spine to limit her movement. With Larissa now a shadow of her former terror, he moved in for the final blow.

Gripping a tangled clump of coarse hair, Rowan yanked her head back until her wild, bloodshot eyes met his unyielding stare. Dangling the collar bomb inches from her face, he taunted as she emitted a distorted, desperate "NO!"

In one swift, brutal motion, he forced the collar into her maw, secured the ends behind her head, and slammed his finger onto the detonation button.

Stepping out of harm's way, Rowan watched as Larissa's monstrous head erupted in a shower of violent shrapnel. Her lifeless body collapsed with a guttural, meaty thud, and a sinister plume of smoke billowed upward from the scorched, incinerated flesh.

"Enjoy the afterlife, devil," he murmured as he sank to his knees, a fleeting moment of grim satisfaction washed over him.

But the celebration was abruptly shattered by the distant screams and roars of other Stalkers echoing through the dark corridors. In that instant, Rowan's mind raced with the grim realization that he could not take them all down. With one last, pained glance at Larissa's decapitated remains, he slipped out the door and into the darkness.

Epilogue

It was nearing dawn at the heat-regulated towers perched over the main gate—monuments of vigilance for the mourning guards who stood watch over a desolate, frozen frontier. Although the snowfall had finally subsided, the relentless high winds continued to whip loose drifts, transforming the landscape into a shifting, blinding whiteout. As routine dictated, the guards began their change of shift by exchanging detailed reports from the night, methodically patrolling the perimeter, and lodging fresh lookouts along the narrow catwalks encircling the tower.

"Man, no matter how many frigid shifts I've slogged through out here, it always feels like you're freezing your soul off," grumbled the first guard, shaking off stubborn clumps of snow from her weathered jacket as her breath misted in the icy air.

Her partner, squinting through a pair of battered binoculars at the vast expanse beyond the armored walls, replied with a dry laugh, "Yeah, dragging myself out of that bunk this morning was brutal after last night's wild party. Mitch really torched his system this time." She paused, scanning the horizon, "It stinks Raven Squad had to bail early and miss the madness."

"I've heard the whispers," the first guard remarked more solemnly, her tone dipping into concern. "They say a few good souls might've been lost out there. Credit where it's due—it takes serious guts to face Skin-walkers and Stalkers day in and day out. I've got to swing by Lili's at shift's end to offer my condolences."

"Just be sure to pass along mine, too," her partner shot back, still scanning the bleak horizon with unwavering focus.

With a teasing smirk, the first guard retorted, "Why don't you give her your condolences yourself?"

"I'd love to, but the minute I clock out, the bunk's calling my name again," came the quick and playful reply.

"Seriously? You lazy sack," the first guard jibed, tightening the laces of his combat boots as if to ward off the relentless cold.

"Judge all you want, but until you've juggled a husband and a two-year-old, you wouldn't grasp this life," she quipped sharply, just as a shifting shape caught her eye among the towering snowdrifts.

"You can keep that circus—my lot is perfect, minus the perpetual snow, biting cold, and whatever's out there scheming our demise," admitted the first guard, a wry smile playing on his lips despite the chill. "It does make you wonder, though— what would you be doing in the Old World right about now?"

"Most likely stationed right here, guarding this blasted tower as always," the second guard mused. But then her tone shifted to one of alert curiosity as she leaned closer, "Wait, check this out." She extended her binoculars toward him, her eyes glimmering with anticipation.

"You're pulling my leg, aren't you? It's been months since anything's dared to breach the minefield—not even a stray wanderer," he replied, skepticism lacing his tone.

"Whatever this is, it's threading through the field like it knows every mine," she murmured as she methodically cocked the bolt on her sniper rifle. Inform the communication room that we have a visitor."

With deliberate steps, she exited through the heavy door onto the narrow, creaking catwalk that hugged the tower's edge. Following her rigorous training, she steadied her breath, zeroed in on the solitary silhouette wavering in the storm, and meticulously adjusted her aim to counter the erratic, howling winds.

For over a decade, she had manned this post, vigilantly watching over a labyrinth of mines whose placements had long since blurred in her memory. The figure before her, initially suspected to be a rogue Stalker, slowly reveals itself. Gently, almost mournfully, she began to caress the trigger, preparing to end the creature's wretched existence with a calculated squeeze.

Softly, she began a countdown, "Three... Two..."

"Sara, hold your fire!" The command rang out as her partner burst through the doorway with the binoculars held tight to his face. "I think that's Devil Squad's missing member!"

A hush fell over them as she whispered, almost to herself, "What in the hell happened to him?" Slowly, her grip slackened and she lowered her weapon, watching sadly as the familiar figure—Rowan, now unrecognizably altered—faded into the swirling wintry gloom.

Afterword

Post Impact 10 years
  December 25, 2063
  Dear Felicia

Little has transpired since my previous entry, aside from finally receiving the generator I had been requesting from Mitch for weeks. Now, we can resume our research into creating a stable vaccine. This moment has been a long time coming—I've been waiting for this opportunity. A reliable vaccine could halt the mutations in individuals with B+ blood type and potentially even reverse the effects in those already transformed. The potential outcomes are limitless.

I almost overlooked mentioning that group of bandits Buirke brought in last week. They've shown themselves to be both resourceful and unexpected. They were the ones who managed to fetch the generator for us. Mitch decided to send them after it, seeing it as a way to gauge their combat abilities. I know, very much in line with military thinking, right? But for once, he was justified in his choice; they proved to be highly competent soldiers.

Unlike many who had been wandering the White for an extended period, they managed to retain their sense of civility.

For a band of outlaws, they exhibit surprisingly good behavior. Their leader, while not the most empathetic individual, carries himself with a certain decorum. I must confess that I misjudged them at first; however, given the unusual circumstances, I hope you can understand my initial skepticism.

I spoke with Rowan, their leader, and I could see the anger simmering beneath his surface upon discovering the extent of EVE and the exposure his team had faced. Honestly, I thought it was premature to share this information with them. Yet, despite the unsettling news, he handled it better than those who had come before him.

People have mentioned that he's a skilled leader who can keep his cool in tough situations. Does that remind you of Marcus? Regardless, I'm starting to think he and his team could be a valuable asset to Haven. Yet, as with all things, only time will reveal the truth.

Yours Truly,
  Orion

We'd Love to Hear From You!

Thank you so much for reading this book—it means the world to us. If you found it helpful, inspiring, enjoyable, or just entertaining, would you take a moment to leave a review? Your feedback not only helps others but also keeps us motivated to create more valuable content for you.

Here's how you can leave a review:

1. Scan the QR code on this page, to go directly to the review page.
2. Or, visit your Amazon Orders page, find this book, and click "Write Product Review."